The Invisible Weevil

Mary Karooro Okurut

FEMRITE Publications Limited
KAMPALA

FEMRITE Publications Limited
P O Box 705
KAMPALA, Uganda

Printed in Uganda by Monitor Publications Ltd.

ISBN 9970 9010 2 8

Dedication

To the memories of my father and mother, Rose, Abigail,
Justus and Jane.
You were such lovely visitors in all ways.

Acknowledgements

Thanks to:

Stanislaus K. E. Okurut, for efforts without which I might never
have written this novel.

J. P. and Hatsuko Mwesigwa, for their wise counsel.

Emmanuel and Dora Karooro, for their ever sustaining help.

Kaata and Flora, for the folk tales.

Betty Sherurah, for her sisterly friendship.

Rosemary Kemigisha, for her positive entry into my life and for
tirelessly, proofreading the manuscript.

The family of the late Canon Yokana Banyenzaki, for their
unwavering support.

Mrs Schola Watuwa, for her principled stand which has seen me
through a lot.

And also to:

The Monitor newspaper, for having serialised part of the novel.

Goretti Kembaga, for typing the manuscript and Hope Keshubi, for
typesetting it, and for much much more.

Prologue

As the Fokker 45 made a descent, Genesis turned to Nkwanzi and softly touched her hand. She jumped as if she had been touched by a live wire. She had been deep in the saddest of thoughts imaginable.

He turned big, spotless white eyes towards her. His lips were cracked and his skin had peeled off, standing out like fish scales. Hurriedly, so as to take her eyes from his gaze that had begun to haunt her, she called to the air-hostess.

"Madam, please give me some vaseline to put on his lips."

"Sorry, I've no vaseline. Just cold ponds," she replied in a crisp air-hostess voice.

"That'll do, thanks." Anything. Anything to distract her mind and attention from that gaze which would for ever be imprinted on her mind. But Genesis was no fool. He sensed that she didn't want to look at him. Gently, in a hushed whisper – his voice was no more than that now – he said,

"Nkwanzi, I only wanted to tell you that I looked out of the plane and saw Kaaro town," and he pointed out at the buildings.

She was amazed that he could recognise the town. The doctors had told her that in his last days, which were a few now, he would be in a state of half-consciousness. Maybe there is some hope yet, she thought to herself knowing inwardly that there was none.

Expertly, the pilot landed the plane smoothly. He must have had Genesis in mind as he made that gentle landing. 'God bless you Captain,' she prayed as they touched the ground.

And then she saw the sad group waiting for Genesis. His father, some of his aunts, one or two uncles and an assortment of other people. She quickly noticed that her mother-in-law was not around. She had probably stayed at home to prepare a room for Genesis. Nkwanzi hurried out of the aircraft to warn them.

"Now get one point straight. None of you should weep or show signs of grief. Genesis has been told that he'll be going back to the hospital. So for heaven's sake, don't show any emotion that may lead him to think he is dying," she said, the terrible word, 'dying' causing her untold grief.

She could see the group registering the message but already some of them were weeping and trying to control the sobs that threatened to wreck their bodies. She felt with them what they were going through; having the knowledge that Genesis was dying and yet having

1

to face and hide it from him. She had lived with it for four months and every minute of those months, a knife seemed to pass through her heart. She tried hard to smile at Genesis, pretending that things were all right.

"But Nkwanzi," Genesis had told her after an unguarded moment, "why have you started to smile like a *muzungu*? The smile is only on your lips and does not reach your eyes!"

As Nkwanzi looked at the small group which had come to take him home for the last time, she knew each one of them was thinking about their love for Genesis. Watching the air-hostess getting him out of the plane, she again felt that tightening in her chest. Genesis was gently put on a mattress in the car and slowly driven off. Nobody was talking and most eyes were wet. What saved the situation was that there was so much dust on the road that everybody was rubbing their eyes, pretending to be getting out the dust.

The sad party moved slowly towards home. Genesis' last journey home. Weakly, he would point out certain landmarks to Nkwanzi in a whisper. "Look, there's Kanyinasheema," as he laughed weakly. Kanyinasheema is a very small hill in the county of Sheema. Its name literally means 'the mother of Sheema'. It stands out, small, rounded and proud in an expanse of plain. Genesis and Nkwanzi had fallen in love with it because of its unique nature and on many an evening, they had gone and sat there to talk about the future. Again, he raised his bony, emaciated hand and pointed out,

"We've now reached Ekyenkokora". The *ekyenkokora* is a tree with a branch shaped like an elbow.

As they journeyed homewards, Nkwanzi recalled how they had passed through this very terrain of hills and valleys on their wedding day, five years ago. It had been after a heavy afternoon downpour. The sun had just appeared and everything looked fresh and green; the hills had just had a bath. Genesis and Nkwanzi felt their spirits uplifted then. They had been driven slowly in a Volkswagen because the new government had just ushered in an era of sobriety, an era where lavish spending was frowned upon. To have been driven in the luxurious Merecedes Benz would have been out of harmony with the new way of living. And they had kept on squeezing each other's hand, smiling fondly at each other as if they had just met although they were being tormented by what had happened to Nkwanzi that morning.

And now, on his last journey home, the hills looked hostile and dry. It was during the hot, dry season. One could literally 'see' the

2

oppressive heat shimmering in the air. The sun relentlessly sent down her naked heat, without a cloud cover. During such a dry season, the wind would start howling in the trees very early in the morning. It made it almost impossible to prepare a meal as the wind would blow the fire far away from the cooking pot. During the dry season, ill health was at its peak with people suffering from high fevers and most deaths occurred then. Matters were not helped by people setting bushes ablaze at night. The people believed that burning the dry grass would ensure that new and healthier grass would grow.

However, this bush burning soon becomes a vicious way of punishing enemies. More often than not, neighbours who had quarrelled over a small piece of land would stealthily go at night and set each other's bushes ablaze. Each family suspected who had done it but they did not have the courage to face each other in accusation as both parties would be guilty. In the latter years, people slowly begun to accept the teaching of the administrators that burning bushes was bad as it led to soil erosion. Moreover, the animals would have nothing to graze on.

As this lesson slowly sank in, the elders stopped bush burning. But the young people – mostly ruffians – took it up. Up to now, they still do it even though there is a law against it. These incorrigible youth steal themselves out at night and with one stroke of a matchstick, they torch the dry grass. They run back to their homes and feign sleep. If an alarm is made by a neighbour that his grass is burning, the naughty young men who did it are the first to go to his aid. With huge branches, they try to beat out the fire if it has not spread too far. The naughty young men join the old men in condemning the fire-setters.

"Some of our young men are really evil. How can they set bushes on fire?" they condemn, while at the same time smiling to themselves. But eventually the elders came to know the truth and were heard saying: "We're moving with the very boys who torch the bushes. These rascals are like thieves who steal millet and then later join those hunting the thieves. The thieves themselves lead the hunters saying: 'This is where the millet was taken. Here are some grains..'"

Therefore, setting the bushes ablaze was another cause of discomfort during the dry season. The heat from the fires would add on to the already stifling dry heat from the sun and one would feel as if hell had let loose its all-consuming fire.

Just like on their wedding day, Genesis kept squeezing Nkwanzi's hand now. He would do so when pain gripped him. She would squeeze his hand gently, reassuringly to let him know that she was hurting with him. Beads of perspiration kept on making their way to his forehead and upper lip and however often she kept on wiping away this sweat, it would reappear.

They reached home. Most of the group had started weeping when they sighted home. When Nkwanzi saw their wedding hut, her throat constricted but she kept a tight grip on herself. Then she saw the old woman, her mother in-law whom they fondly called Kaaka. Nkwanzi felt a great sense of relief coupled with sadness when she saw her. Relief, because she knew Kaaka would help her share the pain, sadness because she knew Genesis' pain was Nkwanzi's, and her pain, was Kaaka's pain.

Many married women have problems with their mothers-in-law. But Kaaka and Nkwanzi got on very well. Nkwanzi loved Kaaka as her own mother and Kaaka loved Nkwanzi as her own daughter. Kaaka came to Nkwanzi and they embraced. Once again, the perfume of moth-balls from her clothes gave Nkwanzi comfort.

"*Bacureera*," she said. She always called Nkwanzi *Bacureera*, a name which was given to her on the morning after the wedding. It means a woman who is quiet, calm and recollected. "*Bacureera*, let's take him inside."

"Kaaka, you're too weak yourself. Other people'll lift him," Nkwanzi told her, gently.

Genesis made an effort to stand up but fell back weakly on the mattress. A group of strong men came and lifted him.

"Take him to their house. It's prepared," said Kaaka.

They all moved towards the wedding hut. The two-roomed hut was round and grass thatched. It had been painted blue outside and white inside. It was neat with beautiful mats and goatskins on the floor. The bed was also beautifully laid out and Kaaka had put her *suuka*, a big cloth worn on top of a dress, on top of the bed. Genesis was put on the bed and Nkwanzi removed his sandals and covered him. He immediately fell into the sleep of exhaustion. Kaaka called Nkwanzi to the adjoining room and when she got there, she found her father-in-law, old man Runamba, seated on a stool.

"Tell us child," started Kaaka in a fearful whisper. "What is it that has eaten up our son? What manner of disease has made his eyes hide in their sockets and his ribs stand out like *askaris* on a parade ready to be counted? What plague is this that has even power to make the head shrink?" She paused for a few minutes then painfully asked, "Is

4

it this new disease we hear about, this disease which is still taboo to us? Is it the disease which even the white man has failed to find medicine for?"

Nkwanzi looked away as the old ones looked at her with fear, waiting for her to confirm what they already knew. She swallowed. Hard.

"It's the disease."

There followed a long silence which was broken by Kaaka.

"But when and how did our son get it?"

"I can't tell when he got it. This plague, they say can stay in a person's body for many years before coming out," she replied tactfully evading telling them how he got it. Genesis had made her swear to keep it a secret.

There was another long silence.

Then Kaaka said, "I know what it is. I know what this plague is. It's like a weevil. The weevil eats up a bean. When you look at the bean, you think it is healthy. Then when you open it, you find that the weevil ate it up a long time ago and inside, the bean crumbles to dust. It's nothing but dust inside. I hear that even after death, this weevil keeps on eating the bones of the dead so that when the box of the dead is opened, there is only dust. Oh my son, he has been eaten by this weevil!" And she broke down and sobbed.

Nkwanzi knew the bit about the virus eating up the dead was not true but what was the point of explaining it to the old woman at this difficult moment?

"Why, why did it have to happen now? My son came fighting with the new army. The army brought peace to this land which had been torn apart by the weevil of bad leaders for many years but at least we are no longer ashamed to say we belong to our land. Although now, some parts of our land are also at war and I believe that even now, there are still some bad leaders. Like the victorious fighter who is killed in the hour of victory, my son has fallen at the last hour. God above, why did it have to be our son? And at our hour of victory?" cried out the old man.

Kaaka sighed heavily. "Mwami, do not ask, 'Why did it have to be my son?' Every child is somebody's son, somebody's daughter. A big fear grips us. We're back to the garden of Eden and Adam has fallen again. Adam has fallen again and we all have to pay for his second fall. This disease which we still fear to mention; this leprosy has taken us back to the first book of the Bible and the beginning of the world.

5

This disease has struck badly through the very food of life. The serpent has struck again and has cut off the breasts of mothers. A mother's breast has been rendered useless and mothers now weep together with the barren. Child, if an elder wanted to curse a person who had wronged him, the curse would be: may you see *baaya*. Do you know what *baaya* is?"

"No, Kaaka. In fact, I have always wondered what it is," Nkwanzi replied.

"*Baaya* isn't a frightening animal or thing. It's a happening so terrible that it makes you shake and wonder what we're doing in this world. This is what we're seeing. We're seeing *baaya*... When you bury your children like we're doing these days instead of your children burying you, that is *baaya*. We have seen *baaya*."

She paused and stared blankly into space.

After a while, she resumed. "Oh, how we're gripped with fear! Our eyes are constantly on the road from the big towns. Day after day, cars bring to us the shrunken, wasted forms of the seeds of our womb. Our withered, wasted seed stare at us with the silent, white eye of death and helplessly we watch as they wither and fade away like floating leaves in the noon-day heat. They wither and fade away in our arms and in dying, we die along with them but remain breathing." The silence hung heavy. "The graves. They look like potato heaps in the banana plantations..." She paused again. "Last year, when the grasshoppers fell, I caught a calabashful and dried them. I harvested millet, prepared it, and sent the flour and grasshoppers to him. And I said to him, 'Son, eat of this year's grasshoppers and new millet' for they mean the beginning of a new year. Rwenzigye, to see that you'll not eat of this year`s grasshoppers and eat of my new millet!" she said, her voice breaking.

The old man broke the silence.

"An ant met her colleague carrying a dead body. 'Why are you carrying a dead body alone?' it asked. 'The one who would help me carry it is this very one who is dead,' the other replied. In the end, we the old ones will have nobody to bury us."

Again the silence hung heavy. Then it was torn by Genesis' dry cough. Kaaka and Nkwanzi dashed to the room. Oh that terrible dry cough! Whenever Genesis started coughing, Nkwanzi would wish that she could cough for him. There were in fact many a time when she would unconsciously start coughing on hearing him cough. Kaaka held Genesis' chest until the coughing subsided.

Then she whispered to Nkwanzi, "*Bacureera*, please allow me to hold my son once more in my arms. He is so small, he reminds me of when I used to put him on my breast when he was a baby. Daughter, let me hold him close to me again and baby him."

Nkwanzi nodded, Kaaka's sorrow making her turn away. She had brought an assortment of herbs and put them in a gourd near the bed and with these, she massaged his head, chest and legs. For a long time, she whispered words to him which she alone could understand. She oiled him with a mixture of fresh ghee and herbs. She had prepared a honey syrup which she gave him to soothe his throat. After some time, Genesis fell into a peaceful slumber with a smile on his face. Kaaka came out.

"He has come home," she said.

"He has come home," echoed the old man.

Dusk begun to fall. The village slowly became quiet and still. The stillness was broken by the low mooing of cattle as they were being brought back for the evening milking, their udders full. The lone cry of the *akafunzi* bird as she invoked her curse of:

May you die of cough
May you die of cough

was coming from the valleys. The dove also sang her 'I sent you for the mortal and you brought me the pounding stick instead'. At such an hour, the silence of the sick and the silent seed of the womb clutch the hearts of the occupants of the smitten households.

Kaaka and the old man moved towards their kitchen. They entered and drew near the fire. She pushed the old man's stool towards him and he got out his pipe and started smoking. She sat on her goat skin quietly, sometimes pushing the firewood and rekindling the dying embers. Seated like this, they spent the night half asleep, half awake. Each lost in thoughts of their son whose calendar was about to be ripped off. Not a word passed between them. Only intermittent sighs of lost souls.

Meanwhile, word had gone around that the patient had been brought home. By the time the chicken went to roost, most of the neighbours had gathered. The women came with their mats and wrappers, ready to stay the night by the patient's bedside.

. Frightfully, they whispered amongst themselves, "It's the new disease that is eating up Rwenzigye. This disease is bad. Our children go to work in the city. There, they don't get enough money to come and visit us. They only come at Christmas. Now this disease is bringing them home to us when they are shrunken and finished. This disease is bad." And the women held their cheeks in the palms of their hands and stared into space.

One neighbour who had all along been jealous of Runamba's family was very happy that Genesis had been brought home to die. He told his wife,

"Ee, so even people who live in *mabaati* houses are beginning to die! Those with *diguriis*, are they also going to become part of the dust? He, he, he! I thought it's us only poor people who die. And this disease, which is afflicting Runamba's son, I hear comes from having intercourse with everybody. You know how Runamba's family is. They have been sleeping with everybody, he, he, he! I hear the boy is so thin you can look through him. I hear all the time, he's passing faeces on himself and has to be cleaned by somebody. The ones with *diguriis* can't take themselves to the latrine. He, he, he!"

His wife was not amused.

"Mwami, it's not good for you to laugh when Runamba's son lies dying. Moreover, you should not say that the family is suffering because they have been sleeping with too many people. Does it mean that they have been committing adultery more than other people? How do you know that our own children don't have it? Many young people are dying, the coffin is revolving in homesteads, please don't laugh."

"The disease isn't there. It's just witchcraft. Now don't you see Runamba's son? Runamba took my land. I told him he'd pay for having stolen my land. Is he not paying now?"

"What land did he steal? Just a hoeful of soil which you always said was yours."

"Woman, I don't want you to enter things which you don't know about. Runamba's son is afflicted with the disease sent by me. They will all perish one by one! Me, I will only go there to eat meat at the funeral. I am sure they will slaughter three bulls for the funeral, he, he, he!"

She kept quiet. She knew when not to add another word. But she knew it was wrong and evil of her husband to laugh at their neighbour's misfortune. Deep at night, when her husband was already snoring in the youngest wife's bed, she crept out and went to sleep with the other women by Rwenzigye's bedside.

8

In the morning, when the birds chirped out their greetings, the women folded their mats and went back to their homes. They picked their hoes and went straight to their gardens. Kaaka came and sat on the verandah of the hut and asked Nkwanzi in a hushed whisper, "How is the sick?"

"He slept well."

They went in and prayed quietly. After praying, they went outside.

"I was worried about the night. The ninth hour of the night is always the worst. That's when people's souls are taken away and yet, funny enough, that's also when most babies are born. And if, in the dead of night you listen carefully, you'll hear many groans. That's when people's hearts break and their spirits are whisked away," Kaaka said.

Nkwanzi felt a shiver run through her.

"Did you sleep at all Kaaka?"

"Not much. Most of the night, I was thinking about my son. I thought about how I fondly held him on my breast when he was a baby like I did last evening. I thought about how I gave birth to him."

"Kaaka, you have never told me about his birth. Why don't you tell me now that he is still asleep?"

"Let us sit near where we can watch him while I tell you the story of how I gave birth to him. But I cannot tell you the story of his birth without telling you about my own life as a girl and how I met your father-in-law."

Nkwanzi said that was fine and they sat inside the hut.

Chapter One

Kaaka and Runamba

Kaaka composed herself, and in her soft, gentle voice, she began her story.

"I was born in Mpororo in the years after the *omujungu* had just come to our part of the land. When the *abajungu* came, people ran away from them. I remember the first time I saw one, I screamed and ran to my mother."

'Maama, Maama, Maaamaa!'

'Child, what is it? Why do you scream and shout as if you have seen a dead body?' she asked shaking me. Meanwhile the whole village had collected. The noise I had made was enough to wake up the dead.

'What is it?' everyone asked frightened.

"I was breathing badly and could not talk properly. I had to wait for my heart to stop beating like a drum and then I told them."

'I was going to the well. Then I saw a man without a skin.'

'What?' everybody exclaimed.

'Yes. The man had no skin. I looked at him and the pot dropped from my head and broke. I was too frightened to move. And that thing, the man without a skin, kept looking at me and smiling and tried to tell me something which I couldn't understand. When he tried to talk more, I found my legs and ran back here.'

"There was a hushed silence. Many of the people dismissed my story as that of a small girl who had just been frightened maybe by a wild goat. But a few others said I must have seen something really frightening which they should go and see. They told me to lead them to where I had seen it. Since we were many, I did not fear to go there. We started moving towards the well. Even those who had said I had not seen anything joined us. Many were laughing loudly at nothing but as we neared the well, silence fell on the group."

'Where did you see it?' asked the village elder.

'There,' I said pointing to a spot in the bush.

'Aa, we're wasting time. There's nothing here,' said one young man. Then all of a sudden, he screamed, turned around and started running. Everybody else turned around and started running back. When they reached the village, breathing hard, the elder asked the young man.

'Did you see it?'

'Yes, it was a man without a skin,' replied the young man and fell down half-dead.

"It was later that we learnt this was *omujungu* and that his skin was not like that because he had peeled off the black top, like a snake takes off its skin but that God made him like that. When he came, he started church schools in our village and my father said I had to go there and learn the wisdom of the master. My father was a chief. He ruled over many hills.

"Before the time the *omujungu* came, my mother used to tell me that people would walk for very long distances, up to the waters of the salt lake and get salt, bring it and exchange it for skins. Other people went to get iron from Buganda which they could exchange for skins. Many people were eaten by animals while on their way to Buganda to get this iron. There is a particular place called Malongo where my mother told me there were a lot of lions. On their way to get the iron, the travellers would stop to rest in Malongo. At night they would light a big fire to keep themselves warm. Then the king of the lions would see this fire. He would get very annoyed and start roaring:

Who is lighting a fire in Malango?
Who has lit a fire in Malongo?
I will put it out!
I will urinate in it!

And the poor travellers would get so frightened that they would scatter in different directions and the lions would eat many of them.

"Even though my father was a chief, he did not spoil us. He never allowed any child to say I am not going to do such and such a job because I am the child of a chief. Both men and women did a lot of work in the gardens. After gardening, they would go home with firewood. The women would then start to cook while the men went to drink." Kaaka sighed. "Child, times have changed and it is good. Many people never used to know who their real fathers were and they did not care. There was a custom that if one's brother came to visit, the one visited would leave his bed and wife for his visitor. All the visitor had to do was plant his spear in front of the hut where the woman he wanted was."

"Kaaka, you mean the wife could not refuse to go to bed with her brother-in-law?" asked Nkwanzi.

11

"Refuse? Refuse? Child, what's the matter with you? How could the wife refuse when it was supposed to be her duty?"

"Suppose she didn't love – I mean like – her brother-in-law?"

"Those are your words. How could she not like her brother-in-law? The brother-in-law is there, she's there. This liking or not liking is for you people. But because of the Blood of Jesus, when the *omujungu* came, he told the people that it was sinful for them to sleep with their in-laws and that they would burn after death if they continued. Many people repented and left the custom. But there are people now, who are still practising the custom. That's one reason why this weevil is killing many of our people. Whenever men came back from war, some of their brothers would say: 'I'm so happy to see that you've come back alive and that you've fought so bravely for our country. I've nothing to offer you apart from my wife. She's yours for the whole month'."

They both kept quiet and became gloomy, each lost in her own thoughts. After a few moments, Nkwanzi took Kaaka back to life in her father's family.

"Yes, I was talking about the way we used to live. Whenever a boy woke up in the morning and said: 'Last night I heard mice eating maize' or 'Last night I heard the cat drinking milk,' then the parents would know that the boy was now big enough to stay in his own house. It would mean he was now alert to what was going on in the house even to the extent of knowing when his parents were engaged in the act of making children. So the parents would tell him to build his own hut in the compound. Again, there was a bad custom which Jesus' blood washed away. Whenever one of the boys brought home a bride, the father of the boy would be the first to sleep with her to 'see what the cows have brought'."

"And of course, Kaaka, the bride wouldn't refuse?" Nkwanzi asked.

"How could she? It was the custom."

"When my breasts were beginning to become like small berries, I joined a church school and we were taught a, e, i, o, u. Later, I also became a teacher and taught other boys and girls a, e, i, o, u, and also how to count. We used to count using sticks and stones. Whereas before we had been exchanging things like salt for skins, the *omujungu* brought money and we started buying instead of exchanging things. He also put a *Diisi* to look after matters of running the villages. All the *Diisi* were white men. They used to wear big hats, shirts which had no arms and their trousers only reached the knees. They would put on *stokingi* to cover both their whole legs. Since the *Diisi* could not speak our language and since we did not know theirs, they picked those to help them talk to the people. Many of these interpreters grew very rich because of deceiving people.

"It was like this: the *Diisi* would talk to people and say: 'You must pay taxes so that we can build roads, schools and dispensaries.'

"Then he would tell his interpreter to say it in our language.

"The interpreter would tell us: 'The *Bwana Diisi* says each of you must bring a goat, chicken, millet, milk and cassava for him tomorrow morning. All these things must be brought to my house by 8:00 am tomorrow. I'll pass them over to him. Whoever fails to bring them will be put in prison.' Early in the morning, everybody would take these things to the interpreter. These interpreters grew very rich until the *Diisi* found out their trick and threw them out of their jobs.

"After a few years, when I was ten and five, the *omujungu* came to put *naikondo* in our village. He came with some of our men and started drilling the *naikondo*. They would work the whole day through. In the evening we the village children, we would all go to where the *naikondo* was being made.

"One evening, while I was there, one of the young men working asked me if I could bring him a calabash of cold millet porridge. He was a strong, tall, black man who never seemed to get tired. But that evening, he looked so tired and hungry that I pitied him. I rushed home into my mother's hut and poured a full calabash of porridge, hid it in a banana leaf and took it to him. He gulped it down as if he had not drunk anything for days. Wiping his mouth with the back of his hand, he thanked me. He went back to work and I noticed how his back was glistening with sweat and how his muscles tightened with power as he dug. After he had finished his work, he came out of the pit and asked me where I lived. I pointed to my home which was just across from where they were digging.

'I'll come to greet your parents later and to drink more of that nice porridge,' he said.

"I almost told him that I was not sure whether he would be received by my parents. Who would I tell them he had come to visit? We were not allowed boy visitors that time. I still believe boys shouldn't visit girls.

"But he gave me a smile which made my heart beat fast and his white teeth shone against his pot-black gum. I looked down and told him he could come and greet my parents. He came when the cows were being brought in for milking. He sat with my father and told him

13

he was a sub-grade teacher but now that the children he was teaching had gone home to rest, he was making some little money working on the *naikondo*. My father took an instant liking to him. He liked people of hard work. The visitor, whose name, we learnt was Runamba, was to become my future husband, your father-in-law.

"Every evening, he would come and sit and talk with my father. Despite the fact that there was a big age difference between them, they would converse as if they were the same age. My father even found out he knew Runamba's people. My mother would go on with her work and occasionally halt to listen to their conversation, laugh a bit and go to cook. Runamba kept coming home. When they completed making the *naikondo*, he came to bid us farewell. I felt very sad that he was going.

"Runamba then cleared his throat. 'Chief,' he begun. 'I'm going away, but with your permission, I beg to be born into your family,' he ended on a strong note.

"My father creased his brow. 'Son, I don't understand what you're saying.'

'What I'm saying is simple, chief. I want to be born into this family by becoming your son-in-law. I want Kengyeya for my wife. I want her to come and cook for me and be the mother of my children.'

"My father kept quiet for some time. Then he spoke. 'This news comes as good news. I know your family. Your grandfathers were men to be proud of. I have talked to you for many an evening. You're a boy after your father. I'll talk to my old woman and the men of the clan and we'll finalise the marriage.'

That same evening, your father-in-law asked me to escort him as he went. I could only take him as far as the end of the Kraal. Once there, I stopped. Your father-in-law coughed and then said: 'Kengyeya, I've known you since we started digging the *naikondo*. I've watched the way you keep your eyes down like a good girl who does not love men. You are also shy, which is what a good girl should be. I've listened to your gentle and soft voice, the voice of a truly good woman. Kengyeya, I've admired the gap in your teeth, your milk-white teeth and your buttocks which are as rounded as those of a calabash. I've admired the dark patch on your face. And your eyes which look like those of a heifer. Kengyeya, you borrowed beauty from a leopard. And I've decided to take you to my home, so that you can cook for me, warm my bed and produce many sons for me. I've already talked to the old man. He thinks I'm the right man for you. When matters are finalised,

14

I'll come to take you as my wife.'

"I kept my eyes down as he talked. I picked pieces of grass and kept on chewing them. I kept on rubbing my right foot over the left, then the left over the right. He then gave me a bangle. Trembling, I extended my arm and he passed my hand through the bangle. I looked into his eyes; I would be the mother of his children. He stood quietly looking at me as I chewed off the nail from my small finger. Then he coughed and went away. I returned home.

"When I reached home, I went straight to the kitchen to help my mother prepare the evening meal. She noticed the bangle on my arm and looked happily at me, with tears in her eyes. I smiled back with tears in my eyes too although I was feeling shy.

'Tomorrow your father's sister will start coming to talk to you about things to do with a husband,' my mother said.

"I nodded assent.

"When everything had been finalised, your father-in-law came and paid the cows and brought goats and beer. I went to his home when night was falling. We reached my new home where they had prepared a big feast which lasted for many days. I stayed inside the enclosure around the hut for one month, weaving baskets and mats. I became brown and fat. God heard your father in-law and I and my stomach begun to swell. I produced five children within five years. All of them were girls. All my in-laws told your father-in-law to get another wife since I was producing only vegetables for boys.

"Your father-in-law would have married another wife but because both he and myself had entered the new religion and got saved, my husband could not get another wife. He followed what the *omujungu* had said. The *omujungu* had said it is a sin to have more than one wife. He had said it is a sin to drink banana beer. Therefore, because we had followed what he told us, my husband stayed with me."

"But Kaaka," Nkwanzi interrupted. "I only object to polygamy but drinking banana beer isn't a sin. Look, he says it is a sin and yet at Holy Communion, they serve their wine!"

Kaaka ignored her and continued.

"During the time when I knew I was ready to get pregnant for the sixth time, I stole myself and went to the medicine man so that I could give birth to a boy. He gave me some herbs and said that I should drink the herbs before meeting my husband and I would give birth to a boy. Unknown to my husband, I drunk the herbs and also prayed. I got pregnant and my stomach became bigger and bigger than the rest

15

of my stomachs before."

At this juncture, Genesis was rocked with a heavy fit of coughing. The two dashed inside. Kaaka held his chest while Nkwanzi wiped his sweating brow. Genesis coughed so much and yet no phlegm came from his throat. When the fit of coughing was over, Kaaka went out and Nkwanzi bathed him and gave him a few drops of Ribena which he drunk with much difficulty. She brushed his hair. His hair had been very kinky and hard before. But now, it had become soft and wavy like that of Somalis.

"How ironic life is," she thought while brushing the hair. Genesis had wanted his hair to become soft. Now it was the sickness which had, in a cruel twist of fate, made it soft! When she thought he had now fallen asleep, she made to move out quietly but he called out to her, "Nkwanzi, I fear to close my eyes in sleep. When I do, I feel that I'm falling into a bottomless pit."

"Genesis, try to imagine a beautiful situation. Then when you fall asleep, it's that beauty that you'll dream about."

He smiled and fell asleep and she tiptoed out.

"How's he?" Kaaka asked.

"He's sleeping again. But he told me that he fears to fall asleep because he dreams that he's falling into a bottomless pit."

"He told you that?" asked Kaaka in a shocked whisper.

"Yes, why do you look shocked?"

"His time is drawing near," she sighed heavily.

"You mean he's about to die?" Nkwanzi asked fearfully.

"Let him sleep," she said. There was a brief silence.

"Now, Kaaka, as he sleeps, continue telling me about his birth."

"Yes. Where did I stop? Yes the increasing stomach. I was seven months pregnant when the locusts came. It was one hot afternoon and I was seated on a papyrus mat on the verandah, weaving a basket and softly singing to the life inside me. And I spat on my stomach so that I shouldn't give birth to a thing which was neither a woman nor a man. I started imagining that since the stomach was so big, maybe I was going to give birth to an elephant. I recalled a woman who had just given birth to two creatures which looked like twin elephants. Whenever I thought of how she managed to push out the tusks, my head would stop working.

"I was lost in these thoughts when I felt an insect hit my cheek. I brushed it off and it fell. I noticed that it was a locust. I had ever seen dried locusts which my mother had kept for many moons. I made

16

a clucking noise and the chicken came running. and they started pecking at the locust. Somehow, I have never liked watching chicken pecking at something live, tearing it apart. So I turned away from them, my stomach feeling funny. There were children playing in the compound. All of a sudden, they became very happy and made a lot of noise, "I've found one! There's another one here!" Then they ran to me and showed me what they had caught; a handful of locusts. The children were happy and run to roast their locusts. I never gave the insects another thought. The following day, as we went to dig, a few more locusts flew from the grass at our approach.

'The children will be happy,' we said. Indeed they were. They caught about a hundred, roasted them and munched away happily. These were too few for us adults to eat. Nobody thought about them again.

"The following day, I woke up in the morning feeling a bit sick. I did not go to the garden. As the sun came out to spread her warmth over the earth, I got out my mat and went to sit outside. I started weaving my basket and again my thoughts strayed to what sort of child I would produce. I was still lost in these thoughts when suddenly, the sky darkened. I looked up to see where the cloud had emerged from. Then I saw the cloud coming slowly from over the hills. I was puzzled and frightened. This was not the rainy season. If anything, it was the seventh month of the year which is usually dry. This is a time when the millet fields are being prepared. The grass in the fields is collected and burnt. The rains always come on the fifteenth night of the month of August. The morning of the following day, people go out with the millet seed to sew. So when I saw that cloud, I knew that it could not be a rain cloud. Other people started getting out too. We just stood not knowing what to think or do. As this dark cloud moved close, we started screaming.

"One of my sisters-in-law fell on the ground and started wailing and clawing at the soil, 'I know it is the end of the world.' Then while still on her knees, she started confessing, 'Please, God, forgive me all my sins and take me well. Forgive me for having stolen potatoes from my co-wife's garden, and for having told a lie against her so that my husband could beat her.' She went on creating sins which she had not even committed! The whole village was in an uproar, abandoned babies wailing, dogs howling. Truly, the end of the world had come.

"Most of the people now remembered Rev King's words which he used to read from the Bible: 'Soon after the trouble of those days, the

17

sun will grow dark, the moon will no longer shine, the stars will fall from heaven and the powers in space will be driven from their courses..." [Matthew 24: 29-41]

"Now everybody was regretting why they had not listened to the words of Rev King. But then nobody had really ever listened to him as he preached. Every time he was preaching, each of the listeners was thinking about this *omujungu's* physical features. If they cut him, would his blood also be red? What was the colour of his urine? Did he also go to the latrine to empty his bowels or being *omujungu*, he had no feaces? Therefore, since many people had not really listened to the Reverend's good words they were now regretting."

Kaaka paused and then said, "Go and see whether the patient is breathing well."

As Nkwanzi was going to check on Genesis, another neighbour came and they went in together. This neighbour on looking at Genesis started weeping and saying, "Oh death is really cruel! Look at Rwenzigye's arm!" and she lifted the skeleton that was Genesis' arm.

"Look at his arm! As tiny as a reed. These bodies of ours are only good when we are oiling them. Look at him! Very near the grave. He's dead, it's only his heart that is disturbing him. Why don't you give him a mug of very cold water so that he drinks it and his heart breaks? I tell you he's already dead. Don't you see he can't look at a person straight in the eyes?"

Nkwanzi made signs to this woman not to talk like that in the presence of the patient. Genesis was awake and was looking at this woman, hearing and understanding every word she was saying. Nkwanzi felt like murdering her. This reminded her of an incident when her friend Lydia had received news that her child was very sick. She had boarded a taxi to take her to her home. On the way, the man seated next to her had noticed her agitation and inquired about her source of misery.

Lydia, glad to get a shoulder to cry on, poured out her heart to this stranger who had shown her compassion, "It's my daughter. I left her with my parents and now I've just got a message that she's very sick," Lydia had said tearfully.

"Oh dear! I'm sorry for you. If they sent you a message that the child's very sick, then it means that she's already dead," he had said calmly.

Lydia had given a shocked grunt, but the man continued unperturbed as if he was narrating an exciting event.

18

"Yes, you know these people in the village. They'll not tell you that a person is dead. They'll only say the person is very sick, when he's already dead. Oh dear, please accept my condolences. Your child's already dead! Here, have one hundred shillings as condolence money from me."

This was precisely the same attitude this woman was exhibiting towards Genesis. Nkwanzi got hold of the woman's hand and took her aside.

"Now, please understand. The kind of words you said aren't fit conversation when you come to see a patient. Do you understand?"

"Oh, I understand all right. I had heard the rumour before. The whole village has heard it. You people are hiding your patient. You don't want people to come and see him," she said then walked out murmuring to herself.

What was funny was that such a woman did not mean any harm by talking the way she had about Genesis.

It was just their way.

***

Nkwanzi came out and Kaaka asked her how the patient was.

"He rests. We had reached where the locusts came..."Nkwanzi reminded Kaaka.

"Oh, yes...I had reached that day when the sky was covered with a dark cloud and everybody thought it was the end of the world. Many people regretted why they had not taken heed of Reverend King's words.

"Had I known comes afterwards," came to many minds at this critical hour. The situation of panic was saved by the old man, Boona whom many said was more than a hundred years old. He heard the commotion outside and crawled out of his hut. The whole earth was dark and yet there was no rumbling thunder in the sky. He shaded his eyes, looked towards the horizon and recognised a situation he had witnessed twice in his life: the locusts had come. He crawled back into his hut, dragged out his drum and sat it between his legs. He mastered all his vigour and drummed.

"Even amidst all the noise and bedlam, people heard the drum. Everyone ran to old Boona's compound and sat down. By now, it was difficult to see anything because of the locust cloud. Everybody was scared but to their utter amazement, old Boona was laughing! The chuckle started in his throat, occasionally punctuated by small bouts of coughing and slowly turned into deep rumbling laughter. People turned to look at each other, all thinking that at long last, he had cracked up and gone mad.

"One young man whispered to his neighbour: 'It's the prospect of his going to the roaring fire that has finally made him insane because it is not a secret that old Boona has committed many an immoral act in his time.'

"This was said in a whisper because nobody could criticise old Boona openly. The man was known to have a bad tongue.

'My children,' begun old Boona with a trace of laughter still in his voice. 'I know that most of you think that my head's not proper because of what's happening but you're wrong. I'm only laughing at you. Next time, you should follow what the reverend *omujungu* tells you and be prepared for the day of judgment. Now what you see approaching as a dark cloud are locusts!'

"Then everybody jumped up in jubilation. The locusts had come! Those delicious insects. They could only be compared to grass hoppers. They were so tasty that even a story was told of a bride who disgraced herself by eating them. It went like this: A handsome young man brought home a very beautiful bride. 'At last my son has brought home a flower both in heart and looks,' remarked his father. Everybody agreed that it was so. For sure this was a woman who combined beauty and good manners. Every man's dream.

"Now her mother-in-law showed her all the food and cooking utensils.

'But for my husband, your father-in-law, you must prepare locusts. They are for him alone. You must never give them to anyone else.'

"But when the time came for the bride to fry the locusts for her father-in-law, the aroma was so good that she could not resist the temptation to swallow one. She looked right, left and behind, eyes darting here and there. Nobody was around. They were all out in the field digging. She swallowed one quickly. She didn't even feel it burning her throat.

"But I didn't get the taste because I just swallowed without chewing,' she thought. Another quick dart of the eyes. Another locust pop into her mouth. Crunch, crunch. Very tasty; best thing she had ever eaten. And so the habit continued and everyday she ate more. The more she ate, the more she wanted. This went on until the father-in-law started noticing that the locusts were getting fewer every meal.

'There must be a thief in the house and we must catch him,'

stormed the father-in-law.

'But how can there be a thief when everybody is in the garden digging?' queried his wife.

'I don't understand it either,' said the bride looking innocently bewildered. 'Maybe there is a ghost in the house.'

"Late that night, the bride's in-laws conferred together. They did not want to involve her in their plan because they were ashamed to reveal that there was a thief among their relatives. The bride would laugh at them.

'I have a plan to catch the thief,' said the father-in-law.

"Kakwisi, the dog was to hide and catch the thief. After everybody had gone to dig, he hid himself up near the roof where the firewood was kept. Then he saw the thief stealing the locusts, and to his amazement, the thief was no other than the bride!

"The bride saw Kakwisi and was desperate. 'Please, please,' she pleaded, 'have some locusts and don't report me.'

'No, no, thank you. Dogs in general and me in particular don't eat locusts,' replied Kakwisi and with that, he ran off to the field where the people were digging and sang:

You people who are digging,
You people who are digging,
Come and see it is the bride eating locusts.
She said Kakwisi have some
And I said, no; dogs don't eat them.

"There was amazement and shock! The beautiful bride? But they knew it had to be true.

"Father-in-law said, 'A good looking person cannot be without a fault. When he doesn't steal, he commits adultery.'

"They all agreed she must go. By the time they reached home, she had already packed her things and left in shame and embarrassment.

"So you can see how locusts can be delicious," Kaaka concluded.

"Kaaka, even if I had been that bride, I would have eaten them."

"Child, those are your ideas of these days," she said and continued. "The people were jubilant. Locusts had come. They gathered sacks and sacks of them. It was like harvest time and the crop was yielding more and more seed. But by the time the last lot were picked, the land was almost completely bare. No green could be seen anywhere and to get a leaf was like looking for water in a desert. Moreover, most houses had collapsed under the heavy weight of these locusts. Many children had their ears bitten off by the same insects and several animals died from the bites. Locusts are terrible. They eat everything in their path, including soil and wood. And they are always excreting. Every hop a locust makes, it excretes and then eats more. What had started as a celebration almost turned into mourning. The land was almost plunged into famine. What averted this tragedy was that the people always kept three granaries of millet to be touched only when there was famine.

"It was during this week of excitement and tears that I gave birth to a pre-mature son. The pregnancy was only seven months old. When I first felt what appeared to be labour pains, I could not believe it. I thought that locusts had made my bowels soft. I felt like emptying my bowels at night and went behind an ant-hill. I pushed and pushed but nothing happened. There was pain in my lower stomach and I could feel some sticky substance going down my thighs. I then knew I was in labour. I could not even stand, so I pushed and pushed and the child was out! I called out in a loud voice. My husband rushed out with a lantern, waving a panga.

'My God, if it's that son of a harlot trying to climb you, I will chop his body into small pieces,' he threatened in a terrible voice only to find me with a shrivelled looking thing between my legs.

'Quick, call Ndiinga to come with a knife,' I panted.
Ndiinga came running and expertly separated the child from the cord.

'He has been taken out of bed too early. However, we know how to deal with him,' said Ndiinga. She was the one who had delivered all the children in the village.

"The baby was wrapped in warm skins and put in the middle of millet husks for two months. The warmth is just the same as in the mother's womb. We named the baby Rwenzigye because he had come during the time of the locusts. For the Christian name, we called him by the first book of the Bible: *Okubanza* because he was our first son. But now the name is in your *Inglishi* and I can't pronounce it. How do you say it again? Jinissis?"

In spite of her sorrow, Nkwanzi burst out laughing.

"Kaaka, you failed to learn the pronunciation of the name long ago."

"And so child, that's how your husband was born. They say a bad name bewitches its owner. Rwenzigye is a good name. I don't know why...," and her voice trailed off.

Nkwanzi saw a figure approaching and went to see who it was. She was both happy and sad when she saw him. It was Mzee, Genesis' best friend since their primary school days. She rushed into his arms. He rocked her gently to and fro. For a long time, they could not talk.

"Take me to him please," Mzee said breaking the silence. Quietly, they went in. Genesis was looking at the wall, counting his fingers. "Genesis," Mzee called softly. Genesis turned his completely white eyes towards his best friend and a smile lit up his emaciated face.

"Mzee!" and he spread out what was left of his arms for Mzee who went and embraced him, and thumped him on the back.

"Mzee, I've got the 'insect' but I feel strong. Don't despair for me."

Nkwanzi saw tears form in Mzee's eyes. She turned away and left them alone.

Mzee came out after some time.

"He's sleeping," he said.

Nkwanzi brought millet porridge for Mzee.

They sat quietly for some time, each lost in their own thoughts. Then Mzee broke the silence,

"I heard about Genesis' sickness. I came immediately but I didn't know that he had deteriorated so fast," he paused. "Nkwanzi, I know this is difficult for you. Genesis sick with this damn ACQUIRED!"

Mzee's coming took Nkwanzi back to her childhood, early school days, the first time she met Genesis and their life together.

Chapter Two

Childhood

Genesis' home was about ten kilometres from her's while Mzee's was much further away. Her father, whom they called Taata, was a very strict man and they all feared but loved and respected him at the same time. He always insisted on everybody participating in keeping the home neat. He used to tell them never to jump over any litter in the compound or anywhere else but to pick it and throw it away. Nkwanzi recalled one incident when he called all of them. Trembling, they wondered who had done something wrong this time. He was seated on his stool on the verandah with his cane dangling menacingly on his lap.

"Now, what rule do we have here about pieces of paper scattered about in the compound?" he asked with suppressed anger.

They all kept quiet and looked at each other.

"Have you gone deaf and dumb? Answer!" he roared as he hit the cane on a nearby tin making everybody jump with fright at the ensuing noise. "Since you have refused to answer, I will send you on a task." They held their breath. "Go and pick all the pieces of paper in the compound and bring them here. I am giving you five minutes. Come back before this saliva dries," he said as he spat on the verandah.

They all dashed to the compound.

"Do you know, actually the place is littered with pieces of paper?" shouted Nkwanzi's brother Tingo. They picked about five pieces of paper each and dashed back to Taata. All their eyes rivetted to the saliva on the verandah which was mercifully still there.

"Nkwanzi, unfold your papers."

She was puzzled. They were supposed to throw them away!

"I said unfold them!" he roared.

Hesitantly, she unfolded the first. She was surprised to see half a cent in it. The second and third pieces all contained the same half cents.

Taata told each child to unfold their papers. They all had money!

"You can see how foolish and irresponsible you are. I deliberately littered the compound with these papers. But in your foolishness, not heeding my words to keep the home neat, you merely stepped over these papers not knowing that you were stepping over money. And if you don't heed my words when you are still young, that is how you will miss good opportunities in life. Don't you know that a stick is bent while it is still young? Give me my money and go."

They dragged their feet feeling a great sense of loss.

Another time, they heard him shouting for the girls to come quickly. They looked at each other and wondered what wrong they had done.

"Come here quickly, before this saliva dries," he roared as he spat on the verandah.

They dashed to where he was. The ominous cane rested on a tin.

"Nkwanzi, go to your bedroom and bring what you think is wrong there." She stared at him. "Go!" he shouted banging the cane on the tin.

She dashed to the bedroom and looked around for the 'wrong' object. She could not see it. She went back and told him she had not seen anything wrong.

"What! Come, I will show it to you," he said as he dragged her by the arm to the bedroom. "And what is this? Bathing water I suppose?" he asked as he moved the basin of urine with his foot. Nkwanzi trembled.

"Bring it."

She took the basin and trudged after him. Her other sisters looked at the basin, as if hypnotised. How on earth had they forgotten to pour it away? Whose turn had it been anyway?

"Come and bend your heads here," he ordered. They did so. He poured a portion of the urine on each head. "Leave it there again tomorrow. I'm sure you've enjoyed washing your hair. Go."

They went away, heads bent but laughed as soon as they were out of his earshot.

"Serves us right," they said.

Taata always insisted that both boys and girls had to do the same household chores.

"I don't want to hear this talk of this job is for boys, that job is for girls. You have to do the same work. The world is changing."

And so work like peeling *matooke* and covering it with banana leaves was supposed to be girls' work. But because of Taata's ruling, the boys had to take turns with girls in doing it. Winnowing millet, grinding and mingling it was another chore which was traditionally for girls and women but Taata made sure the boys did it too. The girls too would do such work like splitting firewood which was supposed to be for the boys. Later on in life, the boys especially appreciated the fact that Taata had involved them in such chores.

He always cautioned them against greed.

"A greedy person is evil. That person becomes a thief in the long run."

As a guard against greed, they were not supposed to eat raw food like sweet potatoes or cassava or roast them. The rule was that they wait for meals and not eat in between. One day, Tingo was caught with a roasted potato and got it rough. He was happily going to eat his potato when all of a sudden, he sighted Taata seated on the verandah. Quickly, Tingo put his hands with the hot potato behind him. He couldn't turn back; he had to pass in front of Taata. Taata noticed his unease and his shifty eyes and became suspicious.

"Come here," he called.

Tingo went and stood before him while the hot potato burnt his hands.

"Spread out your hands!"

Tingo remained rooted on the spot.

"I said spread out your hands!" Taata repeated menacingly.

The ever-ready cane was visible. Taata got it and banged it on the tin. Tingo jumped a few inches in the air and spread out his hands in front of him.

"Very interesting that object in your hand. I suppose it is a piece of soap. Come here," Taata said as he got the hot potato and rubbed it on Tingo' arms. Tingo howled in pain.

"You will roast potatoes again, won't you?"

"No,Taata. Forgive me." And indeed he never roasted them again.

Whereas Taata was this tough,Maama was the opposite. She was as gentle as a dove, enjoining discipline in a firm but gentle manner. If she thought Taata was being too cruel to the children, she would call him to the bedroom and tell him so. "Do you want to kill the children? I am not against your disciplining them but like the beating you have just given them was too cruel."

Taata would never say that he was sorry. But when he realised he had been too harsh, he would buy a pen or a ball or some gift and give it to the child he had been over harsh with. That was his way of saying he was sorry.

Before Nkwanzi started school, she was always following either Maama wherever she went or her sisters or Matayo, the herdsman. Matayo was a very pious man and used to take the children along as he went to herd the cows. He was always with his Bible, all of it underlined in red.

"Why have you underlined all the words?" Nkwanzi asked.

"Because they are very important. You can eat these words, they are more important to your life than food," he replied.

She did not understand how words could be more important than food but let it be.

Matayo would read them stories from the Bible, stories so sad that they would make them weep. They really enjoyed the stories. Other times, he told them folk-tales. Nkwanzi particulary liked the one of Kahiigi the hunter. Many times, she begged him to tell them the story and he would proceed and tell it in a very interesting manner.

"A long time ago, there lived a man called Kahiigi. He married a wife and they got many children. He lived in the same compound with his father and mother. One day, when Kahiigi had gone out to hunt, an ogre came and ate up all his family and when Kahiigi came back late in the evening, tired, there was nobody to welcome him. He looked around for his family but he only saw blood everywhere and he knew the ogre had eaten them.

Feeling terrible, his eyes flashing like lightening, he whistled for his three fierce dogs and went to hunt the ogre. For many moons, Kahiigi and his dogs hunted for the ogre. They climbed mountains, crossed rivers and lakes. They walked through forests which had a lot of evil beasts and vipers that walked on their stomachs. The three dogs followed the smell of the ogre and after many moons, they found it sleeping in a cave.

Kahiigi speared it over and over again. Before it died it warned Kahiigi:

"You have killed me. But when I die, I will become any other thing, a beautiful thing. You will buy me and I will eat you. I will transform into a beautiful woman, you will marry me and I will eat you. I will be a beautiful stick in the market, you will buy me and I will eat you. I will turn myself into a pipe. You will buy me and I will eat you. I will become a beautiful shirt, trouser or hat. You will buy me and I will eat you. I will transform into a beautiful cow. You will buy me and I will eat you.

The ogre died. After that, Kahiigi was very careful not to buy very beautiful things because whatever beautiful thing he saw, he was afraid that it was the ogre.

One day in the market, he almost bought the most beautiful handkerchief. Then as he was about to pay, he remembered and said,

'Oh, this might be the ogre!' And he left it. Many beautiful girls tried to marry him and he would almost agree. Then he would remember and say, 'Oh, this might be the ogre!' and refuse. He went through many temptations but did not fall for any of them. Another day while in the market, he saw a very beautiful cow. Kahiigi`s heart went to it. He was determined to buy it. His relatives, who knew about the ogre, advised him not to buy the cow but he said, 'Ah that ogre is dead.' And he bought the cow. His three dogs kept on barking at the cow, they sensed something evil about it. But Kahiigi took the cow. Everybody who met him said it was the most beautiful cow they had ever seen.

Then one day, when Kahiigi was cleaning it, and singing to it softly, slowly it turned into the ogre and tried to kill him. The three dogs which were always near their master started biting it. As the ogre turned to kill the dogs, Kahiigi got his spear and pierced it over and over again. Before it died it told him, "Cut my hoof and everything of yours which I ate will come out". And it died. Kahiigi did as the ogre had said. From the hoof, Kahiigi's father, mother, wife, children, cows, goats, sheep and everything else the ogre had eaten came out.

Kahiigi and his family lived happily everafter."

The children clapped happily.

Taata and Maama liked and trusted Matayo a lot. Every Sunday, he would put on his well kept white *kanzu* and together with the family, they would go to church.

One evening after he had finished milking the cows, he called Nkwanzi.

"Nkwanzi, come. There is a beautiful bird with its small ones in the nest. I want to show it to you so that you can see what beautiful things God has made."

She was happy. To go and see a beautiful bird with her small ones was her idea of ultimate happiness. She trotted after him into the grazing fields. When they reached a thicket, he gathered a few herbs and rolled them into a ball. He then gave her a small portion.

"Chew it. It is medicine for your worms."

She took the ball and popped into her mouth hesitantly. It was bitter. She wanted to spit it out but he put his hand over her mouth.

'No. Don't spit it.' Just keep it there."

She had no choice but to keep it there anyway, what with his hand clamped over her mouth. When he removed his hand, she asked, "Is this not tobacco?"

"It's medicine."

She was not so sure but remembered Maama telling them it was a sin to chew tobacco. She did not have long to think about it for she begun to feel very dizzy. The world was rotating and dancing around. Turning and turning madly around.

"Please hold me. I'm falling," she cried.

She felt his comforting arms round her before she could fall into a very deep hole. She knew she was dying. She started vomiting, retching over and over again. Gently, he put her down on the grass and gave her water from his skin bottle.

"Wash your mouth."

She did.

"Drink some."

He splashed some water on her head and some on the face. She begun to feel better though still a bit dizzy. He got her from the grass, held her on his lap and started rocking her gently to and fro and she felt good and sleepy. He was softly singing an old lullaby in her ear, a rabbit's song to her child:

> Suckle and I hide you, my little friend
> Suckle, my little child
>
> When I happen to die, oh my little one
> Hide under the stone, my little friend
> And eat grass like a cow, my quiet child
> And suffer like an orphan, oh my little child.

He kept on singing softly in her ear. Then she felt his hand move down and remove her panty. She felt him gently touch her *shameful* and wondered whether he wanted to wash her like Maama did ... They had been told that the private parts were the *shameful* whose real name they should never say.

He started carressing her *shameful* and singing faster and faster. The cow smell on him grew stronger. As he massaged her *shameful*, he took out a hard object from his centre and started hitting it against her baby thigh. His singing was now no longer soft and controlled but broken and harsh. He held her tighter until she thought he would crush her body and then she heard him cry out with much anguish, "Maama!" Then a warm liquid shot up from his hard object. He trembled and gave small spasms as if he had been bitten by ants and then the earthquake that had shaken his body slowly came to a halt.

29

He sighed, got out a dirty cloth and cleaned off the thick liquid that had stuck on her thigh. She wanted to look into his eyes to get some meaning of what had happened but he averted them and did not seem to want to look at her.

"Little one, don't tell anyone about the herb and our little game. It's our secret. Understand? None should know our secret."

She nodded agreement. She would never tell anyone. Not even Tingo. It was good to have a secret with a big person.

For a whole week, Matayo avoided her. Then one day as they sat in the kitchen while Maama cooked the evening meal, he remembered her. They were all seated in the warmth of the kitchen, the only light available was the dim fire. The food was ready and only a few thin pieces of wood were burning to keep it warm. Matayo was seated on a stool in one corner where he was hardly visible, humming beautiful hymns. All of a sudden, he called out to Nkwanzi.

"Nkwanzi, come and we lead the others in this great hymn." Her happiness hit the sky and she run to him, and he lifted her on to his lap. In his strong voice, he boomed out:

Jesus I still recall the day
I committed my life into your hands.
You became my personal saviour
Therefore let me praise you.
   Oh happy day
   Oh happy day
   When Jesus washed my sins away

Matayo would sing the solo and everybody would join in the chorus. Meanwhile, Matayo's hand was recreating their secret. It moved slowly to her *shameful* and started the stroking. He sang faster and faster and his hand moved faster and faster up and down and his breath came faster like whistling wind before a storm breaks. He panted, he sweated and he sounded like the big male cow before it climbed the female one ... And then when she thought he would surely burst, he gave a cry which only she heard in her ears and said "Maama!" It was as if he was under intense suffering and he groaned and sounded spent as he panted, "Thank you Jesus."

"Hallelujah," replied Maama.

Then he put her down.

"Let me go and rest. Goodnight all and God be with you," and went out without another glance at Nkwanzi.

"That man is touched with the spirit of God," sighed Maama as she pushed the firewood to the centre.

Matayo would ignore Nkwanzi for a few days until she asked him, "Are you going to put me on your lap and sing to me tonight?"

He put her on his lap and sang for her many more times. But one night, he did not only stroke her *shameful* but also tried to push a hard object there which gave her so much pain. Then as she was going to bed, Maama said she was walking funny, with legs apart. She took her, lay her down, parted her legs and looked at her *shameful* and screamed. Nkwanzi heard her calling Taata and tell him something in whispers. They took her to a doctor who also parted her legs and touched her *shameful* but not in the same way as Matayo. She heard the doctor mutter under his breath, "Pig. To do this to a mere baby!" She heard him go and tell Maama and Taata that the beast that had done that to her had given her a disease called gonorrhoea.

"I'll kill whoever it is," Nkwanzi heard Taata swear.

"I'll do it before you do. Even the Bible says a man who defiles a child should have a huge stone tied round his neck and thrown in the lake so that he has no grave," Maama said.

"You're both good people. If you find out who the pig is, take him to the police. We are lucky though, that he did not go very far otherwise she would be all torn down there."

Maama took her aside and asked her which man had been touching her. Nkwanzi told her everything. From the tobacco to the songs.

"May God be with us," she prayed weeping. The following morning,Nkwanzi saw policemen taking away Matayo. They had tied his hands behind him and were pushing and beating him.

"Matayo!" she called tearfully but he never turned to look at her.

Maama saw Nkwanzi and said, "My child, do not weep for him. He's the devil. Any man who touches your *shameful* isn't a human being but is the devil hiding in a person. If a man ever tries to touch your *shameful*, tell him that you will report him to us. You understand?" She nodded understandingly. At least Maama had talked to them a lot about the devil.

"But Maama, can somebody sing Jesus and still have the devil inside?"

"Yes child. And that's the worst devil: the one who tries to hide in Jesus."

31

Chapter Three

School and home

When Nkwanzi was ready to start school, Taata took her to a girls' school. In those days, co-education schools were very few. It was generally believed that if girls studied side by side with boys, the girls would get spoilt and become *malayas*. This in fact proved untrue in the later years.

Experience later revealed that girls who studied with boys knew how to deal with men better, especially those who wanted to exploit them. In the primary school, the teachers were quite strict. This strictness instilled a sense of discipline among the students. Some of the teachers were harsh though. The Mathematics teachers were particularly harsh or was it because most students did not understand the subject? They would give them a few hours in which to cram the multiplication tables, maybe an evening. The following day, they would be ordered to recite them. On one particular morning, the teacher was extraordinarily harsh.

"Goora, come in front and recite the multiplication table for the number six," shouted the Mathematics teacher. Goora, Nkwanzi's best friend got up trembling. She went to the front of the class and stood rooted to the spot, speechless.

"Well, what's the matter with you? Start. Six times one is ..." the teacher prompted.

Goora seemed to have lost her speech. She looked at the teacher like a frightened rabbit. The teacher's cane rang out, the impact of cane on buttocks resounding in the classroom.

"Stupid girl! Recite the table!" he shouted.

Goora just looked at him, dumb-founded. She could not utter a word.

The teacher, enraged caned her again. Nkwanzi cried uncontrollably.

"You!" the teacher called out to her.

"Come here. You are weeping for nothing? Well, I will give you something to weep for. Recite the table for the number six."

Nkwanzi had written the tables on the palm of her hand. Turning in such a way that she could steal a glance and look at her palm, she slowly recited the damned number six times table.

"Six times one is six
Six times two is twelve
Six times three is eighteen...
And six times twelve is seventy two".
"Great girl. Everybody clap for her". Teacher said.
The class clapped.

"Good Nkwanzi. Now you can go and sit down."

As she walked past him, he suddenly pulled her skirt. She tripped over and fell down. Teacher roughly hoisted her up.

"Think you are very clever, do you? Show me what is in your sweet palm," he said with an evil glint.

"Come on, open your palm," he said between clenched teeth.

Somehow, she could not spread out the palm. It seemed as if her hand had lost all motion. She could only stare at the enraged teacher, her hand clutched in a fist. He hit her fist hard and it uncurled and he saw the multiplication tables. He looked at her hard and long and her eyes fell to the ground. There was a hushed silence in the classroom. "I can't even punish you. You're beyond repair. You're a thief, a cheat," he hissed. "Get out of my sight, you scum! My cane is too precious to touch your vile body."

He sent her out and shouted at her that as a punishment, she should go to his house and fill his drum with water. The drum was no stranger to the pupils. To fill it, one needed about one hundred litres of water. This would not have been such a big problem if the well was near the school. But the well as in most parts of the land, was in a valley. Climbing the steep hill from the valley was nothing to joke about, one had to stop and rest about four times. Even then, one could only afford to rest if there was another person also fetching water. This was because the water pots were so huge that one needed another person to help in putting the pot on the head.

She went to teacher's house and started on the impossible task. As she was wondering how she would be able to put the pot on her head, she heard Goora's voice behind her. Hearing Goora's voice, half of Nkwanzi's problem was already solved. The task seemed lighter.

"Why Goora! What did you do again?" she asked her as they embraced.

"Nkwanzi, Serpent heard me speak vernacular." Serpent was teacher's nick name. " The punishment is to fill his other drum with water."

In school, they were supposed to speak only English. Woe to

whoever was heard uttering a vernacular word! This made them think their mother tongue was bad, inferior, primitive... They set off merrily for the well, filled the pots and started the task of climbing the hill. After pouring the water in the various drums, they ran downhill for the second pot and after ran home, their shadows already beginning to lengthen along the path. They were so engrossed in their conversation that they did not see the group of boys laying ambush for them. The boys would put a long stick across the road and dare the girls to jump over it. If a girl dared do so, they would beat her up.

"The boys! Let's run," Goora screamed. Before they could run far, the boys caught up with them and started raining blows on every part of their bodies. But the group that had descended on Goora suddenly got it rough. Goora had her big needle for basket making. She got it out of her bag and started stabbing her attackers. They took off in shocked disbelief. The thugs attacking Nkwanzi did not let go. She was on the ground crying in pain. Then out of nowhere, a voice came from heaven.

"You thugs, stupid idiots! How dare you keep on waylaying and beating up innocent young girls who have not harmed you? Brutes! You aren't even men. Real men don't beat women. Mzee, come and give me a hand", called out the angelic voice. The Mzee person did not need a second calling. He came and together with the Angel, whipped Nkwanzi's attackers almost senseless.

When the brutes had all managed to crawl away from the battle field, her rescuer came and said gently, "Get up, little girl. These thugs will never hurt you again." She got up slowly, with the help of his hand and stood facing him. She simply said thank you to him and his friend Mzee. They appeared big and looking up at their bigness, she felt a sense of security. The Angel introduced himself as Genesis Rwenzigye and his friend simply as Mzee. The girls also introduced themselves.

Goora and Nkwanzi quietly walked home. That evening's incident of being waylaid and beaten up by brutes was the last. After that, the girls walked home in the evenings without fear of being attacked again. Nkwanzi, while going home in the evening, would look out for their saviours. But whenever she came across them and tried to greet them, they would look uncomfortably around. It seemed they had forgotten all about her. 'Maybe they didn't want her reminded of the painful encounter,' she thought. She kept on wondering why her second guardian angel was called Mzee which meant old man. She later learnt that it was a nickname. He was called Mzee because he looked and behaved older than his years.

Nkwanzi met Genesis again in 1962, the day Uganda got independence ... They learnt about independence one morning at school. The bell rang and teacher told them there was a special assembly. They rushed to the Main Hall wondering who the headmaster was going to punish.

"Could be somebody was caught stealing the headmaster's passion fruits," said Goora.

They sat attentively in the hall.

"I've called you here to tell you that there'll be no school tomorrow," he begun. They all broke out into wild cheering and clapping. No school! That was the best news they could receive.

"What! You clap because there is going to be no school? Let me tell you, the pen is the most important investment in this world. So, be proud that you are in school." They fell silent. "There'll be no school tomorrow October 9, because we are getting our independence. Uganda will become independent tomorrow."

"Sir, what does independence mean?" Nkwanzi asked.

"It means to be free. You know we've been ruled by the white men. But now, we are going to rule ourselves because this is our land. Even now the flag at the administration building is for England which is ruled by the Queen who has been ruling us also. That's why every morning at school you sing:

God save the Queen
God save the King
May the Queen reign
May the Queen reign
For ever and ever
A __ Men".

"But from the middle of this night, the Queen's flag will be taken down and the one for Uganda will go up there instead. That is what independence means. So clap because we are going to be free."

The whole assembly clapped.

Later that night, Nkwanzi heard Taata telling Maama about it.

"Me, I don't want this *dipendensi*. What's wrong with the way the white man has been ruling us?" asked Maama.

"The white man also has been doing some things which aren't good

35

for us. For instance, we pay six shillings every year to the Queen. That's a lot of money. And then, they think they're better people than ourselves as if they don't go to the latrine. I hear that in Kampala city there are three different latrines. One for the white men, another for the Asians, and the third for the black people. Why? That shows they even think their faeces are better than ours! The latrines for those white people are always locked and when they want to use them, they are given the key. The place is very clean, and it is us who are told to keep it clean. If a visitor comes here, he should not think he is better than ourselves."

"Ee, now I see it," said Maama.

Some of the things the children understood others they did not. But they liked the word 'Independence'.

"*Dipendensi, dipendensi* tomorrow," they chanted as they played in their beds.

The following day, very early in the morning Taata went with the boys. Nkwanzi heard a goat cry and came out and peeped from the corner of the house. They were dragging away the goat *Kitanga*, the one with white and black spots. That meant they were going to kill it. She started crying because she loved that particular goat. Maama found her weeping. She asked her what the matter was and Nkwanzi told her. She admonished her.

"Don't bring bad luck to us by mourning for an animal. If you go on crying, you'll not even eat the meat. You can't eat something for which you have mourned. Today is a big day. We're getting *dipendensi* and we must eat meat."

Nkwanzi stopped crying.

Later, Taata told them to get ready. They dressed in uniforms and went to the bus stage. They boarded and the bus went towards the big town where the king lived. They waved to Maama until they could not see the home anymore. It was as if they were going to a far off land.

They reached the town and walked up a steep hill. *Taata* was a fast walker and they kept on running after him. There were many other people going up the hill. Nkwanzi saw Genesis and her face lit up with happiness. But he did not seem to recognise her and he soon got lost in the crowd ... Soon they saw a big, beautiful building.

"Is that a hospital?" Nkwanzi asked.

"No. That's the king's palace," answered Taata.

How beautiful the palace was! It was a house on top of another. Everybody was made to line up and they stood until the sun scotched them.

When they thought they could not stand anymore, an *askari* came to the verandah and shouted, "*Tention!* The King and Queen are coming. Everybody will march before them and give them salute. Turn your eyes towards them."

There was the sound of many drums and then the King and Queen came. Nkwanzi's attention was caught by the Queen. She was dressed in the most beautiful gown Nkwanzi had ever seen, purple with gold and she had a crown on her head. She was tall with a smooth black skin, small waist and very big buttocks. Nkwanzi thought a child could sit on those buttocks and travel many miles without falling off. Nkwanzi had always thought Maama was the most beautiful person on earth but the Queen was more beautiful.

"*Tention!*" shouted the *askari* again. "The King and Queen are here. March." They marched past them and saluted them. "*Eyees, light!*" shouted the *askari*.

They looked at the King and Queen who looked at them from above. Oh how Nkwanzi wished the Queen could look at her! As if she had read her mind, Nkwanzi saw the Queen smile at her. Nkwanzi looked behind to see whether it was really her the Queen was giving a shiny smile or the person behind. But when Nkwanzi turned, she saw the Queen's smile following her. Nkwanzi almost burst with happiness.

"I'm *dipendent*," she said to herself.

They reached home in the evening and found Maama seated in the compound.

"Are you *dipendent*?" she asked.

"Yes, Maama," they chorused.

They were so hungry they made a bee line for the kitchen. By the fireside were sticks of roast meat. Tingo picked one and sunk his teeth into it. Nkwanzi picked another and did the same. Meanwhile, Maama had also come to the kitchen. Busy with the meat, they did not see her looking frantically at the remaning sticks that lined the cooking place.

"One of you has picked your father's tongue! Bring it back quickly!"

"Taata's tongue? Maama, what tongue are you talking about?" Nkwanzi asked between mouthfuls.

"It's you, Nkwanzi. You're eating your father's tongue. Here, bring it quickly," she said as she snatched the stick of meat from her.

37

Nkwanzi was too hungry to let it go. She took off. Maama hoisted her *kikoyi* and ran after her.

"Nkwanzi stop. Bring back your father's tongue!"

She could not catch her, what with her *kikoyi*. Nkwanzi ran on but realised that the whole household was running to catch her. Tingo was in the forefront but it must have been because he wanted to eat the tongue himself, not because he wanted to rescue it for Taata. The servants too were panting after her and Rukamba, the dog, had also joined the chase probably thinking Nkwanzi was part of the chasers. Well, since she had already demolished three quarters of the tongue, she reasoned that she might as well eat all of it so that if she were punished, which was for sure, it might as well be for a full crime.

Before she could take the last bite from the lush tongue, the chasers caught up with her. Maama snatched the balance of the tongue from her.

"Child," she panted, "never eat tongue. It's for the owner of the house. It's only eaten by boys and men, women and girls never eat it."

"Maama, what happens if a woman or girl eats it? Does she die?"

"No but she becomes proud and thinks she should speak like a man. It's only a man's tongue that should speak loudest in a home, not a woman's. A woman speaks once, a man twice. A man is the head, a woman is the shoulder and the two can never be at the same level."

"But really, Maama, I can eat it because I'm independent."

"Don't start with your nonsense. The tongue is for men and that's final."

"Yeah, yeah," said Tingo clapping wildly.

"Shut up you," Nkwanzi shouted at him. She was annoyed because she had lost good meat and also because Tingo was going to boast over what Maama had said.

***

Meanwhile, reports were coming in from all parts of the country about how people had received independence. Some lay in the middle of the road and refused to move declaring that they were independent. Quite a number of them were run over by cars and died shouting that they were independent. In Kampala city, white men were made to carry bananas on their heads and Ugandans laughed at them. Some of the whitemen were forced to carry Ugandans on their backs. Yes! Ugandan was independent...

***

Four years after Independence, the children came home from school one evening and found Taata and several of the neighbours seated in the compound. They looked worried and sad. Something was wrong. Tingo and Nkwanzi decided to sit under a nearby tree and hear what they were talking about.

"Things are bad in Kampala. Very bad," Taata was saying. "Only four years after we got *dipendensi*, in Kampala our ruler, *Puresidenti* Opolo has fought with the Kabaka of Buganda, Opolo sent many of his soldiers to go and fight the Kabaka of Buganda. The soldiers killed so many people, the blood of the dead flowed like a river. They looked for the Kabaka himself to kill him. But he ran away to the land of the European. The soldiers stole all his property and they are now living in his palace," narrated Taata.

"Eeh, things are bad," said the neighbours.

"Yes they are. Now, President Opolo has said the kingdoms are no more. I fear this is the beginning of very serious problems not only for our ruler Opolo, but for the whole country. All right, not all of us loved our kings, but there are many who loved them. The Baganda in particular loved their king very much. I can't see how they'll ever love Opolo again. And Opolo is ruling from their land, how will he manage? This is the beginning of very serious problems for us."

"You're right. I know not everybody loved these kings. You know that, for instance, here it is said that our own kings who were Bahima hated us, the Bairu. It is said that, even when the Europeans came, they seemed to have preferred these Bahima to us, Bairu. They thought the Bahima were better looking than ourselves because they have sharp noses like the Europeans."

"There're stories that our kings here do not spit on the ground. A Mwiru is called and the king spits in his mouth! They also say that the king's spear cannot stand on the ground. They call a Mwiru and the king's Spear is pierced through a Mwiru's foot and it remains there and is only removed when the king wishes to use it. Should the Mwiru fall with that spear in his foot, he'll be killed instantly."

"But are those stories really true? These may be lies. Moreover, there were many Bairu chiefs whom the Bahima used to respect."

"I've never seen those things with my own eyes. They could be lies. Be that as it may, there are also stories like that about other kings. I hear that even in Buganda, there are also people who do not like the

39

king because of the things they say he used to do. They say that sometimes when he wanted to make sure that he could shoot the gun properly, he would order for a person to be brought and he would practice by shooting at this person!"

"Eh, eh! I'm sure that is a lie! Still, whatever bad deeds they are supposed to have commited, the kings were holding their people together. After all, not everybody can like you. They've been removed badly."

"My only fear is that things which start in blood end in blood. As you know, life is funny: things never stay the same, they always change. Now Opolo has said our kingdoms are to be no more. After many years, maybe when we have already gone back to the dust from which we came, another ruler will come and say: let the kingdoms come back."

Nkwanzi wept. The kings were no more! That meant the Queens were no more either. The beautiful Queen would no longer stand on the verandah of the house which was on top of another. And where had she put her crown?

Nkwanzi went and peeped at Maama who was busy in the kitchen. She peered at her face which was lit by the flames which were licking the cooking pot. She thanked God that Maama had not worn a crown because since she did not have it, nobody could take it away from her. Maama was indeed the most beautiful person in the world.

Chapter Four

Girl and boy

Nkwanzi met Genesis again during the Christmas festivities of that year. Christmas time was always a colourful occasion. The Christmas festivities really started with the coming of grasshoppers in mid-November. The elders would know the night the grasshoppers came. They would say that they could hear the chorus of the whistling of millions of insects. Nobody knew where they came from. Most people just believed that God sent them from heaven to signify the closing of the year.

The entire village would get up before the sun radiated her rays to earth. The women would get the calabashes kept for putting in the hoppers as they caught them. Each member of the family got a calabash. As soon as there was enough light to sort the grasshoppers, the entire family would set off for the fields. The search always started when there was still dew on the grass. At that time, the hoppers would be glued to the grass because of the dew. But when the sun began her upward journey in the sky, the heat would send the hoppers flying. And then it was impossible to catch them. It was left to the energetic children to run after the flying insects.

There are brown grasshoppers which look like dry grass. Then there are green ones which are as green as the leaves and grass. Then there are those whose colour is a mixture of green with streaks of purple. Whenever one catches a grasshopper during the search, one blows air on it and depending on its name and the catcher breaks out into a declamation.

Welcome, welcome
The brown one
Which a girl eats as she is going to the well.

The hopper is dropped into the calabash which is then covered with a grass cover.

It was during one of such grasshoppers catching days that Nkwanzi met and talked to Genesis after years since the rescue operation. She had been searching a bush for an elusive grasshopper when she imagined she saw a sleek green snake. She screamed and jumped in fright.

41

"What is it?" asked a concerned voice.

"I...I...thought...I saw a green snake," Nkwanzi answered tremulously.

"Where?"

"There in that bush."

"Let me see."

"Be careful."

"I will."

He got a long stick, approached the bush and turned it inside out. Nkwanzi held her breath. She feared and hated snakes, and was sure they were the devil himself. Maama used to tell her so.

"See, there's no snake. It's only some green cloth," he said as he held up a cloth at the end of the stick.

Nkwanzi moved backwards. She thought she saw the so-called cloth wriggle at the end of the stick. Her brave rescuer laughed.

"Still think it's a snake? No, no. Here, see," he said as he got hold of the cloth and crumpled it in his hand and threw it away.

She laughed with relief.

"Why, if it's not little Nkwanzi! My, I'm always rescuing you. It seems you may need me around for the rest of your life."

Both of them laughed. Nkwanzi recognised Genesis and was happy to see him.

"But Nkwanzi, you aren't small any more. You're almost a woman now and a beautiful one at that. Whoever gave you that name was right. Nkwanzi means beads and your eyes are just that – beautiful beads," he said admiringly.

She looked down, shyly.

"You're also a man."

He laughed.

"Why don't we meet in the evening at that famous tree?"

"Well, if it isn't too late in the evening."

"It will not be. I'll see you then," he said as he walked away whistling.

The day flew by. Nkwanzi was filled with feelings which she did not understand. As evening approached, she told Maama that she was going to Goora's to borrow a book.

"Don't stay there too long. You know there is a rumour that Taabu, that brown man, these days turns himself into a lion and eats people."

"Really Maama, you don't believe that nonsense, do you?" she said as she run to meet Genesis.

On the way, she met another dreaded group of men: the workers in the electricity board. These men, whenever they were putting up an electric pole, would mouth the worst obscenities. And when a girl happened to pass by, the obscenities would double. All the girls felt embarassed at this vulgar behaviour. There were also many men who would make vulgar gestures when they saw girls. 'Really, can't girls be left alone?' Nkwanzi thought with disgust. She resolved to report such men to the village chief, should they ever say anything vulgar in her hearing. She run very first and was out of breath by the time she reached the tree. Genesis was there waiting. They greeted each other shyly. Then both of them became tongue-tied. The silence was broken by Genesis.

"You know what, Nkwanzi, let's go to your friend, Goora's home. There are a lot of people there. We can go and converse in a corner."

Nkwanzi agreed. Soon they were at Goora's home where the people were busy serving *tonto*, the local beer. Nkwanzi just recalled that Maama never approved of Goora's mother brewing the alcohol. She used to argue with Maama.

"But, Maama, why do you think it's shameful for her to brew? She does not even drink it. She only sells it and that is how she maintains the whole family. So where is the sin?"

"My child, the Bible tells us that bad things do not kill only those who practice them, but even those who welcome them. Even if I don't drink it myself, I would be sinning if I served it in my house. Have you not realised that I do not allow people to smoke in my house? Smoking is a sin. If I allow them to smoke in my house, I'll be sinning too," she explained.

"Since Goora's mother gets money by brewing beer, Maama, I suppose you think that God doesn't welcome what she gives in the church during the collection? "

"That's what the Reverends tell us and we don't question what they say. Brewing is a sin. And child, sin is sin. Drinking is as much of a sin as brewing, stealing or killing. There's no smaller or bigger sin. They're all sins."

"Maama, I don't agree. Take something like telling a harmless lie. Surely you can't say that it's the same sin as killing?

"You see child, there's no measure for sin. There're no weighing scales for it. Lying is a sin. Killing one person or very many people is a sin. Therefore, you'll be punished for what you call an innocent lie the same way as the one who killed whether one person or more.

Child, there's no small sin. That which you call an innocent sin is like a weevil. It will eat you from inside until your whole person crumbles like a bean eaten up by a weevil. Today, you'll tell what you call an innocent lie, tomorrow you'll add on. You'll make it a habit to tell lies until your whole life's a lie," Maama cautioned.

At Goora's home, Genesis and Nkwanzi found a lot of customers. Unfortunately, Goora was not around. But her father was there, hopelessly drunk. He kept on singing snatches of obscene songs together with his habitual loafer. One old woman called Nkwanzi aside.

"Daughter, you've grown! Have you ever tasted *tonto*? Have some. It's good for killing the worms in your stomach. Come on, take some," she offered.

"No, I can't, thank you," Nkwanzi said declining the offer.

"And why can't you? Because you come from a saved home? That does not stop you. Even the Bible says that a little beer is good for your stomach. Come on, don't you remember that even the son of God in Cana in ..."

"Oh, I know about it."

"Here, have a sip," offered the old woman.

Although Nkwanzi was tempted to taste it, she could not stomach the idea of drinking from the same calabash with the old woman. The old woman was not the only one drinking from the calabash using the same straw, it was a big group.

"If they can give me a little in a cup, I'll drink it," she said.

"Oh hear her! How can you drink it from a cup? It's not tea. And why do you educated people think that we're lepers? Why can't you drink with us? The reason we use the same tube and calabash is that none can poison you that way. Here, get a cup for her."

They got Nkwanzi a cup and she poured some *tonto* from the big calabash and gave it to her. She tasted it cautiously.

"It's bitter."

"That's why it's medicine. All medicines which cure are bitter."

Actually of late Nkwanzi had been having bad stomach aches and may be this *tonto* could cure her. She decided to take a little, which she sipped slowly.

"There's a true girl of the village. Drink up and have more," said her friendly companion.

Nkwanzi called Genesis and offered him the drink which he took without hesitation. They drunk two cups and by the time, they finished, Nkwanzi's tongue had become loose and she had joined in the talk, arguing and laughing with Genesis. Life was good. They even joined in the singing. Nkwanzi developed a hi-cup and Goora's mother told her that it was time for them to go back home. They went singing snatches of songs and as they got near her home they parted. They promised to meet regularly. Nkwanzi was so happy that she did not know she had reached home until she saw the usual group of people that used to come and listen to the radio every evening. Not many people had radios those days but her father had one. In the evenings, people from other homes would come home to listen. Apparently the group had not heard her singing. They were busy listening to listeners' favourites – a programme that featured music. She could not by-pass them without greeting them. Cautiously, trying to steady herself, she approached the group.

"Good evening elders," she said as she genuflected in greeting. When she bent a little, she lost her balance and fell forward, bringing down with her the table on which the radio was. The radio flew off, scattering the cells on its unplanned voyage. Everybody got up and showed concern. Nkwanzi was too stunned to get up immediately. Now, everybody was going to realise that she was drunk.

One of the elders, with concern, started hitting his chest,

"Eh, Mr Erinesiti, why didn't you tell us before that the child has got the falling disease? My own son had it. Whenever people gathered together to feast and make merry, my son would fall. But I gave him medicine and he is now all right. If you had told me about your girl, I'd have cured her long ago. Poor girl! And she's so beautiful and clever! But now who'll marry her when they hear that she has the falling disease?" lamented the old man.

What! They thought she had epileptic fits! They would spread it immediately and Genesis would get to hear about it and would stop being friends with her! But even if she had the fits, would it have been her fault? Nobody invites disease. She got up quickly.

"I don't have fits. It's just that I have malaria and when I walked in the sun, I became dizzy," she said sulkly.

Taata helped her up and told them that actually, Nkwanzi had just had malaria. But Nkwanzi saw him gnash his teeth. He realised what had happened. Nkwanzi knew that night or the next morning, she would get her punishment. Maama who on hearing the commotion had come, led her away. She genuinely thought it was malaria. She went and put her on her bed and brought three blankets and covered her. She then brought her a glass of milk. Nkwanzi did not feel like drinking it at all but she forced herself. She took a sip and grimaced.

"Drink all of it child. You'll feel better," Maama urged pressing the glass on her lips.

Nkwanzi gulped down the contents. Immediately she finished the milk, she started vomiting. The first vomit hit Maama in the face. Nkwanzi saw her recoil with shock. The whole room now smelt of *tonto*. Nkwanzi kept on retching.

When it was over, Maama looked at her.

"You mean you drunk *tonto*?" she asked, her face a mask of anger and hurt. Nkwanzi kept quiet. "You, Nkwanzi, whom I knew to be following in the footsteps of Jesus? Your father will kill you."

"I'm sorry Maama. They said the it can cure stomach ache and I've been having this ache really bad."

Maama sighed.

"Your sister should come and clean up this before your father comes. But the whole house is already smelling. May God help us."

Nkwanzi's sister came and cleaned the whole place. She kept on asking,

"Tell me Nkwanzi, was it sweet? I would also like to taste some. Did you enjoy it?"

"Oh shut up! Stop asking me stupid questions. If I enjoyed it, then why did it make me sick to the extent of vomiting? Get away from here. You're just irritating me."

"I'm going but Taata will for sure not be amused."

Her sister was annoyed because Nkwanzi had not taken her in as her confidant.

That night, there was absolute silence in the house. It was as if somebody had died. Everybody avoided Nkwanzi. Even Agatha, who usually slept in the room with her, did not appear. Nkwanzi could hear her father walking up and down in his wooden sandals – clonk, clonk, clonk.

By 6:00 am, everybody was already up. Taata was seated on his stool at the verandah.

"Call Nkwanzi here," he ordered.

Maama came and told her and Nkwanzi followed her, trembling.

"Mukyara, why did your daughter go to drink and ashame us? Why did she behave like a harlot?" he burst out.

Maama kept quiet.

"I'm asking you, Mukyara. Why did your daughter go and drink

46

tonto?" he roared.

Maama still kept quiet. She always kept quiet when Taata was in such a mood.

"And you," he turned to Nkwanzi. "I'm not going to beat you. You think you're now a big girl. Let me tell you, you're still a child. And as long as you're under my roof, you'll live according to the rules I set. This is your punishment. For all this holiday, you'll not step out of the house. You'll only go to the garden to dig and you'll not even go to the well. If you step anywhere beyond that, you'll no longer be my child. I've spoken," and he got up and left.

Nkwanzi was happy that at least he had not caned her because his cane was terrible. But on reflection, she wished he had caned her. It would have been a better punishment than confining her to the house and garden. That meant she would not see Genesis and Goora at all! She begun to regret why she had drunk the *tonto*. She started devising ways of how to meet Genesis. Ah, but it was the Christmas season, and she was liable to meet him somewhere. But unfortunately, he did not turn up at the church. Nkwanzi was so disappointed that she lost all interest in the usually beautiful singing at the church on Christmas.

***

Nkwanzi did not see Genesis again for almost a whole year. When she met him, funny enough, was when she was having a crisis again. She was then in primary seven. That day, she got up when she was not feeling too well in the stomach.

As she was about to run to school, she felt an urgent need to go to the latrine. She dashed there and realised that her problems were caused by diarrhoea. After cleaning herself, she looked at the piece of paper and was shocked to see it covered with blood. Scared, she got another piece of paper, cleaned herself and looked at it. Again blood! She run out of the latrine screaming, "Maama, Maama! I've got dysentery!"

Maama came from the kitchen, scared too.

"What do you mean dysentery? How do you know?"

"Blood's coming from my behind," Nkwanzi wailed.

In the meantime, all the workers, brothers and sisters had formed a circle round her. They were all frightened. Dysentery was a terrible disease. The previous month, it had killed a neighbour's child. Moreover, it was known to be highly infectious. Nkwanzi could see

47

some of the workers already moving away from her, thinking any close proximity with her was enough to infect them with the dreaded disease.

"But where did you eat half-cooked posho?" Maama asked.

It was widely believed that one got dysentery from eating posho that was not ready.

"I don't understand at all where I could have got it from. We haven't eaten posho at school for the past two months."

"Anyway, go to the latrine again and check whether the blood is coming as you ease yourself," Maama said.

Nkwanzi rushed back to the latrine. It was the same story. She came back crying.

"Maama, there's more blood."

"Let me just put on a *kikoye* and take you to hospital."

Within no time, Maama was ready. They left people at home worried and sad. Maama sent somebody to go and tell Taata who had gone to the market, to come home as the situation was alarming. As Nkwanzi walked to hospital, she begun to feel sad. She thought she was going to die and the thought frightened and saddened her. Genesis, who was going to tell him that she was very sick and dying?

As they walked on, she kept on praying silently, asking Jesus to forgive her her sins and take her well. When they neared the hospital, Maama stopped suddenly and asked, "Nkwanzi, are you sure the blood is coming from your behind where you pass out faeces? Are you sure it's not coming from your, your ... where you urinate from?"

Nkwanzi was embarrassed, confused and annoyed.

"Maama what do you mean? The blood is coming from my behind and not from my *kooko*."

As she grew up, they started reffering to private parts as *kooko* rather than the *shameful*. Her friend Goora had told her to stop referring to private parts as *shameful*. She had said that there was nothing shameful about it. Instead, she said it was better to call it *kooko*. But Nkwanzi wondered how *kooko* was a better word when it actually meant animal!

They reached the hospital and soon the doctor called Nkwanzi. He had a form in front of him. He asked her her names. Nkwanzi told him. He then asked her religion. She got frightened. Why was he asking for her religion unless she was dying and he wanted a religious person of the same denomination to give her last prayers? She hesitated. He asked her again, impatiently.

48

"Doctor, is it because I'm dying and you want to call somebody to pray for me before I die? Is that why you want to know my religion?" Nkwanzi asked him while trembling with fear.

"Look here, young girl, I ask the questions, you give the answers, not the other way round. You understand?"

Nkwanzi understood all right.

"Now, what's your religion?"

She told him. Then he asked her to take off all her clothes and lie on the couch. Nkwanzi felt very embarrassed. How could she allow another person to see her naked? Worse still a man? Would he not make her pregnant by touching her? The doctor became irritated.

"Young girl, take off your clothes. There are other patients waiting to see me."

Wishing she could become a small insect so that he could not see her, Nkwanzi shyly took off her blouse and remained with the skirt and underclothes and lay on the couch.

"Take off everything, your panty as well. I told you to take off all your clothes," he told her angrily.

Really, her panty as well! Nkwanzi had never undressed in front of anybody. Not even Maama had seen her naked since she was five years. How could she take off her panty in front of this man then?

Impatient with her, he said, "If you don't want to take them off, get dressed and go home and die there," and threw the blouse at her.

At the word die, Nkwanzi quickly took off her skirt and panty and as quickly covered her *kooko* with her hands. The doctor did not seem to be bothered by her nakedness. He touched her stomach. Then said,

"Open your legs and spread them wide."

"What?" she asked mouth agape.

"I said, 'open your legs'. You're stubborn young woman."

Instinctively, Nkwanzi closed them tighter. The doctor then roughly flung one of her legs here and the other one there and pushed his gloved fingers inside her *kooko*! Suddenly, something snapped somewhere inside her. Some kind of mist clouded her eyes and the doctor's face became Matayo's – the herdsman who had done *shameful things* to her years back. The doctor became Matayo and Nkwanzi smelt the cow smell on him. He was massaging her *shameful* and his chest heaved up and down and he snorted and grunted and made the noise of the male cow when it is about to climb the female cow. And sweat run down his face, saliva dripped from his mouth and mixed

49

with his sweat and he licked the mixture with his tongue which hang out like that of a thirsty dog. Soon, he would get out his hard object and do what he had done to her so many years ago.

Nkwanzi panicked and screamed, "Matayo, stop! You're a devil hiding in Jesus! Maama, Maaaamaa, come!"

Maama rushed in.

"What is it? Doctor what is happening? Is my child dying?" Maama panted as she rushed to her.

Nkwanzi held Maama tight and wept uncontrollably. The doctor looked at her strangely.

"Why didn't you tell me your daughter is a mental case?"

"She isn't. What did you do to her?" Maama asked suspiciously.

"What do you think I did other than examine her? And then she started raving and calling me Matayo. She's sick up here. You better take her to a mental asylum."

Maama visibly relaxed.

"Oh, she must have remembered a man called Matayo who did bad manners to her very many years ago."

"I see. Well, she can dress up and go. Put this cottonwool between your legs and then put on your panty," he said to Nkwanzi.

She did not understand what the cottonwool was in aid of but did as she was told. She dressed without looking at the doctor. He told her to go out and said Maama should remain behind so that he talks to her. Nkwanzi went out and the doctor closed the door. She stayed near the door to hear whether he was going to tell Maama that she was dying.

"Your daughter doesn't have dysentery. She's having a menstrual period. You better tell her how to take care of herself." Nkwanzi did not catch what Maama replied. She was feeling terrible. She had heard the big girls talk about periods. That meant she was also a big girl. It meant she was going to become pregnant! My God! She was already pregnant! That accursed doctor impregnated her by pushing his fingers there! In any case, she thought getting a period meant going to the latrine and urinating out the blood. But this blood which kept flowing! Maama came out and looked at her with a strange sad look.

"Let's go home," Maama said.

They went back home. Maama immediately sent for Nkwanzi's paternal aunt whom they fondly called Ssenga.

Ssenga came and Maama said, "Nkwanzi, you're now a woman.

Your aunt is going to talk to you about how to take care of yourself in your new situation."

Nkwanzi was happy that she was going to talk to Ssenga. She was completely free with her. Nkwanzi loved Maama so much but somehow, she could not discuss with her, for instance, what the doctor had done to her. And of course, discussing such an issue with one's father was totally out of the question.

Nkwanzi brought out a mat and put it under the shade of a tree. For more than an hour, Ssenga talked to her about the menstrual period and all it entailed. She talked to her about becoming a woman and Nkwanzi confided in her the humiliating experience she had gone through at the doctor's.

"Daughter, you're now a woman, you have seen the moon. From now onwards, be careful not to allow any man to sleep with you."

Nkwanzi was shocked that Ssenga could even think she could do such a thing.

"Really, aunt, do you think I can sleep with a man?"

"Daughter, don't quarrel. Listen carefully. Men and boys are crafty. They can trick a young girl like you. Worse still, they can try to rape you or even you can like a boy so much that you want to sleep with him. Don't. Because when you become pregnant, he will leave you immediately you tell him. If a man ever tries to rape you, pretend that you are giving in. Even sing a little song. Praise him and then when he is about to penetrate you, raise your knee and hit his manhood and testicles, hard, very hard. Squeeze the origin of his seed: the testicles. Squeeze them hard and he will cry for his mother. Do you follow daughter?"

"I follow aunt. The only fear I have is that he can get so annoyed he will plot to kill me."

"Have no fear. Such a man will fear you in such a way that he'll never get the courage to attack you again. But this forced intercourse is becoming too common these days. In our days, it was not there. I'd advise you young girls to always carry *empindu*, that sharp pointed instrument used in making baskets. Then in the event of a man forcing himself upon you, pierce him with it. Pierce him deep until the son of woman calls out for his mother," she spat out with gritted teeth. Nkwanzi had never seen Ssenga looking so fierce. A dangerous fire burnt in her eyes reducing them to mere slits and as she talked, she held an imaginary *empindu*, in her hand and stabbed the empty air repeatedly, viciously.

"Yes," Ssenga continued. "These are bad days: men are doing what used to be taboo. Daughter, things are bad and this is why I'm saying always have that *empindu* and stab such men. Stab, stab, stab!"

"Stab, stab, stab," Nkwanzi repeated after her aunt stabbing the empty air herself.

After spending themselves stabbing imaginary rapists and defilers, Ssenga sighed. She wiped sweat from her face and waited for her panting to cease.

"Daughter, make sure your menstrual blood is never seen. Always bind yourself well when you are in the moon. It's a dirty, careless woman whose blood is seen on her clothes. It can be an accident but make sure you never have this accident. Keep your thighs tight. For the day you get married everybody will know whether you kept yourself for your husband or whether you allowed yourself to be used like a well by men. This will be known because after your husband has slept with you on your wedding night, he'll come out with the white sheet both of you slept on to show everybody if you had ever known any man or not. If you are a virgin, they'll see blood on the cloth. Your people will be proud of, you, it'll mean you're a good woman not a loose one. That's blood to be proud of, the blood of purity. Your mother'll be given a beautiful cow. But if your husband finds that other men have ploughed in his field before, if there is no blood on the sheet, then your husband'll cut a big circle in it. He'll come out with it and everybody'll see the big hole in the middle of the sheet. That hole will mean the hole in the middle of your womanhood. It means men have bored a hole through you and you are open like this," and she made a circle by joining her fingers together. "Daughter, do you understand?"

"I understand Ssenga. And I'll keep myself well. But there's one question I'd like to ask you. What about my husband? How will I know and let the people know whether he has kept himself intact and that there's no hole in his manhood? How do I find out whether he has shed blood when we sl-sle-slee-sleep together? Or if he hasn't bled, how do I know so that I can cut a big hole in the white sheet to show the people?"

"Child, what do you mean? Men are supposed to practice these things before marriage so that they know what to do."

Nkwanzi kept quiet and Ssenga continued with her talk. By the end, Nkwanzi felt mature.

Tingo who had noticed Nkwanzi talking to Ssenga came to ask her what they had been talking about.

"What were you talking about for so long? Please tell me," he pleaded.

"We were talking about things to do with mature people. You're just a small boy. Wait for your turn to come. Then you'll get somebody to talk to you."

"You mean you're now mature?" he said as he laughed in mockery.

"You can laugh as much as you wish but I can assure you I'm now a woman whereas you are just a small boy," she said as she turned up her nose with an air of superiority.

"How can you call yourself a woman when you still have small breasts?"

"It's not big breasts that make a woman. There're other things." Nkwanzi said with secret knowledge.

"Are those the things that Ssenga came to talk to you about?"

"Yes, those are the things."

"But I'm also a man. Look at my beard," Tingo said fondly caressing the few hairs that had sprouted on his chin.

Nkwanzi laughed. "Where's the beard?"

"Here, you silly girl. My voice is a man's. So I'm a man not a boy. Moreover unlike you, nobody came to talk to me when I became a man. I knew it. I didn't need anybody to tell me."

"Tingo, you're a boy. Your voice is not even like a man's. It's like a buzzing beatle's voice. One minute it's deep, the other minute it's like a woman's. You aren't yet a man. I'm now a woman."

"All the same, Nkwanzi, let us go and play the tap game."

"No. I can't play the tap game anymore. It's a game for children not for adults like me," Nkwanzi said as she walked off airily.

Tingo stood transfixed, looking after her and wondering whether he'd lost a playmate for good.

It was afternoon but Nkwanzi still had to go to school. She went but halfway, she felt sad again. She sat down under the barkcloth tree and cried. She did not know for how long she sat and cried. Then out of nowhere, she felt a gentle tap on her shoulder. She turned and saw Genesis.

"Genesis! You saw me cry?"

"Yes I did. Now Nkwanzi, what is the matter **this** time?"

"The matter is that I'm now a woman," Nkwanzi said and laughed, cried and hugged Genesis at the same time.

He looked puzzled.

"What does that exactly mean?"

"You wouldn't understand even if I told you. Let's go," she told him kindly.

Slowly, they walked in silence. Nkwanzi felt removed from Genesis. He was nice but he was also a small boy. What did he know? How could he know anything when he could not go in the moon? Blood is important. That is why sacrifices are important. Blood is life, therefore women were the knot of life, Ssenga had said. How could she tell Genesis all this? He would never understand and would think her mad. Nkwanzi sighed heavily.

They parted at the cross-roads, Nkwanzi in deep thought, Genesis puzzled. She did not care whether or not she ever saw him again. She did not even think about it. She was now a woman.

"Nkwanzi, when will I see you again?" Genesis asked anxiously.

She shrugged her shoulders and walked away to look for Goora and tell her about her changed life.

***

Nkwanzi normally shied away from describing any person as ugly. Maama had always told them, "Never, ever call anybody ugly, we're all moulded in God's likeness and God cannot be ugly. But," she added, "ugliness lies in the way a person behaves. If a person behaves badly, then that person is ugly even if on the outside she or he is very good looking."

Many of them had come to the conclusion that Goora's father was ugly because he had ugly manners. He had a big square head and his ears stood out, like those of a rabbit. He had tiny eyes which darted this way and that way like those of an overfed pig. His nose covered three quarters of his face, standing out like a gigantic Irish potato. It was as if somebody had thrown an Irish potato on his face, and it had stuck precariously, flaring up at the slightest annoyance, ready to fall off. He had a big torso, supported by tiny, spindly legs which looked like they would snap any minute. They all referred to him as *Zinje*, short for Zinjenthropas – early man – which they had learnt in history. Nobody would have minded his features if he had been good mannered.

When Nkwanzi reached Goora's home, Goora took her aside and told her in tears, "Nkwanzi, I'm fed up with my father. He is too cruel. You should see the way he behaves the day he buys meat."

"Eh, what happens?"

"To begin with, it's understandable that we eat meat only a few times a year. It's too expensive. But father takes the matter too far. After he has come from the market with the meat, he calls for his knife. He then proceeds to cut up the meat and places each piece carefully on a banana leaf. After counting the pieces, he then gives them to mother to cook. When it's time to eat, we all gather around the basket of millet or *matooke*. Then a big round plate and big wooden spoon is brought for father. He starts getting the meat from the pot, as he counts. In the unlikely event that he finds a piece of meat missing, he goes wild and can even cut a person with a *panga*. But we're all so scared of him, nobody can dare take a piece," finished Goora with a sigh.

"My God! How terrible! And how does he commence to serve the precious meat?"

"That's another scandal. You know there're about twenty children in my home. For five children, he gives them one plate with one piece to share."

"How on earth can five people share one piece of meat?"

" We have to bite the piece in turns. As one is biting, the others watch, eating suspended, scared that the person might bite off a big chunk, leaving very little."

"And what about your father?"

"Oh, he has a plate full of meat like a small mountain. And he snarls and gnarls like a dog as he eats, as if somebody is going to snatch away his meat. Other times, he eats meat all by himself and gives us only its soup."

"It's terrible," Nkwanzi said.

"It is," Goora echoed.

Goora and Nkwanzi talked for many hours. Nkwanzi told Goora of the moon she had seen and how she had become a woman and they shared many more secrets ...

Yes, Nkwanzi felt mature and she refused to carry out Tingo's errands. One of them had been the mean joke Tingo and his friends used to play on the girls. The boys used to have a standard love letter, all written out.

55

It went like this:

> *In the valley of love*
> *Where flowers never fade*
> *My love for you*
> *Will never fade.*
> *P O BOX LOVE.*

Dearest.... (They would leave this space blank).

You are the most beautiful girl that has ever walked this earth. Your face is more beautiful than the moon, your neck is longer than a giraffe's. Your breasts are like fresh, juicy oranges and I long to drink of that juice.

I love you like chalk loves the blackboard.

Please reply in the affirmative before my heart breaks.

Yours in agony,

Tingo (or one of his friends).

They would have many copies of this letter. Then say on a market day, when they sighted a beautiful girl, Tingo would ask Nkwanzi to go and quickly find out her name. This was easy to do. Then he would fill in the girl's name and ask Nkwanzi to deliver the letter. On such days, they could issue out more than ten of this same letter to different girls. And they would have a big laugh over their joke.

This practice made Nkwanzi suspicious of any advances by any boy. Whenever a boy tried to tell her that he loved her or wrote a love chit, Nkwanzi would think of Tingo's revolving love letter and she would think the boy was deceiving.

***

The years rolled on and the time came for Nkwanzi and Tingo to sit their primary leaving examinations. Tingo went for weeks without combing his hair and looking generally shabby.

"Tingo, why don't you comb your hair? You look like Gustava, the village madman!" Nkwanzi exclaimed.

"I've no time to comb. I'm too busy reading," he answeredwith an air of intelligence.

"I am also a candidate but I comb my hair daily!"

"That's you. As for me, I'm too busy."

56

Chapter Five

High school

When the pimary leaving examination results came out, it was a happy occasion in Nkwanzi's home. Both Tingo and her had passed to go to senior one. Taata, who smiled rarely, allowed himself a twitch at the corners of his lips. That was his smile. He was now a proud father. Nkwanzi felt happy because Goora had also made it and they were going to the same 'O' level school. Tingo carried his success a bit too far.

"I'm a senior one boy now and everybody should harken to my call," he would say as he pulled up his collar.

He kept on repeating it until he irritated everybody. But nobody could get annoyed with him because he was so nice and devoid of malice.

The night before Tingo and Nkwanzi set off for their respective senior boarding schools, they had a big supper. Taata killed a goat. Neighbours were invited to come and share the meal with them. It was a great occasion: going to senior school was no small matter. Maama heaped their plates with a lot of meat and Taata did not object.

"Eat, eat more meat and food. You will not have good food at school, so you might as well eat as much as you can," she urged.

After supper, Taata led them in prayer.

"Father in heaven, we are nothing but dust. We thank you that you gave us these our children who have honoured the family, the clan and the whole of Uganda..."

Here, the children giggled. He opened his eyes to see who had dared to make noise during prayers and also to check who had their eyes open. They all quickly closed their eyes and covered them with their hands. But of course as usual, they would peep at each other through the fingers.

"Father, we're insects under your feet and we pray that as you walk over us, do not crush us. Father as these your children go to school, protect them like a chicken puts her young ones under her wings. We ask all this in Jesus' name."

"Amen."

When Tingo was about to leave, he called Maama. "Maama," he began in an emotional tone. "I'm giving you this photograph of mine.

From now, you'll begin to see less and less of me. From the senior school, I'll move farther away from home for higher studies. Then you'll only see me for a few weeks during holidays, after that it'll be for a few days, then later for a few hours. If I go abroad, you may not see me for many years. You'll remain alone with Taata when all of us go away and you'll be lonely as if you never had any children. Whenever you long to see me and you cannot, just take out this photograph and look at it. Here, take it."

She took it and put it in her bra. There were unshed tears in her eyes.

Tingo boarded a bus and went.Next it was Nkwanzi's turn to set off for school. Taata put her on his motorcycle and told her to hold him tight around the waist. He kicked the machine and it spurted into life and they roared off. Maama and the rest of the family waved to her, most of them with moist eyes while she wept openly. Nkwanzi kept looking behind at them until they became small dots.

Soon, they reached the school. They went through the formalities and then Taata said farewell to her. Two big girls approached her.

"Hey, lets take you to the dormitory. Your father isn't going to stay with you," said one.

Nkwanzi felt more lonely than she had ever been in her life. But then she saw Goora and gave a sigh of relief.

"Nkwanzi!" Goora said.

They embraced.

"Alone no more," Nkwanzi said happily.

Goora was with her mother who was holding a bundle of something, tied in not too clean a cloth.

Nkwanzi greeted her.

"I've not seen where my child is going to sleep," Goora's mother said.

They discovered that they were going to stay in the same dormitory and that made them even happier. Goora's mother was attracting attention from the continuing students. She stared at everything and wanted to touch the gadgets she had never seen before. She saw some girls getting water from a tap and ran there.

"Ee, ee! This water, it runs like a man urinating!" she said loudly. Everybody excluding Goora and Nkwanzi, laughed. Then she saw a man cutting grass, using a machine. She took off while screaming: "Ee, eh, save us! The animal is coming to eat us! It's eating grass!"

This was further entertainment for the students, some of whom were kind enough to re-assure her that the machine was not for gobbling people but grass. They reached the dormitory and were shown their respective double decker beds.

"You'll sleep on the upper decker," one senior girl told Goora.

"What, my child to sleep on a mountain and fall down and break into pieces! I'll take her back home. This isn't a bed, it's something else made to make my child see the world dancing around her. Come, let's go back home. There're evil spirits here," she said getting hold of Goora's hand.

All the big girls burst out in laughter and Goora and Nkwanzi felt embarrased. Eventually, Goora's mother left, much to their relief.

Soon, it was time for supper. They went down to the dining room where food was served.

"Where do we wash our hands?" Nkwanzi asked one of the big girls.

"You want to wash your hands? For what?" the girl answered rudely.

"Do we eat without washing our hands?"

"You eat using these," she said thrusting a fork and a knife at her.

Nkwanzi got hold of the instruments. She had never used either of the two in her life and neither had any of the newcomers. She held the fork in her right hand and the knife in the left and tried to cut a piece of meat. Her hands failed to co-ordinate and the piece of meat jumped in the air and landed on one of the girls' head. Both the knife and fork clattered to the floor. The senior girls clapped and cheered loudly at her embarrassment. Somebody picked up the knife and fork and gave them back to her with a sarcastic bow but she had already lost appetite. Meanwhile, the whole dining room started chanting, "A tail with a knife, a tail with a fork!"

Newcomers were called tails.

How Nkwanzi missed home then! Here they were, subjected to this knife and fork mystique. Why did the school not first teach them how to use these instruments when they very well knew none had ever used them?

Nkwanzi was not the only one having a rough time. Nor was she the only newcomer who went without supper that night. There was one 'tail' on another table. She was holding the fork as if it was a defence weapon. And the knife in her other hand which she constantly raised up looked so ominous that one senior girl said, "Eh, this one is a warrior. She has come to finish all of us."

The whole dining hall burst into laughter and chorused, "Warrior, warrior!"

The newcomers went out of the dining hall, hungry and hurt. Goora was almost in tears.

"Nkwanzi, this is terrible! How can they laugh at us like this? Now we're even going to sleep on empty stomachs! And they call it teasing. Teasing! This is torture!"

More was to follow.

In the dormitory, the senior girls were talking excitedly about a film they were going to watch after the lights had been switched off. Nkwanzi got excited when she heard about this film. Soon, the bell for switching off the lights sounded. It was 10:00 pm, time to go to bed. One big senior girl approached Nkwanzi's bed.

"You! Go and blow out the light," she commanded.

Nkwanzi stared at her and kept quiet.

"Are you deaf or just stubborn and arrogant? I ordered you to go and blow out the light!"

Another girl approached. "The commander has given orders. You must follow them."

The bell shrilly sounded a second time.

"Get up and blow out the light. If the teacher on duty comes and punishes us for your refusal to take orders, I shudder when I think of the punishment that we will mete out to you," and she hauled Nkwanzi to her feet.

"Now", blow it out with your breath, like you blow out a candle."

"Blow, blow!" they bellowed.

Nkwanzi just looked at her. A slap on her cheek did it. She sprung into action and started blowing away at the bulb. The other senior girls cheered and clapped.

"Harder, harder!" urged the biggest girl known as Brigadier.

Nkwanzi blew until her cheeks hurt. Meanwhile the other newcomers had all been lined up and told to come and blow harder. Their cheeks would surely have burst if the teacher on duty's voice had not been heard outside telling everybody to switch off the lights and go to bed. One Senior girl switched it off immediately and everybody jumped into bed and pretended to be asleep. Some feigned snoring so well that Nkwanzi wondered whether they were getting lessons in it. After half an hour, there were muffled sounds in the dormitory. Then somebody lit a candle. A lot of activities seemed to be going on. A table pulled, the sound of somebody urinating, water being poured into a cup and stifled laughter.

After about forty five minutes of such sounds, the Brigadier's voice again bellowed out.

"All the tails get out of bed. It's time for you to come to the holy table and receive holy communion. Come quietly and quickly."

Holy table? What was this?

Nobody could afford to stay in bed after hearing that voice. All the newcomers filed out. And indeed, in the middle of the room, there was a table spread out with a white tablecloth. There was a glass with a rusty coloured liquid and a saucer with bits of food of sorts. Mesmerised, they all filed towards the 'holy table'. Nkwanzi had not seen the 'priest'. There she was, complete with white robes. She had spectacles, which were placed on top of her nose and a big wooden cross around her neck.

"Come my children," intoned the 'priest'. "Eat his body and drink his blood and then sing a song of praise."

And one by one, they went and received 'holy communion'. The wine tasted salty and murky. Nkwanzi almost threw it up wondering what stuff it was. The 'bread' was equally nauseating. The senior girls would clap as each one of the 'tails' finished receiving the 'holy communion'. None of them dared refuse: the 'Brigadier' was standing by with a big stick and looking more than ready to hit anybody who refused to go to the holy table .

When their initiation ceremony was over, they learnt bitterly that the 'wine' had been urine and the bread food droppings. All the 'tails' threw up. Goora and Nkwanzi were in misery after this incident.

"What is good about being in senior? It's hell," Nkwanzi cried.

"Next year, I'll make the tails suffer worse than I have," swore Goora.

"But Goora, what's the point of making innocent tails suffer the way we've done? Your revenge is directed in the wrong direction. If you were to take revenge on the seniors who made us suffer, it would be understandable."

"The culture is that we must make next year's newcomers suffer."

"It's wrong. It's wrong." = moral vocabulary here

"It's the tradition. It's right, it's right."

"Well, I won't do it to those poor innocents next year," Nkwanzi declared.

After a few days, she got a letter from Tingo. Culture of violence of the country. Nkwanzi can see the culture itself is corrupt

St Peter's High School,
3rd February, 1968.

Dear Sis,

I hope you are fine. Well for me, I am not at all fine. The way I was looking forward to joining Senior! But all my happiness has been dashed to pieces. The first night, the senior boys paraded all the new comers and each senior boy picked a "Servant". We were then given the rules for the servants. These are as follows:

1. A servant must make his "master's" bed every morning, wash his plates, cups, clothes, etc

2. He must collect bathing water for the master in the morning (NB the well is in a valley, about three Kilometres from school)

3. He must surrender all the grab he brought to the "master".

There was an incident that made me tremble. One of the newcomers was ordered by a group of about ten hefty boys to accompany them to the farm. There, the big boys got hold of one of the pigs. They then forced the small boy to have sex with it! Most of us are still sick when we think about this incident. And what is absurd is that these practices are called "teasing" the newcomers! What sort of teasing is this? This is madness!

I hope what we have gone through is not what you have gone through too. I will keep on praying for both of us.

Your loving brother,

Tingo.

God! Was Nkwanzi shocked! What they had gone through compared to Tingo's ordeal was nothing! In later years, the practice of 'teasing' got worse. Some students even got beaten to death in the name of teasing which later came to be termed bullying. Why the head teachers never put stringent measures in place to halt this evil beats all imagination.

The teachers too had their own problems when it came to being teased by the pupils. They were called all sorts of nicknames. One particular teacher, called Rose, had it rough. Rose was brown. Everybody admired her brown colour so much. She was the envy of the school especially of her fellow teachers. Then, out of the blue, Rose's fate changed. One day, a newcomer to the school said, "That teacher is as brown as *bogoya.*"

And from then, the name *bogoya* stuck to the teacher. Whenever she came to class, she would find sticks of *bogoya* on her table. The whole blackboard would be full of drawings of the banana. The students would start chanting in whispers: "*Bogoya, Bogoya.*"

Soon, the students started putting *bogoya* on the verandah of her house and on her doorstep. *Bogoya* peels were strewn all over the compound. Rose started by asking the class about who had put the bananas on her chair and drawn them on the blockboard as well. Silence.

" I repeat: who put these ... these ... things here?"

Silence.

"Then form one line outside, all of you. Out. Out I say!"

And they would form the line and she would give them a stroke of the came each. But they would make fun of her and start giggling. Moreover, the whole school would be watching from the windows of their classes. They would all whisper: "Bogoya, Bogoya" and the incessant noise sounding like the hiss of a spitting cobra would get to her head. When she knew she could not take it anymore, she approached the headmaster and told him about the problem.

"Just laugh it off. Laugh as if it is the biggest joke of the year. Then they will leave you alone. But if you continue to show them that you mind, they will increase what they see as their torture tool."

She tried to laugh it off. But her laughter sounded hollow even to her own ears. The students intensified their sadistic teasing.

Rose used to like taking evening walks. She would go when it was cool and walk to the nearby hills. But now, the walks were also becoming torturous. Whenever she set out to go for a walk, some of her students on their way to the well would sight her. Then one student would shout at the top of his voice: "Bo - oo - oo!" another would hear and pick it up: "Go -oo - oo" and a third would round it up - "Ya - aa - aa!", laughter would follow. And the hills would pick it up in instalments, send it down to the valleys and the whole world seemed to join in the echoing, mocking laughter.

It seemed nature itself had joined in the conspiracy to turn Rose into a wreck of nerves. This new method devised by the students to say the nickname in installments almost sent her mad. One time, while in the staff room, one of her colleagues was going to call the Shamba boy that "Boy, come here". No sooner had she pronounced the letters "Bo -" than Rose got up with hysterical excitement. She thought the teachers had joined in to ridicule her too. Really this was becoming too much! Unable to stand it any longer, she eventually asked for a transfer and went to a distant school.

The months rolled along and soon, it was time to go for the Christmas vacation.

During the final assembly, the headmistress warned them.

"You're going for vacation. Use the time to help your parents. Don't play around with boys otherwise you'll become harlots. Whoever misbehaves during vacation and I come to hear of it, I'll expel her from school. And you," she said pointing to a small girl, "you still have the habit of wetting your bed. If you haven't stopped the habit by next term, you'll be sleeping in the pig sty."

The small girl was embarrassed. When the assembly was over, Nkwanzi called her.

"Doesn't the urge to go and urinate wake you up?"

"No it doesn't. In fact whenever the urge comes, I always dream that I am walking with my friends. In the dream, I feel like urinating. So I tell my friends to wait for me while I go behind a bush and start urinating and the relief of the urine flowing out is a beautiful experience. Then when I finish, I look down only to see the patch of my urine slowly becoming a lake around me. The water becomes cold and makes me shiver. Then I actually wake up and find that I have urinated on the bed," cried the small girl. Nkwanzi was sympathetic but did not know what advice to give.

Nkwanzi's father came for her on his motorcycle and she reached home and bathed in the family love. Tingo was coming a week after. She had some little money which she used to buy half a kilogram of rice. She would make a beautiful rice dish for him.

The day he was to come, Nkwanzi got up about six in the morning. She had sorted the rice the day before. By 7:00 am, she had put the rice on the fire. For more than four hours, she lovingly turned the rice this way and that. Tingo would have the best dish in his life. She boiled it until Tingo arrived at about two o'clock in the afternoon. They sat in the kitchen, on a mat as usual, but Tingo was given a chair and a table to sit on. He was now a senior boy. He looked uncomfortable though and seemed to have wanted to come and sit down with the rest. Maama had made millet bread for him and she asked Nkwanzi to get him a fork and knife.

"Maama, I can't use a fork to eat millet. I'll use my hands," he said.

Maama looked hurt. She wanted him to feel his new status. Tingo understood.

64

"Maama, don't worry. I don't have to use this fork. I'm still part of the home and I have not changed."

"Maama, Tingo will not eat millet. I prepared a special dish for him," Nkwanzi said.

"Well, bring it then. He must be hungry."

Nkwanzi went and brought the rice and served Tingo. He thanked her, took a mouthful of the rice and then she saw his face crease with perplexion. He tried to eat more but obviously, something was wrong.

"Son, what's the matter? Why aren't you eating?" Maama asked.

"I'm not feeling hungry and what I've eaten is enough."

"Now you are behaving like those *abajungu* who eat very little."

"Actually those people don't eat little food. They eat every minute, eating small things. Then by the time food is ready, they are already full and eat little. But Maama, I'm all right."

Even though he said he was all right, his eyes told a different story. A story of hunger. Later on in the afternoon, Nkwanzi asked him why he ate so little of the delicious food she had prepared for him.

"By the way Nkwanzi, what sort of food was it?"

She gaped at him.

"What do you mean what sort of food was it?"

"Well to be honest, I could not tell what it was."

"What, you mean you could not tell that it was rice?" Nkwanzi asked hurt.

"Rice! Good God, it did not taste like rice at all. Nkwanzi, are you sure that's what you prepared?"

"Really, how can you ask such a question? Of course it was rice. I bought it with my own money. And I prepared it from early morning till you came. I spent such long hours preparing a dish for you and you say you could not even tell what it was!"

Tingo laughed. "You know what? That was the problem. Rice is never boiled for such a long time. Thank you for the kind thought though."

Then Nkwanzi understood his disinterest in her dish. She took him and gave him sweet potatoes and he walloped everything.

"By the way, there's a boy at school who knows you and he has sent his greetings," he said when he had finished eating.

"Who's that?"

"Genesis Rwenzigye. Nice fellow."

"Oh that one. Well, how's he?"

"All right."

Nkwanzi did not ask him any more questions about Genesis. She was not interested in him anyway. Genesis was not yet done with, though. He wrote to her a few days later.

20.8.1968

Dear Nkwanzi,
I would like you to be my pen friend. Please say yes.
Genesis.

Nkwanzi considered the note. There was no harm being his pen friend.

21.8.1968

Dear Genesis,
I have accepted to become your pen friend.
Nkwanzi.

Soon after, she recieved this letter from him.

24.8.1968

To my dear pen friend Nkwanzi,
How are you?
I would like to come and visit you on the 30th of this month.
Am I welcome?
Your pen friend,
Genesis.

Nkwanzi was not sure how he would be received at home, but Tingo solved the problem for her.

"I'll say that he's my visitor," he said.

They started preparing how they would entertain the visitor.

On the appointed day at 11:00 am, their guest arrived. They had been outside waiting for him, welcomed him and led him to the sitting room. Tingo went for tea and proceeded to serve it. No sooner had he finished than Maama entered the sitting room. On seeing Maama, Genesis put his cup down and got up.

"How are you, Nyabo?" he greeted her politely.

Maama looked him up and down.

Genesis, thinking Maama had not heard his greeting repeated it. She ignored him completely, turned to them and asked with suppressed fury, "Who is this boy?"

"Maama, he's my ..." begun Tingo.

"He's my pen-er ... " Nkwanzi too begun.

"I'm the son of ..." stammered Genesis.

It was as if Maama had heard nothing.

"You Tingo and Nkwanzi, who told you to bring out my visitors' cups? Who? I want the visitors' cups taken back and put in their cupboard."

They looked down. They were embarrassed beyond description. Genesis however understood and said they had to accept what their parents told them. He could not stay for lunch and they escorted him. 'A good thing he hasn't stayed for lunch. Maama would have asked us who had given us her plates for visitors!' thought Nkwanzi grimly. This incident made Nkwanzi develop some pity for Genesis. She felt an anger towards Maama. How could she have ashamed them like she did? However, Nkwanzi did not want to annoy Maama. Time for going back to school was getting closer and if she annoyed her mother, she would not be given most of the requirements like a lot of groundnuts and soyabeans to take to school.

***

First term of second year begun badly for Nkwanzi. The headmistress seemed to have a particular dislike for her and called her to the office.

"Nkwanzi, I understand you were met in town when it was past midnight. You were very drunk and singing on top of your voice. Moreover, you were walking hand in hand with a man," she charged.

Nkwanzi was shocked and she shouted, weeping.

"Really Miss Smith, I don't even drink. How then could I have been drunk?"

"Don't give me any of your tears. That's what was reported.

Nkwanzi walked away, looked for Goora and told her about the incident with Miss Smith.

"It's because she wants you to get saved. If you don't, she'll create more and more stories about you," Goora said.

"But really, Goora, I've always said you can't force one to get saved. I thought salvation comes spontaneously. You have to feel something urging you. I've never felt it. So, how can I get saved?"

"Why don't we attend their Christian fellowship? Then you can act being saved. Moreover the headmistress and all the teachers will like you if you say you're saved. What have you got to lose?"

"But I'll be deceiving God and myself. I can't do that!"

"You can't deceive God. He knows and understands human beings. You wouldn't be deceiving yourself either because you would know what you were up to. Anyway, I'll go and act saved. Maybe then I'll be made a prefect. My parents will be happy." Goora kept on insisting that they should attend fellowships. At long last, she managed to convince Nkwanzi. That Sunday after supper, they went for the fellowship. The headmistress' eyes lit with happiness when she saw Nkwanzi.

"Now, it's time for confessions and testimonies," announced the leader for that evening.

One small girl in senior one got up.

"I want to thank God for what he has done for me this week. And I want to confess my sins. Yesterday, I stole a spoonful of sugar from Lucy's drawer. The other day, I stole some groundnuts from her drawer. I confess to the sin of theft and greed. I ask God to forgive me."

She sat down trembling. The group clapped and sung: 'Tukutendereza'.

Goora giggled. "Those are not sins," she whispered.

"Actually they are. A small sin leads to a big one. It is good if such a girl can confess her small sin," Nkwanzi replied.

"You sound like my mother!" Goora exclaimed.

"Shh," whispered Nkwanzi.

Then Zabulooni, the cleaner got up.

"I also thank the Good Lord for what he has done for me this week. He has caused the good rain to fall and the good sun to shine. But I want to confess to the sin of lust. On Wednesday, the devil tempted me and I slept with the cook's wife," and he wept.

The cook flinched and his wife looked down. The group shook their heads and burst into Tukutenderezza. When they finished, Zabulooni went on with his confessions:

"I've had this devil of lust ever since I was a small boy. I want God to forgive me. Yesterday, the devil led me to sleep with a chicken," he cried.

Members burst into Tukutendereza. They were more vigorous this time. When they finished Zabulooni still had the floor.

"The other day, I lusted after ..."

Oh God, Nkwanzi prayed, let him not say he lusted for a cow or a goat! Really this was becoming too much.

Nkwanzi pinched Goora and whispered, "I think the old man is making up all these sins."

The headmistress never allowed Zabulooni to complete his third confession. She got up resolutely and said,

"You can see what the devil can do. Let us pray for our brother Zabulooni so that he can be fortified against further temptation," and there was a renewed burst of *Tukutendereza* followed by a fervent prayer for Zabulooni.

One by one, the students got up to confess about how they had pinched somebody's salt, stolen a handkerchief from so and so, a rubber, a ruler or pencil. Then suddenly, Goora got up slowly and moved to the front of the chapel. She stood and faced the gathering.

"For the first time in my sinful life, I've also seen the light and from this moment, I've accepted Jesus as my personal Saviour. As I sat there listening, an Angel of the Lord with huge wings, dressed in white appeared to me. He asked me to open my heart to Jesus and I did. Sisters, I've been the worst sinner. I'm not even worthy to stand before you," and she broke down and wept.

The gathering thundered *Tukutendereza*.

"No...ow... now, al that...ha...t...that...I leave behind," she wept as she sat down.

Nkwanzi gave her a pinch and whispered, "You're really an excellent actress.. For a minute, you sounded so genuine that I begun to wonder ..."

Gently, Goora pushed Nkwanzi's hand away and turned her tear stained but admittedly changed eyes towards Nkwanzi.

"Nkwanzi, I'm not pretending. When I came for fellowship, it was to pretend. But then God did touch my heart and I feel a different person. I've committed my life to Him."

Well! Wonders never cease! Somehow actually there was a new look on her, a calmness, a serenity ... Nkwanzi scratched the nape of her neck uneasily ... She was brought out of her deep thoughts by a quietness in the chapel. She looked up and found all eyes turned towards her, looking expectantly at her.

Nkwanzi looked down and whispered, "Goora, I do not feel anything. I can't go there to confess."

"If you don't feel anything, please don't go," she whispered back.

Nkwanzi looked at Goora in wonder. Indeed this was a new Goora.

The headmistress, tired of waiting, stood up.

"Since there're no more lost sheep or since those sheep think they are not lost," she said casting a weary look at Nkwanzi. "We shall go on with the fellowship."

Then the chemistry teacher, whom they had nicknamed Equation, got his guitar and in his deep voice, started singing. His voice was a soft caress on the mind. It soothed like a stream of quiet waters as it ripples through the hills and valleys. His eyes wore a glazed ecstatic look as if indeed he was in paradise. His deep, sonorous voice whispered into their young minds:

> And Lord Jesus, when I look up
> And see your wondrous face
> Gentle and full of Grace
> The pearl gates open
> With Angels ready to welcome me
> Me – a poor sinner
> Then I know that it is only in you
> That there is life.

All their bodies started swaying, caught up in a movement which they could not resist. And as Equation sung, he would call out softly, "If you feel Jesus knocking at the door of your heart, do not resist. Now is the time to open. Come hence, do not fear, the Lord is calling out to you."

And the girls, as if in a trance started going in front. Slowly, like somnambulists, tears streaming down their cheeks, they went towards Equation and surrendered themselves to God. Nkwanzi too found herself getting up, holding out her hands. The music was touching a chord in her heart, making her feel funny, but nicely funny. Goora was visibly happy for Nkwanzi.

"Now's the time to open the door of your heart. Jesus is knocking; don't fear. And on judgement day, He'll call all of us by name. The whole world, He'll address all by name and say: Zabulooni, you're welcome, welcome Joshua ..."

How beautiful! To know that He knew all of us by name!

Then all of a sudden, the magic was shattered by a rude shock.

Zabulooni's gigantic wife started screaming.

"I hears them! I hears the son of God! He say Joyce, you are welcome. He call me by name. He call me!"

As Nkwanzi watched the screaming woman, she woke up as if from a trance. She was frightened and yes, a bit disgusted by it all. She knew within that crowd there were many who had genuinely given their lives to God but also knew there were pretenders in there. She ran out of the chapel as if the very devil was after her only to see Zabulooni's wife on her heels shouting, "Jesus He call me by name." Nkwanzi doubled her speed.

"Nkwanzi, Nkwanzi, come back! Don't run away from the Lord! That's His power at work. And you're now saved, remember? Come back!" Goora shouted, running after her.

"I'm not coming back and I don't want to deceive God that I'm saved. It was the music which deceived me. I'll get saved when I feel that special something that you felt," she shouted back.

She dared not look back lest like Lot's wife, she got turned into a pillar of salt! Some of the girls who became saved then remained so up to the present day. And it has helped them to lead exemplary lives. Many however, fell out along the years.

Chapter Six

Drop-outs and survivors

The second year went along smoothly. Then tragedy struck in the third year. During the second term, Goora begun to behave funnily. She became very moody and always snapped even if asked something simple. All of a sudden, she would not go to the dining hall.

"But really Goora, what is it with you? If it is, malaria, let us go to the sick bay. You should go to the dining and eat," Nkwanzi told her.

Goora broke down and wept.

"I don't know what's wrong with me. I've had three injections of chloroquine and swallowed eight tablets of the same so far but the fever persists."

Chloroquine! Nkwanzi hated the medicine and was not the only one who did so. In fact for most of them, the fear of swallowing bitter Chloroquine tablets was more than their fear of malaria.

"When I smell food, I just want to vomit. That's why I cannot go to the dining hall," she cried.

Her condition deteriorated. She became so thin and light skinned. Then one morning the school nurse came and took her to a clinic in the trading centre for a more thorough examination. Nkwanzi waited for Goora to come back to the dorm but she did not. She went to the nurse.

"Nurse, where is Goora?"

The nurse gave her a queer look.

"Go and read your books and forget about her."

"What do you mean I should forget about her? Is she dd-dde-ddea... dead?"

Nkwanzi was getting puzzled and frightened. 'May be Goora was dead or dying,' Nkwanzi thought in panic. That evening she kept loitering around the sick bay because she was very sure that Goora was somewhere in there. Then about 7:00 pm, the school van came and parked at the sick bay. The headmistress got out and said, "Come this way". And Goora got out of the car. She wore a blank look. Hiding, Nkwanzi somehow managed to follow them. She stood eaves-dropping at the window and she heard the headmistress tell the nurse, "Keep her under tight guard. You know such a girl can easily commit suicide. Keep all medicines away from her."

The headmistress walked out. Nkwanzi crouched in a corner of the sick bay and tried to make herself small and invisible. From her vantage position, she saw members of staff standing in groups of two or three, holding their cheeks in the palms of their hands. For sure, Goora was dying.

When it became pitch dark, Nkwanzi tried the door of the sick bay but it was locked. Desperately, she went from window to window whispering.

"Goora, it is me. Open for me."

Eventually, a small voice answered one of the knocks. Goora's voice sounded frightened but relieved.

"Nkwanzi, how nice it is to hear your voice! How did you know that I was here?"

"I kept on following you. But Goora, tell me quickly. Are you dying?" Nkwanzi asked, her heart pounding.

"No, no. I'm not. Not yet anyway".

Relief flooded over Nkwanzi.

"Then what is it?"

"It's a long story."

"Tell me the short of it."

There was a long pause. Then she said, "Nkwanzi, let me see whether the nurse left the key somewhere. You know she is dead drunk!" Goora laughed.

It did not take long for Goora to get the key and open the door. "I got it from her. She's dead drunk," Goora whispered and they giggled. Goora led Nkwanzi to the room where she had been put. The night was so cold that they were shivering and their teeth were chattering. Goora led Nkwanzi to the bed and pulled back the beddings. "Here, let's get inside for warmth," she said.

Nkwanzi did not need a second calling. She went straight inside to the warmth and they cuddled against each other for more warmth.

"Goora, what's it?"

Goora kept quiet for a long time, looking at the ceiling.

"It's worse than death."

"Anyway, what is it that's worse than death?"

Goora kept quiet. Then in a flat voice, she let out the words: "Nkwanzi, I'm pregnant."

"You're what?" Nkwanzi shouted in terror.

"Shh! Not so loud. You'll wake up the nurse. I said I'm pregnant."

Nkwanzi started weeping. Indeed this was worse than death. How would Goora face her parents and the people in the village? How terrible!

"But who ... who ...?" Nkwanzi started to ask.

"Equation," Goora said with a deadpan face.

"Eh-what? Equation with his angel voice which almost took me to paradise?"

"Yes, it is Equation who did it. You know how poor I'm at Chemistry. He told me to go to his house some months ago so that he could teach me Chemistry. Then he did it. I could not stop him because he is teacher. He said if I screamed, he would kill me. I did not know until today that my illness was caused by pregnancy. You know, Nkwanzi, I'm telling only you. If he knew that I told anybody that he is responsible, he would kill me."

"But he should be exposed and his certificate torn! Why should he go on working when your life is ruined?"

"But if his certificate is torn and he has no job, how will he look after the ... the ... baby ... that is if I decide to produce?"

"And you think he will look after the baby? Forget it. He will even deny that the baby is his. In fact if I had authority, even school boys who make their fellow school girls pregnant would be taken out of school until the girl delivers. It's unfair that such boys stay in school and the girl's expelled."

"What's worse is that after producing, we're not even allowed to go back to school. They say we would be a bad example to the other girls. After I've produced I should be able to go to another school and study. But you find people looking at you as if you're a prostitute or the first person to get pregnant outside marriage. As if you drunk the pregnancy from a glass of water or made yourself so," Goora wept with frustration. In a small frightened voice, she asked, "Nkwanzi, what am I going to do? I'm so scared. My parents will kill me and the whole village will laugh at me."

"Goora, there are girls who have got rid of such pregnancies."

"Yes, I know. There's that woman in town. She does that. But I'm scared that I may die. But then giving birth to this baby is also another death!"

"Have you heard about the methods she uses?"

"Yes. They are several. One I hear is that she pushes a hanger inside..."

"Oh, that's terrible! I already feel stomach ache. Not that one!"

"Then I hear that she can push a small stick... "

"No please, even that is horrible. Anything to do with pushing an object inside should not be considered. It's horrible."

"Then I hear if one takes thirty six chloroquine tablets, the baby comes out."

"Ah, chloroquine is horrible and I'm sure thirty six tablets would kill you. I've heard about other medicines which can do it. Like drinking a cow's urine every morning for a week. That one is harmless even if the idea of drinking cow urine is nauseating."

They went on discussing the different alternatives. In the end, they concluded that abortion was just too dangerous. It was better to have the baby than risk losing one's life. At 5:00 am, a shrill gong sounded. That gong usually went when there was to be an assembly.

"Nkwanzi, you know what? I'm going to run away. I'm not going to wait for that assembly where they will tell the whole school that I'm pregnant and drive me to my parents."

"But where will you pass? There is barbed wire all round the school and a gate keeper."

"I've little money. I'll give it to the gate keeper and tell him not to talk. I'll tell him to tell the headmistress that because I'm a crook, it seems I had instruments with which I cut the barbed wire. The gate keeper can go and cut the wire for evidence."

Nkwanzi agreed with Goora's plan. The shame of making Goora stand in the assembly would be too much. At least Nkwanzi was happy that Goora would not be there to be humiliated. The students assembled in the hall. The school van came screeching and everybody turned to look out with fearful eyes. That van driving towards the assembly hall always meant that the "prisoner" was inside. Nkwanzi sighed with relief.

"Once again Satan has struck at one of us," the Headmistress begun. " Once again, one of you, instead of taking her body as the temple of God, has used it as the devil's house. Goora, a Senior three student has not only disgraced herself and her parents but has disgraced the school as well." She paused for a long time. The girls started whispering that maybe she had been caught with the night watchman. Actually the headmistress was genuinely sad for she considered the students as her own children and wanted the best for them. "Let Goora be brought in," she announced.

Nkwanzi smiled to herself. Lost in her pleasure at knowing that Goora had escaped, Nkwanzi did not see Goora being brought in by the nurse.

"And here she is," said the headmistress. Nkwanzi turned and indeed Goora was standing on the platform, looking down.

"Goora!" Nkwanzi shouted in disbelief.

She did not realise that she had stood up. The girl seated next to her tugged at her skirt and she sat down.

"Yes, she's here," said the headmistress fixing Nkwanzi with a hard stare. "You thought your plan of making her escape would succeed, did you? How foolish of you." The headmistress turned to the school. "This girl isn't only loose but she's also corrupt. She tried to bribe the night watchman with money from her men so that she could escape. God helped us because the watchman is saved and refused her dirty money."

Goora smiled to herself. This watchman was also pretending to be saved! She offered him money. He said no. He wanted sex not money. She spat at him and told him that she would rather die than sleep with him. He led her back to the nurse.

"This girl's corrupt beyond imagination. After the watchman had refused her dirty money, she offered him her body."

The whole assembly pulled in their breath in shock. Nkwanzi looked at Goora. Goora looked back at her and in her eyes, Nkwanzi read denial. Nkwanzi sat back and sighed with relief. She knew Goora could not have debased herself to that extent.

"This girl is pregnant," another hushed shock. "We're, therefore, taking her to her parents. She's expelled from school. And it's our motto to weed out all vermin from the school. We must keep it clean. If any girl's suspected of immorality, she'll be expelled straight away so that she does not infect the others. Please let no one of you get into such a situation."

Poor Goora! She wanted to shout out that it was that bastard, Equation who was responsible. And he was there looking holier than St Peter. Sure, he had solved his lustful equation for a few minutes. And poor Goora's equation would remain unsolved for ever. Goora shuffed to the van and it took her. The girls stood in groups of three to five talking in hushed whispers. Nkwanzi went back to bed and covered herself thinking about what awaited Goora in the village. The weather became chilly and dark clouds hovered in the sky. After a week, she received a letter from Goora.

Nkwanzi my dear,

Since I have been able to go through this ordeal, I will go through anything in life.

76

The van arrived home in the evening. As usual, there were customers at home drinking tonto. Oh my dear Nkwanzi, how my heart beat loudly! I was so scared and ashamed!

As the van stopped, the revellers also put a halt to their drinking. They knew something was wrong. Cars which reached people's compounds were very rare. I saw my father stagger a bit as he came towards the van. The teacher who had escorted me stepped out with the letter from the headmistress.

"Please, I would like to speak to Goora's father."

"You are in his presence," my father, who was obviously drunk, answered with authority.

Teacher looked at him with distaste. He took my father and I aside. By then, mother had come and joined us.

"What's wrong?" she inquired her face creased with worry.

"Your daughter is pregnant," he announced with apparent pride.

There was a moment of shocked silence. My mother stood with her mouth half-open, the word pregnant stuck somewhere down her throat.

Then pandemonium broke out. For a fleeting instant, my eyes made contact with those of my father. Drink had fled from there to be replaced by a glitter of insanity. He turned on the teacher and gave him a blow that staggered him into the van. I caught myself laughing quietly.

'Serves him right. Rejoicing over my misfortune,' I thought. The driver seeing the turn of events drove off fast. My father then turned to the revellers, "Get out of here, out of my house! Did I invite you here? Coming to laugh at me," he froathed as he broke calabashes of beer, threw the contents in the eyes of the drinkers and kicked after them.

His hands then landed on the stick that was used on Kajeru, the stubborn cow. He picked it and beat everything in his way: chicken, the cat, the goats, everything live.

And finally, he came to me. He first tore my uniform into shreds, meanwhile gnashing his teeth and shouting obscenities. He started reigning blows on any and every part of my body.

"Harlot of harlots, queen of harlots. Wasting my money. Ashaming me! I will kill you today!" He beat me until I could not feel the blows of the stick anymore. My mother pleaded but her pleas fell on deaf ears.

"She inherited her harloting ways from you," and he started beating her up too.

My small sisters were around and they started crying. He beat them up mercilessly too.

"You are also harlots," he spat. "And from today, no girl from this home will go back to school. No v....a shall step in school again."

Oh the obscenities Nkwanzi!

77

How I cried. I cried for myself, my mother and now my small sisters. The home was gone. The situation was worse than if somebody had died ...

He chased all of us from home and we crawled to my uncle's home. But Nkwanzi, what is uppermost in my mind is what will be the relationship between the child and myself? For sure, I will not love it because I hate its damned father! Nkwanzi, Nkwanzi, I am lost ... lost.

Mother later suggested that the only way out for me is to get married to a man of many villages away from home where people will not know that I am already pregnant. It did not take long to find a husband for me. A short stump of a man, with mean, cruel eyes was organised. He came to take me away one chilly evening. He had rolled his torn trousers and the calf of his leg stood out like the head of a hammer. The flesh of his buttocks peeped out of two gaping holes in his trousers. His whole body seemed to be a granary of dust – I doubted whether it had seen water in the past decade. His nails were torn and had obviously not been cut for a long time-maybe his teeth doubled as the razor blade. When he opened his mouth to speak, I looked into a long, dark tunnel – endless. His teeth were coated with the millet of yester- years ...

Nkwanzi, our people, have no money but at least they are clean. But this creature! How in heaven's name would I be able to hold this creature in my arms and call it husband? But I had no choice ... After all, it was doing me a great service by marrying me! It was now speaking – almost unintelligible words, eaten up and muffled – something that passed for speech.

"Lets go," it said cruelly. "I will bring the dowry at end of this month."

I got my small bundle of clothes and followed it with tears streaming down my cheeks. I could not keep the creature's pace. It kept throwing a curt "hurry, hurry" at me. Half walking, half running, we reached my new home at about four in the morning.

It went and knocked on the door of a house whose form I could not discern.

"Woman, open," it commanded.

A form opened the door. We went inside. It was pitch dark. Wherever I stepped, my foot would come in contact with a warm body.

"Light the reed," it ordered the form.

The form struck a match which illumined the house briefly. The house was a one roomed affair. At the flash of the match stick, a number of bodies moaned, mumbled and turned in their sleep.

The woman had meanwhile lit the reed which she held up and peered at me closely.

"Make room for where we are to sleep," it ordered. The woman told three children to squeeze closer and make room for "your father and the bride."

Bride! I cringed.

The children moved.

"Sleep," my 'husband' commanded.

I lay down on the grass covered floor. The woman gave us a threadbare blanket.

The "groom" pushed one part of the blanket to me. I pushed it back. I did not care whether I covered myself or not. I was too exhausted to care, my whole body ached. Then I felt the "groom's" hand move roughly between my legs. My God, in the presence of these children and his wife! Roughly, he threw my legs apart. I gritted my teeth and creased my brow waiting for the worst. I could not refuse.

As a sharp pain seared through the centre of my very being, the stench from the "groom" mixed with pain and humiliation made me dizzy and mercifully, I fell into a semi-unconscious state ... It seemed like an eternity before I woke up. The sound of thunder woke me up and I covered my ears as it tore the sky. Flashes of lightening lit up the dark interior of the house and I wished it could strike me dead ... And then the downpour came – in torrents. It was as if we were sleeping in the open. The grass thatch was full of holes and soon, we were drenched to the skin.

When the torrent became a drizzle, my 'husband' told me roughly to get up and go to dig. With difficulty, I got up. I went outside. He threw a hoe at me and ordered me to follow him to the garden. Following him with difficulty, I went to dig.

Nkwanzi, that is my home now. My 'husband' has four wives and about thirty children. I am just an addition to the free labour in his house. Labour that neither complains nor is paid ... the unpaid labourers.

Nkwanzi, goodbye. I hope we shall remain in touch.
Goora

Nkwanzi and Goora never got in touch again for decades – she fell by the wayside. Nkwanzi remained lonely throughout 'O' level. In the holiday prior to the last term, her father brought a teacher to talk to her and Tingo about their future – and give them 'career guidance'.

"We shall start with you, Nkwanzi. Now, what subjects do you want to concentrate on?" the teacher asked her.

"Biology, Chemistry, Physics, Literature, Geography and History."

"Good. Some of those are good subjects for a girl. But I want to help you. You see, you are a good girl. A girl from a good family. By the time you reach 'A' level, men will already be looking at you for marriage. Big men with big jobs. They are already looking at you because you are one of the few clever girls we have. Clever, good mannered and beautiful."

Tingo and Nkwanzi were embarrassed. Why was the teacher saying such things?

"So, with your beauty, good manners and brains, you are going to be the wife of a big man."

Really this was becoming too much!

"But sir, I thought you came to talk to us about subjects which we need to concentrate on," Nkwanzi told him.

"Yes, that's what I'm talking about. Choosing the right subjects will mean choosing the right man for you," he replied unperturbed.

Tingo and Nkwanzi looked at each other, more bewildered than ever.

"So, my dear girl, we have to think about your future. The future for any good girl lies in a good marriage. You must be a good wife. Therefore, the subjects you offer should shape you, mould you into a good wife."

Meanwhile, he had gotten up and was stretching his hands as if going to take a dive at the deep end of a swimming pool.

"Therefore, you're going to take your English Language – she had told him Literature – since you're going to become the wife of a big man. Supposing you were to get foreign visitors in your home, you should be able to speak good English. Your second subject will be home economics. A good wife must be a good cook. You know that common saying. The way to a man's heart is through his what?" he asked Nkwanzi.

She looked helplessly at Tingo who looked more perplexed than her.

"The way to a man's heart is through his what?" insisted the teacher.

"It's through his chest cavity," replied Tingo with authority. He had just learnt about the chest cavity in biology. There was a diagram in Mackean, the biology textbook.

"No, boy. Got it wrong. Nkwanzi, which is the way to a man's heart?"

"It's through his God."

She knew he would be impressed by her religious bit.

The teacher laughed.

"Yes you're right. But we're talking about things here on earth. The way to a man's heart is through his stomach."

What madness was the teacher uttering?

"Yes. If you feed your man well, he'll love you forever. So you must be a good cook. That's why you're going to take home economics. Your third subject will be divinity. A good wife must be a religious wife."

"But sir, if I take divinity, does it mean that I'll be religious?"

"Don't ask stupid questions. Divinity will be your third subject. And there you'll be moulded into a perfect housewife. A housewife who will be smart to entertain the visitors of her VIP husband."

"But sir, with those subjects, what job will I do after completing my studies?"

"What do you mean what job? But you're going to be a big man's wife! Are you so foolish that you haven't been following what I have been talking about? Or if you have to go to work in an office, you can go and learn typing. Those subjects are good enough for you. If you have to work at all, you'll be a secretary."

"But, sir, I want to be a lawyer."

"What? Girl, are you mad? Be a lawyer? And argue with your husband? Look here, your father called me here to guide you. And I've done that. Those are the subjects you'll take. And that is final. Now, you," he said turning to Tingo. "You'll become a big boss. So you have to do tough subjects. You'll concentrate on commerce, economics and political science. You see, you'll become a Permanent Secretary or a Minister. That's why you need Political Science. For commerce, you need to know about trading. You have to make money and commerce plus economics will teach you how to make money. Is that clear?"

"It's very clear. Thank you, sir," Tingo's face was creased in smiles.

"You can do carpentry on the side so that in case you fail to go to university, you can be a carpenter. Or you can learn driving and you become a driver. But you'll pass and become a big man with those subjects. Any questions?"

"But sir, I also want to be a big woman!"

"You will, through your husband."

And with that, he dismissed them. Tingo begun punching the air with his fists. He was very excited.

"You know, Nkwanzi it's true. I'll become a big man. With those subjects, I can't go wrong. I can imagine myself seated at the back of a black Benz with an *askari* in front. And when the Benz stops, the *askari* opens the door and salutes me. A Minister, you know! And everybody will be looking at me with envy, what with my briefcase. Nkwanzi, I'm happy."

81

"Well I'm not and don't show off to me."

"Why, what's the matter with you? The teacher said you're going to be a big man's wife. Doesn't that ..."

"Oh go to hell with your big man's wife idea! Why do you think I'm studying? I too want to use my knowledge to work like you."

"Oh come on. But when you're a big man's wife, you'll also sit in the back seat of the Benz and the *askari* will..."

"Oh shut up. Shut up, shut up!" Nkwanzi screamed at him.

And when the 'O' level results came, she had passed well. She was happy that she would go to study in Kampala city for her 'A' level. Unfortunately, Tingo did not perform well and ended up in a technical school to study carpentry.

Chapter Seven

Coup d'etat

In the middle of the night of January 24th 1971, Genesis was dreaming about the dry season. He was walking after his father as they herded the cattle in search of water. The sun sent her fire relentlessly on earth, there was no cloud cover and Genesis was alarmed that any time, the earth would catch fire. The hot earth scorched his naked feet. Stepping on it was like walking on live charcoal.

Skeletons of cattle littered the caked earth and the further they trudged on, the more skeletons they saw. The meatless jaws of those carcases seemed to hypnotise Genesis and his eyes would get glued to them. Then huge black vultures would descend and pick on these jaws and cackle away. Genesis would try to avert his eyes to no avail.

Then all of a sudden, he could not see his father anymore and he panicked, breaking out in a cold sweat.

"Father!" he screamed only to be answered by the mocking echo of his own voice, "Father, father," the echo replied in a high pitched crescendo.

"Cackle, cackle," barked the vultures.

The thirst began to claw at his throat. He started swallowing his thick saliva at an alarming rate and within no time, his mouth was totally dry.

"My God! My well has dried up!" he said as he went on his knees and poured out his heart to his maker.

"Father in heaven, if I don't get water to drink this very minute, I'll soon become like those skeletons. Please cause it to rain so that just one drop can fall on my tongue."

Suddenly as if from a long distance, Genesis heard the rumbling noise of thunder. Miracle! He knew that God had answered his prayers. Kneeling down in the dusty road, he stretched his tongue out to catch the first raindrop. Another clap of thunder rent the earth and sky and he woke up with a start to find himself stretching out his tongue and panting like a dog. What he thought was another clap of thunder shook the whole structure of the hostel. So the thunder was not just a dream after all. It was going to rain. This was going to be quite a heavy thunderstorm. Several of the students were by the windows, looking towards the city wondering about the ferocious thunder. Genesis joined them.

The hostel was situated at Old Kampala Hill – one of the seven hills then, that the city of Kampala was built on. The hostel was packed with students to capacity. As Genesis struggled to get a place in between the closely lined up beds, another very sharp clap of thunder threatened to tear the earth asunder. All the other students jumped out of their beds.

"What sort of thunder is this?" they asked.

As they were wondering what all this was about, the headmaster walked into the hostel. His house was nearby. The students were relieved to see him and crowded around him.

"Sir. Sir, what sort of thunder is this?"

"It is not thunder. That is the noise of heavy gunfire. Such gunfire signifies very serious trouble for the country," he said.

"What trouble do you think is brewing up for the country?" asked Genesis.

"It's most probably a coup."

"A coup?" chorused all the others. "What on earth is that?"

"A coup means taking over government using force of arms. Normally, it is the army which does so," the headmaster explained.

He was interrupted by heavy shelling and the sound of continuous gunfire. This latter noise sounded like corn being popped in oil and later the students named this particular noise pop-corns. The headmaster spoke over the heavy 'thunder' and told the students to take cover under their beds.

"Take cover, take cover all of you. Stray bullets can come through the windows any time."

The students had never heard the words take cover but hearing the tone of steel and command in the headmaster's voice coupled with the unearthly noise outside, they all meekly went under their beds. Occasionally, controlled sobs of fear could be heard from under the beds. The situation worsened when the loudest bang of all boomed out. The windows of the hostel shattered into pieces. The students now knew for sure they were dead. Most of them cried out for their mothers – always the first and last cry in times of both ecstasy and pain. The headmaster himself, frightened out of his wits, threw himself under the nearest bed. When the noise subsided, he got out his head cautiously, feeling it to see whether it was still intact.

Even though the circumstances were grim, he recalled a much talked about incident of a man who was swimming in a river and was attacked by a hippo. The man who thought he had escaped the hippo, swam and as he neared the shore, shouted out to the people that he had escaped being sawn into two by the vicious hippo. He swam on and people came congratulating him on having survived. He stretched out his arms and the people stretched out theirs to pull him on shore. They pulled and got the shock of their lives. The lower part of the man was missing. What had been swimming was the head and chest with the heart still beating. Everybody ran away and left what was left of the man to sink to the bottom of the river!

Then, there was the tragedy of fatal accidents. A victim of such an accident sighed with relief and said, "That was a terrible accident but thank God I survived it", and then died after that.

Mzee got up cautiously and looked towards the city. There was heavy, black smoke everywhere.

The headmaster had come with a radio which he now turned on. Marshal music filtered through. Then a voice came on, speaking slowly, very slowly, almost like a child learning to talk.

Ziz is a speso announce. The government spokesman wishes to informs all the piploz of this greet county, zata za Uganda armed force led by his exellenta Major General Duduma have tooks over the government. Ze new President will swear at ten hocklock dis hafternoon. End of specso announce. By government spokesman.

"I suppose by saying the swearing in ceremony is at 10:00 pm, he means 4:00 pm," said the headmaster.

Most of the students were holding their ribs in laughter at the spokesman's bad English.

"But who is this Duduma?" asked the students.

They attentively listened to him, some of them understanding, others merely looking at him with big eyes of miscomprehension.

"Duduma is the army commander. To begin with, it is the colonialists who found him when they were recruiting Africans to fight in the second world war. They looked for tall, strong, illiterate people who could obey orders without questioning. So, Duduma entered the force and later on Opolo used him to fight his battles, especially the one of the Kabaka of Buganda. Duduma brutally quelled the rebellion in the Kabaka's palace and Opolo was pleased with him. Opolo being from the northern part of Uganda wanted a person who would be loyal to him to head the army. According to Opolo, he would rather trust

Duduma who was also from the north. So, he made him the army commander."

After the explanation, the headmaster told them they could go to the city to see what was happening. He cautioned them to be careful and to move in groups. They set off.

From all over the city, soldiers seated precariously on jeeps, lorries and all manner of vehicles streamed into the city singing songs of victory. They called out to the civilians to join in the celebration.

"*Saasa to na overthrew ditator* Opolo! The killer is went! Hurray!" they chanted as they gulped down alcohol.

Many of them did not know how to drive. They would grab cars from people who had held big posts in Opolo's government and try to drive them. Cars were veering madly around before smashing into buildings. Many cars were wrecked and many soldiers perished. As the two friends walked along, Genesis all of a sudden stopped and screamed.

"My God!" he cried.

"What's the matter?" asked Mzee.

"There is a dd-ead bo-bbody here!"

"Don't look at it. Let's go."

Genesis tried to avert his eyes from it by looking in the opposite direction. Then he let off another nerve wrecking scream. He had almost stepped over another dead body whose eyes stared horribly in death. This one had no legs and the intestines were strewn all over the place. A number of small children were staring at it curiously. A mangy dog with a hungry look licked its hanging lips.

"Those kids should not see such things. Come, let us get some grass and throw it on the body. You know in our culture, in the rare event that you see a dead body in the open, you bury it by throwing some grass there."

They gathered grass which grew by the roadside and as they were about to throw it on the body, a jeep full of soldiers screeched to a halt and a soldier jumped out.

"Halt! Do not covering that dead bodies or any *ader. Dose dey* traitor of Opolo. Kicks *dem*," he said as he cocked his AK 47 and emptied a whole magazine into the inert body. The body danced to the grotesque disco of the bullets. Its mouth pulled back over its teeth, it seemed to sneer and laugh at the irate soldier.

The nearer they got to the city centre, the more dead bodies they met. At one time, they saw a woman's dead body. A baby suckled from the lifeless breast of the corpse. As they stood rooted to the spot, not knowing what to do, a woman who had been walking along with them gave her baby to Mzee. She looked left and right to see whether there was a soldier in site. Seeing none, she dashed to the corpse, got the baby and put it on her own breast and the baby suckled hungrily.

Thousands and thousands of people thronged the city, waving branches and chanting slogans of victory.

"Duduma our saviour, our Messiah, may you live long! You have taken us out of the jaws of death," they sang and danced together with the soldiers.

By late afternoon, everybody was streaming towards Parliament for the swearing in of the 'Messiah'. As the excitement built up, out of nowhere, a soldier aimed his gun at the court of arms at the entrance to Parliament and pulled the trigger. With a deafening noise which temporarily silenced the crowd, the court of arms tumbled down and shattered into a thousand pieces. When the noise died down, the people thundered into applause.

"Our saviours, hurray! You have completely destroyed Opolo's last connection with this land," said one man as he shook the soldier's hand and handed him a fat bundle of bank notes.

"But this is wrong," an elderly man Yakobo said under his breath.

"The court of arms does not belong to any President. It's for the country. Me, I'm leaving. It is lunatics who have taken over the country," he said to his friend, Dombo, who agreed with him but convinced him to stay on. Afterwards, it was realised that it was only Opolo's head that had been shattered. The Court of Arms had remained intact.

Meanwhile, the naked sun rentlessly baked the waiting crowd. People sweated profusely, several fainted but still, they waited. Soon, President Duduma arrived to a tumultuous welcome. He arrived in a jeep, driving himself and followed by about a hundred other jeeps all mounted with the hugest guns they had ever seen. The excitment in the air was so thick one could cut it with a knife. And when Duduma alighted, towering over everybody, the crowd surged forward, each person trying to shake his hand. He wore such a winning smile and his face looked so innocent and friendly that for that alone, he won the hearts of many. He shook as many hands as he could with the crowd surging forward, almost causing people to be crushed.

He was then given the microphone to swear: "I, Duduma, *swaers dat* ..."

After being sworn in, the crowd begged, "Saviour, speak to us. Give us a few words of wisdom."

President Duduma smiled, took the microphone and addressed the nation:

Ladies under gentlemen, Saasa I am bery happy completely and also to stood here and undress you on this suspicious ocazion. I not politician, I professional solder and man of few wards, brief wards. No ambition man your Daddy, buta very good man completely and throughout. Tomorrow, I write to Mr Queen of Engranda. I to told her my country Uganda now stability. Bada man Opolo has wented."

And then he really got worked up, so annoyed that he started foaming at the mouth:

"Opolo he thief, he tribes, drunco, is went to bed with woman completely, he kill, bring kondo, broughts poor. He taxing. I am tell you the true," he said as his eyes danced dangerously. Then abruptly, he switched on his big smile and seemed to relax. *"I, wants to brought you educate. Imagined, even small childs in England more clever than big piploz here. Small childs dere, dey speak Hinglish! And ourself here, big piploz can`t spoke Hinglish! How small childs can spoke hinglish and we old piploz here we cannot? How for childs to be more clever than ourshelves? Dis, I cannot allows. I am sunk you berry much for what have you done."*

There followed thunderous applause. Genesis and Mzee had kept on pinching each other as Duduma spoke on almost unintelligibly.

"Eh, this fellow does not know English, how will he rule us?" remarked old man Yakobo.

"But is it English which rules?" rejoined Dombo.

"My point is, at least the President should be educated!" Yakobo butted in. "English is our medium of instruction whether we like it or not and more so it is our national language. So in our case, it is a mark of an educated person. And I'll be damned if I will be ruled by an illiterate. I'm not even sure your Duduma will rule us peacefully as you say. Things which start in blood usually end up the same way. There are already so many dead bodies so what peace is there?"

That very evening, the looting intensified. The shops were looted clean. Most shopkeepers, the majority of whom were Asians, were told not to worry. They would be compensated by the 'civilised' new regime.

The soldiers, led by the civilians then went on rampage to the residences of people who had held big government posts like ministers, managers of parastatals and the like. These homes were swept clean. Most of such big shots had long fled the previous night, many of them into neighbouring Kenya. The looters took everything – from personal items like photographs to deroofing the houses.

One wife of such a former minister who had fled from her house watched from a neighbour's as her property was being vandalised. Later, she found photographs of her wedding torn to pieces. The looters shat in every room and smeared feaces on the walls and used some of the photographs and certificates as toilet paper. She wept broken heartedly as she knew she would never recover such memories as had been captured in the photographs.

"What had my photographs done against these people?" she lamented.

For months after the coup, an atmosphere of bliss pervaded the city and the whole country pouring in from far and wide and the President's popularity soared. He could talk to the poor and impoverished. He loved children and on many of his trips in the city, he always stopped to greet and give them generous amounts of money. On many occasions, he drove himself in an open jeep to all sorts of places to prove that he had no enemies.

Behind all this, Duduma began to systematically kill right and left. He started killing the people of the deposed President Opolo's region. One morning in one of the army barracks, an early trumpet sounded all the soldiers to a meeting. At the meeting, a captain informed the rest that President Duduma wanted to meet a certain section of the army.

"*Good news are in store for yours,*" started the officer in-charge with a broad smile when all were at parade. "*The President, he want to meet many of you. So we are prepared list ya watu wuyo watayenda to looking the President,*" and the officer in-charge got out a long list and started reading from it. The other soldiers became envious of those who were lucky to be going to meet the big man. Most likely, they were going to be promoted.

As each name was read out, the others clapped with joy for the good luck of the chosen. Others clapped with envy. The list was quite long. When the officer in-charge had read out more than a hundred names with the owners going to the front, there was a sudden air of unease, of fright and apprehension in the hall.

"Do you know, all the names which are being read are from one region! Opolo's region! What does this mean?" whispered one soldier and the whisper spread. Tension and fright filled the air.

"The rest went back. And dose in front, *mwende kwa* lorries," said the officer in-charge.

"Afande, where are we going?" one ventured to ask.

"Why, I tolded you we are goes for tea with de President. President, he good man. He want to show dat he no tribe. He promote even piploz of Opolo." He smiled and they relaxed.

The group of more than three hundred were herded on to tipper lorries. Some of their families had heard the rumour that they were being taken for promotion. The families, filled with joy, came to see them off. As the lorries sped off, the wives and children waved cheerfully.

The soldiers waved back, some with uncertainty. The lorries were driven at breakneck speed, the dust from the murrum road making it impossible for those on top to see where they were going. They drove on and on until dusk and begun ascending a steep hill. At what seemed like the summit, they came to a stop.

"Press the red button," ordered the officer in-charge in a deadly calm, voice. The drivers felt a shiver run through them. But they had to obey orders. They extended their fingers and pressed the red button, in each lorry, hard. They felt the springs of the tippers creek and slowly, like in a slow motion horror picture, the back part of the tippers went into the air and threw their contents over a hanging cliff.

Screams rent the night air as the occupants of the tipper lorries found themselves in space with nothing to hold on to, their arms beating the air like birds whose wings had been severed, before plunging deeper into darkness and emptiness and then they hit the dark, swirling waters of Lake Victoria. Lake Victoria, shaken out of her peaceful slumber sucked them in, her waters angrily lashing out at humankind for sacrificing her own.

The lake birds, their slumber interrupted woke up and flapped their wings in anger, their cry of protest mingling with the human cries of extinction... Lake Victoria took in the children of Adam and Eve and covered them with her cold blanket, enveloping them in an eternal embrace. Then a calmness descended on the waters below once again as the echo of the cries faded away.

"Let's go. And remember, you've seen nothing and dead men don't talk," the officer in-charge barked.

The lorries set off in a single file, their emptiness making them rattle loudly along the murrum road. They reached the barracks at dawn. The wives had been waiting to welcome their promoted

90

husbands back. They all dashed to the lorries.

"*Wamaama*, your husbands *saasa banayenda* for training for five years. When they comed back, they wills be big men. So you pack and waited for dem from your village omes."

Some women were happy, some sad. Five years! That was a long time. But word went round that the men had been killed. Similar operations had taken place in the other barracks and men from Opolo's area mercilessly felled down. A stench of blood hit the country. Duduma's government pretended that nothing was amiss and some people from other tribes shrugged it off.

"Ah!" they said. "We shouldn't blame Duduma for killing those people. They were ruling, their turn is over. Those people are bad. Why do they involve themselves in sabotaging government?"

These people did not know that very soon, Duduma's killing machinery would descend on all the tribes in the country.

Others wept, "This is terrible, what kind of President is this? This is a monster! How can he kill people like this? Innocent people? A weevil has entered our country."

Chapter Eight

Exodus and after

One Saturday when Nkwanzi and her roommate Atim went to the
city window shopping, they came across Genesis and Mzee. They
greeted each other warmly.

"Nkwanzi! My! How you have grown!" exclaimed Genesis.

"So have you," Nkwanzi said.

Nkwanzi introduced Atim.

"Atim, Mzee is a friend. Our homes are not too far from each
other and Genesis is my pen-friend," Nkwanzi said and they all burst
into hearty laughter.

Genesis' laughter was fresh, invigorating, open. Nkwanzi found
herself wishing she could crack some joke and hear his laughter once
more...

"Come and we show you where we stay," Genesis invited.

They went to the hostel. Mzee put the kettle on the boil. He then
mixed millet flour in a plastic jug, poured the boiling water into the
mixture, stirred and millet porridge was ready. He served it in plastic
cups and as they sipped the hot porridge, they discussed events in the
country, the terrible killings all over.

They sat in gloomy silence for some time. The silence was broken
by Mzee's creaking radio. Those days, most people kept the radio on
constantly as any time the "government spokesman" could come up
with an important announcement which was what was coming on right
now. They all strained their ears.

"*Zis iz speso announce. De government spokes-man wisez to informed de
general pubic dat last nights, Presdent Duduma had a dreams. In dis da
dreams, God tolded him; de piploz of Uganda, dey berry, berry poor also. God
tolded de President to tooks dem piploz from poor. God tolded him; give
businesses to poor den poor no longer like so. God saided, get business from
hand of foreign and give to piploz of Uganda. God he saying, you seeing
Asians? Dey milking de cow, de cow Uganda and not gave it foodstuffs. De cow
den grow sin, sin you can looked sru it. Derefore, God saids to President, sent
away dem Asians, gave business to our piploz. Dis God's order.Derefore, the
President, he goodman, he mankind. Derefore, he give Asians much days to
prepares demself to pack and went back to deir ome, Hindia. He give dem
ninety day. Dey to start pack now. End of speso, announce.*"

There was stunned silence which lasted for about two minutes, and then they all spoke at the same time.

"My God, chasing away the Asians..." began Atim

"Christ, this is unbelievable! How..." Mzee was saying.

"Incredible! How can this..."

"Sweet Jesus!..."

"How, how ...?"

The whole hostel was aghast with shock.

"You people, let us dash back to the city to see how people have received the news," suggested Genesis.

"Brilliant idea!" the others chorused.

They went to the stage to catch a taxi. People stood in groups talking excitedly. The Asians were huddled in shocked silence in their shops.

The reaction of the people was varied. Many of them were saying, "This President is the greatest on the African continent. He cares for his people. Now he is giving us riches. We have been just watchers of the Asians as they made money in our land and we grovelled in poverty! Indeed, President Duduma was sent by God."

Others were apprehensive.

"What sort of dreaming President is this? Are we going to be ruled through dreams? We're in trouble. This President is simply a lunatic. How can he give these Asians ninety days in which to quit?"

"But you people, don't despise the man's dream and dismiss it. There are many people who get visions through dreams. It is like many of our herbalists, they get to know the right herbs through dreams. What about the Biblical Joseph? Was he not a dreamer?"

"Let these bloody Asians quit our land. They're a bad lot. Infact ninety days are even too long. They despise us and pay the African workers very little money. Calling us *Boi*! Can you imagine that! Even if an African worker is grey haired and over seventy years, they still call him *boi*. They never mix with us. Holding up their noses and thinking they are more superior. Let them leave us alone and go back to their homes."

"What do you mean they don't mix with us? You probably mean they can never intermarry with us. But we don't have to marry each other in order to show that we've integrated. This thing Duduma has done is terrible and we shall pay dearly."

"Let them go bag and baggage to their homes!"

"Which homes? For most of them, Uganda is the only home they know. Most of them were born here."

Everyday, the government spokesman's voice would come over the radio, "*Today, we wisez to informed the Asian dat dey now left wid 88 day, 98,...75,... 40,...20, ... 10,... 5,... tomorrows, you leaves our country.*"

The morning of the day of the exodus, Atim, Genesis, Mzee and Nkwanzi agreed to meet in the city and watch the proceedings. When they reached the spot for their rendezvous, they decided to go to the airport to see how the Asians were taking off.

The airport was filled with loud wailing. The Asians wept openly, their future bleak. They had been allowed to take just a few belongings. Stories of how many of them had committed suicide abound. It was said that many hurled themselves into LakeVictoria. As another group was about to board a Boeing, Nkwanzi suddenly saw one of the women stand at the entrance. Then the woman lifted her dress.

"Look, look at that woman! What is she doing?" Mzee asked.

"I've also been watching her," Nkwanzi said.

The woman lifted her dress exposing her bare brown bottom. She then bent down and showed her bottom to nobody in particular.

"Eh, she is showing her bottom to Duduma's regime," said Genesis averting his eyes.

"This is a terrible curse. I did not know that Asians too have that kind of curse. When a woman bends over and shows you her bare bottom, you are doomed," Atim said.

"Actually, the Asians may not be having that custom. Maybe they got it from us," Nkwanzi sighed.

The woman then stood up straight, re-arranged her dress, and entered the plane, and the plane closed. Shortly after, it took off.

They shook their heads and went back to the city.

For the next few weeks, the city was awash with excitement. The soldiers and relatives of the rulers were allocated shops and businesses left by the Asians.

"Major Panga *has tooks over the Textile Pactory.*

Captain Kill-me-Quick *is owned the suga planteson.*

Lt Colonel no-Parking *now owned of Diary Milks.*"

The gang of four, as Genesis' group came to be known, went downtown to see how the new business class were carrying on with their newly acquired businesses. In one shop, they found a young man beaming with happiness.

"How much is that blue shirt?" Genesis asked him.

The young man looked at the collar of the shirt.

"Twelve," he replied promptly.

"Only twelve shillings!" they whispered in amazement. That was really cheap.

"What about that green dress?"

The young man looked at some tag on the dress.

"Ten."

Again they were amazed at how cheap things were. With the little money they had, they were able to do big shopping.

As they were leaving, the young owner of the shop said, "*This President Duduma really great. Look me. I no go school but now I am million. Duduma! May God to live him for long and ever.*"

"This man has a point. As he says, he never went to school but through good luck, he's now a millionaire. He's right to thank God," said Genesis.

"I agree but the question is, will he be able to sustain the business?" asked Mzee.

"Well, one hopes so," replied Genesis.

Later when they were wondering how things could be so cheap, they realised that the Ugandan businessmen had in fact made a blunder. When asked for the price of a piece of clothing, they would look at the size and take it to mean the price of the item. With such underpricing, soon the shops were empty. Commodities started disappearing. In the midst of this scarcity, President Duduma still boasted that there were a lot of riches;

"*Saasa, I want to told you zat Mafuta ni mingi. Watu wa Uganda, dey hab got business now, dey hab got money. De piploz now are all mafutamingi.*"

From then on, the class of rich people which had been created by President Duduma came to be known as *Mafuta-Mingi.*

***

The years rolled on and soon, Nkwanzi, Genesis, Mzee and Atim entered university – the one and only university in Uganda then, Makerere University. Genesis and Mzee registered for Political Science. Nkwanzi registered for Law and Atim for Education.

Chapter Nine

University

Makerere University! How it had changed by the seventies! In the sixties, it had been a place of grandeur. The dons used to earn a living wage. Books and journals were available, the bookshop and library were fully stocked. But by the seventies, the situation had drastically changed. Books were vandalised by illiterates who would sell them cheaply to market vendors. It was sad to go to the market, buy pounded groundnuts and have them wrapped up in a piece of paper which one later on found to be from Chinua Achebe's novel, **Things Fall Apart** or Mackean's **Introduction to Biology**. Many times, foodstuffs were also wrapped in government papers on which was written TOP SECRET.

In the sixties, the undergraduates used to have anything up to six course meals but now, there was one standard meal: *posho* and *murrum*. Makerere University had been the best institution to be at in all ways. It had been an ivory tower in every sense. But now, the situation started going from bad to worse ...

Soon after their arrival on campus, Genesis and Nkwanzi started seeing each other regularly.

"This fresher is coming for importation," the other students would say good naturedly on seeing her.

After a few weeks Genesis told Nkwanzi solemnly. "Nkwanzi, you know how I feel about you. I'm now asking you to be the custodian of my heart. I want us to be fiancees."

Nkwanzi felt love well up inside her and she could not answer him. He took her face gently in his hands and made her look into his eyes. Then as gently, he parted her lips with his tongue and kissed her. Nkwanzi returned his kiss with a fire and a passion that surprised even her. Then she felt her knees weaken and sensing it, Genesis led her to his bed and they held each other as if their very lives depended on it. Slowly he took off her clothes.

"My! Nkwanzi! You're lovely!" he breathed thickly.

"I'm too thin!" she replied shakily.

"Honey, the nearer to the bone the sweeter the meat," he said as they melted into each other.

Nkwanzi felt Genesis' hand move down and commence to remove her underwear and a tremor went through her. But in the same instant, she seemed to see a hazy picture of Ssenga and Maama frowning down at her.

"No, please Genesis," she said getting up and holding him at arm's length.

"Nkwanzi, what do you mean?"

"Genesis, I'm sorry but we can't have sex."

"What? You are not serious Nkwanzi. Please honey, come..."

"No, Genesis. I'll not have sex with you until our wedding night."

"What! Nkwanzi, I don't believe this. You belong to the medieval ages! If we can't have sex, how do we call ourselves boy and girl friend and better still, fiancees?"

"No Genesis. No sex till marriage. We shall only kiss."

"But kissing is only an introduction to greater things! We can't kiss passionately and not go on to do the needful!"

"I'll not do that so called needful. It's wrong."

"That's childish. It's only teenagers who hold hands, cuddle and kiss only. Look, most people on this campus are doing it anyway."

Nkwanzi was beginning to get irritated.

"I'm not most people. Look Genesis, we're going to live together all our lives. There'll be plenty of sex. We need to wait for only three years when we complete our course, marry and then have it. Call me conservative but when on our wedding day I put on a white bridal attire, I want that white to symbolise my sexual purity. Moreover, I remember when I got my first period, my aunt said I must stay a virgin until my wedding day. She said the morning after my wedding, a white sheet which my husband and I will have used that night would be brought out and shown to the entire clan of my husband. If my husband found me a virgin, the sheet would be stained with blood. If not, a big hole would be cut in the middle of the sheet to symbolise that my womanhood was like a gaping hole. The sheet ..."

"Oh damn the sheet! Nkwanzi, how can I starve for three years? And especially when I love you?"

"That is precisely why you should wait."

He sighed. Heavily.

"All right honey. I love and respect you so much, I will wait."

"Thank you Genesis," she said hugging him.

As they seriously took to their studies, commodities in shops disappeared everywhere. They took tea without milk or sugar and saltless food. Soap was almost impossible to get while paraffin was a fairy tale.

It was at this difficult time that a *mafutamingi* came into Nkwanzi's life. The name was usually shortened to *mafuta*.

***

One evening, as Nkwanzi and her friends sat on the bench outside the hall, a practice that was commonly known as benching, a black Mercedes Benz came and parked nearby. Out of it came a fat, tall, quite handsome man dressed in a gray Kaunda suit.

"I wonder who that *Mafuta* has come for?" wondered one of the girls.

The *Mafuta* went to the custodian's office. Immediately, the custodian came directly to Nkwanzi and said she had a visitor. Nkwanzi was surprised but went all the same.

"I am yours visitor," started the *Mafuta* extending his fat hand to her. "You looks surprised to seed me. I am goods friend of yours *faaza*. He tolded me you had came to universe so I camed to pays you a visiting. Comes, let we goes to the car and picks your language," he said. Nkwanzi looked uncomprehendingly at him. "I said come and pick your language."

'Pick my language! If any language needed any picking it was his not hers,' she thought with suppressed laughter as she realised he meant luggage.

"I've bringing you a few *tings* as a friend of *faaza* your."

They went to the car and he opened the boot. There was a suitcase and two huge boxes. He took them out.

"You mean, sir, all these things are mine?" Nkwanzi asked him. He laughed.

"Yes of course not. Actually. But *dey* small *tings*."

Puzzled, they lifted the things to her room. He opened the Boxes. There were enough tins of margarine, packets of biscuits and all manner of eats to start up a canteen.

"Sir, what are all these for?" Nkwanzi asked in amazement.

" Of course for yours. I knows the situation in Camps. There is too much of hungers. In order to studying well, you must to eat too well. Me nice man. Me, your *faaza* friend so I helping for you."

Something told Nkwanzi to send off the *Mafuta* packing with his mobile canteen. But then she recalled how for almost a week now, they had not had any tea since there was no milk, tea leaves or coffee. The sugar that there was in the country was being hoarded and then sold at exorbitant prices. It was only the *mafutas* who knew where to buy this sugar and who could afford it anyway. So, there was no way she could refuse this *mafuta's* things. She needed them badly.

Then he opened the suitcase. Dresses, lingerie, platform shoes...

"Do you want me to sell these clothes for you, Sir?"

"No, no, no. Took, took forever," *Mafuta* said with a winning smile.

"But sir, what on earth am I going to do with all these clothes?"

"Don't be like a childrens. Just wears them. You have to be smarty on camps."

"What about my parents? Where will they think I got the clothes from?"

" *Dey* knew already. Don't forgets your *faaza* he make me to look over you, like guardsman."

Nkwanzi took out the clothes hesitantly and hang them in the wodrobe.

"Now, gets ready, gets set and we went. I want to takes you for eating and danced at Imperial Hotels and Lodging."

She had of course heard about the Imperial Hotel. She wanted to go and see what this grand hotel was like. Moreover, she liked dancing. However, she was getting a bit apprehensive about this *mafuta*. What would her friends say if they knew that she had gone out with him?

"But, sir, I hear Imperial Hotel is very expensive."

"Why worried about money? I'm money itself! Money no problem. Get readys and we went and stops calling me sir. You made me sound Mzee. My name was Jackson. Call it Jackie."

There was no harm in having a nice meal. He chose one of the dresses he had brought. Nkwanzi put it on with one of the pairs of platform shoes. He gave her what he called a perfume to spray on herself. She read the words on it: 'Glade air freshner'. She frowned. Was this really a body perfume? But to tell the truth, as a first year at university, she did not know any better. They had been brought up in schools where deodorants and perfumes were unheard of and if a student managed to get one from maybe an elder sister and used it, the teachers on smelling it would tell her to go and bathe it off, labelling her a harlot.

She applied the Glade air freshner and *Mafuta* said, "Mm, you smells goodness". She was not sure. At the back of her mind, she was reminded of insecticide, DDT was the common one those days.

When she looked at herself in the mirror, however, she was quite happy with what she saw. The attire had transformed her positively.

Mafuta acknowledged, "Ah, you looked greatful. You knows, the way I founded you down there, you looking like nun. You were wears that no shape *kitenge.*"

"Please don't insult my *kitenge.* It was my mother who gave it to me and I treasure it." She was not about to allow *Mafuta* to insult her *kitenge.*

"No problem, no problem I was announcing how smarts you looks. Let us went."

Nkwanzi and *Mafuta* reached the parking bay. He moved quickly to open the door of the sleek, black mercedes benz for her. In the same instant, Genesis arrived at the scene. When he saw her, he stopped short in his tracks. Surprised, he stood agape staring at her. Feeling a bit embarrassed, she looked back at him with her eyes a bit downcast. Good God, why was she feeling ashamed and a bit guilty? She had not done anything wrong! There was a moment of silence. The *mafuta,* stood foolishly with the door of the benz halfway open.

"Nkwanzi, you look so different, so – mature and – and... And where are you going?" Genesis asked.

"Oh we are went for eating and dance at Imperial Hotel and lodging," interjected the *mafuta* airily. "And we are got late."

Genesis looked confused, shocked and flabbergasted.

"Genesis this is my father's friend. My father has made him my guardian," Nkwanzi said sounding unconvincing even to herself.

"Oh, I see," said Genesis lamely.

Nkwanzi wondered whether he could see anything. She was getting increasingly embarrassed.

"Mr Jackson, this is my friend Genesis."

"How you young boy? Me no problem," said *Mafuta* extending his fat sweaty hand to Genesis.

Genesis' hand got lost in the soft, massive flesh of *Mafuta's* hands. In one sweeping glance, Jackson took-stock of Genesis from head to toe. Genesis became aware of his neat but obviously worn out shirt, of his trousers which were not exactly fashionable and were a bit worn out on the hem. His shoes told a story of poverty and want. The soles were long worn out and the shoes were in fact facing a funny angle. To make matters worse, Genesis' tooth had just been extracted and he had a swollen cheek which had disfigured his face.

"But thank God I am neat," Genesis told himself and this gave him new courage. "This pot-bellied fellow's collar is black with the grime of his sweat."

And with his new found strength, he stretched himself to his full height and said with forced cheerfulness, "Well Nkwanzi, have a good dinner. And you sir, don't address me as a boy. I am a man. Nkwanzi I will wait up for you."

"Waits for her? Not necessarily. No problem. Dancing to morning. She okay, no sleep, you sleep."

"But Nkwanzi also needs the sleep!"

Mafuta laughed out loud and clear.

'Uncouth laughter, obscene laughter,' thought Genesis.

"She will sleeps. I gives her sleeping doze. Big, big sleeping doze. No problem," and he threw a glance of understanding in her direction and winked at her.

Nkwanzi recoiled from *Mafuta's* stare where she read a lot of unsaid things. He then ushered her into the car and closed the door with much ceremony. He went to the driver's side and inserted a cassette in the player. Loud, blaring music boomed out. It was the obscene 'Jungle Fever' record. Good God, what would her friends and Genesis think of her going out with a *mafuta* who was loudly playing *Jungle Fever*?

Mafuta drove off the Benz with screeching tyres, sending a cloud of dust cascading over poor Genesis' head. The wheel almost touched Genesis' foot and he jumped and stood on the pavement. He stood watching as the black limousine flew off. He wore a bewildered, confused, hurt expression on his face. As they were leaving, Nkwanzi thought she discerned a glitter of something like unshed tears in his eyes. And as he stood there on the pavement, lonely and sad, her heart went out to him. She knew what he must be feeling and pity welled up inside her. There was a frog in her chest. She wished she could get out of that sleek Benz, go back to Genesis' room, boil porridge and eat cassava with him. Then they would read Milton's **Paradise Regained** together.

Mafuta brought her back to the present.

"Hey my darlingest, if you keeps look behind, your byutifull necks pained. Lets went and enjoys. No problem," he said as he put his fat hand over hers and gave it a squeeze.

Nkwanzi quickly withdrew her hand. He got hold of it again and scratched the palm. She snatched it away again. 'These men think women are always there waiting to be scratched in the palm of their hands. I hate men who scratch women in their palms,' she thought disgustedly.

As the black mercedes rounded the corner, Nkwanzi took a last look at Genesis. He stood lonely, with his swollen cheek, the tall tower of the Hall behind him making him look shorter than he was. The sun was setting and it illumed him briefly while casting a long shadow behind him. Then she lost him.

***

Genesis walked slowly to his hall, head, hanging down. He walked lifelessly, like a zombie. There was a group of girls who had been watching the scenario. They wanted to laugh out loud and clear but something held back their laughter. Genesis looked so grief stricken: his grief commanded respect and nobody laughed.

He reached his room, and stood by the window looking out towards the Kasubi Tombs. Genesis envied the dead. Was it not better to die, to get lost in oblivion and become the dust and soil of this earth than to live this kind of life where his very life had been snatched away from him by an illiterate *mafuta*? And he had been impotent, had been unable to do anything to halt the theft of his Nkwanzi. What could he do when that lousy *mafuta* had presented a whole new wardrobe to his Nkwanzi? What could he do when a brand new Benz was used to steer her away? Genesis was lost and knew it.

He got out a copy of **Paradise Regained**, which he was supposed to have discussed with her. Then he threw it away. Without thinking, he got out a copy of **Paradise Lost**. But he could not read anything. The letters got blurred.

Mzee, in a very jolly mood, entered the room.

"Hi Genesis, what're you doing here? I thought you said you were going to have discussions with Nkwanzi and burn the midnight candle. What happened?"

Genesis kept quiet and it was only the slight tremor that seemed to run through his body at the mention of the name Nkwanzi that showed any indication of any feeling. Mzee approached Genesis cautiously and softly turned him around. What he saw in Genesis' eyes made him shudder with apprehension. Infact the eyes were expressionless. There was no feeling in them at all. They were dead.

"Genesis, whatever it is, it can't be that bad. Just think. There must be worse situations in life than whatever has happened to you,"

Mzee paused. Then looking softly into his eyes, he said, "It's about Nkwanzi isn't it?"

He did not need any confirmation. What was it that Nkwanzi had done to make Genesis a living corpse?

"Has she gone with another man?" His question was greeted with silence. "Is he a *mafuta*?" Silence. 'Oh damn it,' thought Mzee. 'The way we have sat here with Nkwanzi and agreed with her that she should never defect to a *mafuta*! Not that there was anything wrong with *mafuta's* but they were just not Nkwanzi's cup of tea.

"Look Genesis, is he handsome? Better looking than you?"

There was a long pause. Then Genesis sighed and said, "Yes, he is handsome. It is most probably that because of money he has put on a lot of weight. Handsome or not, I don't understand how my Nkwanzi could..."

He was interrupted by a knock and Rex, one of their colleagues entered with a gusto of energy. Rex was a half-caste. He was tall and handsome in a ragged manner. He always sprayed himself with a very generous portion of 'Gift of Zanzibar', a very strong, cheap perfume. It was always said that one could tell his whereabouts ten miles away. A typical playboy, he did not care about any body's feelings. The longest he kept any one girlfriend was two days.

"Hi men!" he shouted thumping Genesis' back. He always tried hard to feign an American accent.

"My friend, *howz* things?" he asked getting hold of Mzee's hand and almost breaking all the fingers. He was greeted with heavy silence.

"Hey men, what's it with *yous*? Somebody died or somethin'?"

"Yes. There is a problem and you found us in the middle of a discussion," Mzee said with feeling.

"Not interrupting anything, am I? Okay. I quit. But by the way Genesis, *howz* that chic of yours?"

Genesis winced. It was not lost on Rex.

"Men, she in trouble or somethin'?" he asked suspiciously, coming closer.

"Yeah, she's gone off with a *mafuta*," said Genesis in a flat tone.

"Genesis, how could you?" asked Mzee and gestured towards Rex. Genesis shrugged.

"Men. These chics! They will go with anything that smells money. Men, it is as if you don't give her enough tail, very unfair. It is..."

"Shut up you," thundered Mzee.

"Eh, men easy, easy. What wrong have I done?"

Then in a voice trembling with emotion, Genesis asked, "Do you think he will... they will ...I mean will they sort of eat ... will she sleep with him?"

"No. Nkwanzi is not that type of girl," Mzee answered quietly.

"Men, how naive can you get? Ofcourse he will eat her. Men, be your age. You think a man can take a girl, they sleep in the same bed and nothing happens? Are you crazy? They'll chew the..."

"Shut up! I'll kill you if you don't," said Mzee shaking Rex by the collar.

"All right men, all right. Ok, they'll not eat the apple. They'll play Ludo in bed. I won't say no more," he said with a gesture of surrender then went and slumped sulkily in a corner chair and started tapping the floor with his right foot.

"Genesis, I know Nkwanzi. She will come back intact."

"Men, that's crazy talk. Hey, don't give that crap about that 'type of girl'. You never know what will make her tick. Nkwanzi is an attractive girl. Men, have I lusted for her myself! She has incredible transport, and men her behind is great. Her breasts ..."

Rex threw himself on the bed, moved his bums about talking excitedly while jumping up and down the bed which made obscene, creaking noise.

"Shut up," screamed Genesis and Mzee simultaneously, almost hitting him.

"All right, all right, guys. I won't say another word. I'm deaf and dumb, guys. Blind as well," and he closed his eyes and feigned sleep.

"I don't know what to think. My head isn't mine. I can't breathe properly. Christ!" groaned Genesis.

"You knew what to think until this creep came," Mzee said as he cast a venomous look at Rex.

"If I stay here, I know I'll go crazy. You know, now I can't be too sure that Nkwanzi will not sleep with that louse. After all, she has already put on the clothes he brought! Which means she's already succumbed to the corrupting influence of money."

"Men, I've been in this *kinda* fix before. There was this chic acting like the Blessed Virgin if you please. Gave me all that crap of not screwing until she gets to the nuptual bed. Believed her like the blooming idiot I was. Men, only to come one afternoon and she was happily romping with my roommate. Boy, was I mad! That's when my life in the so called slums started. Brother, them dames down there sure know how to console a jilted fellow or any fellow in trouble.

Those dames in the slums of Katanga and Makivu," Rex said.

"What are you saying? They give comfort?" inquired Genesis.

"Comfort which will give you sleep. Genesis, you need sleep now but it sure will evade you."

Then standing up, he begun to recite Shakespeare dramatically:

Sleep, that knits up the ravelled sleave of care. The death of each day's life, sore labour's bath, Balm of hurt minds, great nature's second course, chief nourisher in life's feast ...

"Don't listen to his madness Genesis," cut in Mzee.

But already, conflicting pictures had formed in Genesis' mind. Indeed as Rex had said, he would not be able to sleep that night.

"Men, it's the only solution for you. Otherwise you are doomed."

"You Rex, what are you? I've always known you're bad but I didn't know you are this evil. Get out," fumed Mzee as he dragged him by the collar of his shirt towards the door.

"Hold it Mzee. Rex has done nothing wrong. Come to think of it, I think he's offering a practical solution. I'll go to Makivu," Genesis stated with calm determination.

"What? Genesis you can't say that. You can't go to those slums. They're death traps. With the frustration you're now having, you'll be tempted to drink crude drinks. The next thing, you'll sleep with its sellers. You know that place is teeming with prostitutes and they've a way of enticing a man ..."

"What's wrong with prostitutes? Men, at least they can listen. And who is not a prostitute anyway? Where is his Nkwanzi if she isn't ..."

"Shut up!" both Mzee and Genesis screamed at him.

"Sorry, sorry lads. See here what I was saying before I touched a raw nerve, those women there..."

"Anyway, he isn't coming."

"I'm going. I'm an adult, capable of taking my own decisions and I know what's good for me," asserted Genesis a bit annoyed as he pulled his jacket on.

"Genesis, you are not going. I cannot allow you to go to ruins. Not as long as I am still alive," said Mzee as he struggled to take off Genesis' jacket.

"Look here, you are not my guardian. Leave me alone. How do you talk of not allowing me as if I first have to get permission from you? You want me to stay here and do what? Want to call a prayer group for me?"

"Well, at any cost a prayer meeting is better, far much better than your going to Makivu."

"The gospel according to St Mzee if you please! Spare me. I've heard it for too long. You know Mzee, right now you remind me of that girl Nkwanzi. Giving me all that crap about staying a virgin until her wedding night and like the fool I am, I swallowed it whole. How I despise myself. God did I swallow it! And that bit about the white sheet. When I think of it, I go crazy!"

"What about the white sheet, men? What did she say?" Rex cut in with characteristic inquisitiveness.

"Genesis, don't tell him. Those are matters which are personal to holder."

Genesis ignored Mzee, opened the door and propelled Rex to move ahead. As they moved along the corridor, with Genesis buttoning his jacket, he started telling Rex about the white sheet. They rounded the corner and both burst into cynical laughter. Mzee stood in the doorway, a sad expression on his face, knowing that after visiting Makivu, Genesis would never be the same again.

"Genesis, please come back!"

"Back, back, back ..." the echo from the empty corridor threw his words back at him with hollow mockery. It mixed with the harsh, sarcastic laughter of the receding figures and Mzee went back inside the room. He stood by the window and looked towards the quietness of the royal tombs ...

Genesis and Rex soon reached Makivu. By then dusk was falling. The sound of loud music and laughter came from every corner. Genesis pushed his index fingers in his ears. Rex led the way to one of the dilapidated, shanty houses and knocked at the rickety door. Printed on a white cardboard paper in red blood and pinned on the rickety door,were the words: **COME ALL YE THAT LABOUR AND ARE HEAVY LADEN AND I WILL GIVE YOU REST.**

A woman opened. Behind her, a naked bulb, covered with blue toilet paper, showed her wide smile.

"Eh, Rex. I haven't looked you for long," she said as she gestured towards two chairs.

"Careful with the chairs. They can give way any time," Rex warned Genesis.

"Brown, I'm here now and I have brought you a friend, Genesis.

106

And Genesis, this is Brown".

"Gene, you welcomed. We shall care you. Haves a glass."

'Eh, this Brown is fast! She has already shortened my name. Although I don't think I like it much. Sounds a bit like Jane,' he was thinking. Brown went behind her curtained bed and came back immediately with a glass full of a clear liquid.

"Karibu" she said and she took a generous sip from the glass and passed it on to Genesis.

Genesis cautiously took a sip, coughed and spat out the contents. Rex laughed. He took a generous swig himself.

"Oh I saw. Gene, he innocent and greenery. Like saved one. I bring pepsi-cola and mixed him."

Genesis took stock of his surroundings. The room looked neat. The bed was immaculately made with spotless white sheets very visible. The walls appeared as if they would crack any time, porno photos from magazines covered the cracks. Another cardboard had more writing. **CHRIST IS THE HEAD OF THIS FAMILY, THE SILENT LISTENER TO EVERY CONVERSATION.**

'The conversations that Christ listens to!' thought Genesis grimly.

"I can see that you are intensely reading Brown's literature. Interesting isn't it? She has a creative mind and is very artistic. And all her literature is religious," Rex laughed coarsely.

"Hmm," Genesis grunted.

Brown handed him the cocktail. Cautiously, he took a sip, liked it and swallowed three fingers.

"Goods. He like the drinks now. I am happiest."

Eventually, Genesis begun to relax. He no longer felt tensed up. He stretched his legs and joined in the conversation. He even began to enjoy the loud music and started moving his body rhythmically. He began to laugh at each and everything Rex and Brown said.

He had not realised that in a chair in one of the corners, there was a human form. The form coughed and stood up on unsteady legs. Genesis looked at it with interest then shock as he realised who it was.

"My God Rex! We are doomed! That is one of our lecturers!" he whispered, the alcohol which had made him high evaporating momentarily.

"Don't worry. Don't bother about him. Even if he sees us what's wrong? This is a public place. He'll not bother about you, let alone see you."

The University don staggered to the verandah, his eyes not

focusing. He shot off a jet and the noise it made as it landed was akin to that made by the Murchison falls. He staggered back, slumped into the chair and began gnashing his teeth.

"Let's scram. I feel terrible."

"Easy man, easy. He is one of Brown's customers."

Genesis watched the don who fell into immediate slumber. Genesis sighed with relief and went back to his glass. The more cocktail he took, the more he relaxed. Eventually, everything in the room begun to get blurred. He did not even notice when Rex stealthily left. He found himself talking freely to Brown. She was a kind, understanding woman. A real mother. Soon he begun to hiccup. She gave him a glass of water and told him:

"Come and sat on my laps."

He did. She then patted him on the back and rocked him gently. Eventually, he started sobbing.

"Don't worried baby. You will be hockey. I will looks after you. You know actually, infact you reminder me of my young *buraaza*," she cooed.

"Yesh Nkwanzi. I know I look like your ... bu ... *buraaza*," he lisped as he ruffled her hair.

She smiled. Now that he had started calling her by the name of some woman, things were going to be easy. That's probably where his problem lay. He would tell her everything and she would console him...Yes, her job was to mend broken hearts for a little payment. She got many strange men, men who had read books on a subject called psychology. Men whose task it was to help a person with problems. But did they need to read so many books in order to understand a human being? She had been with this handsome young man for only a few hours and yet she already knew that his girlfriend had left him for another man. She would help Gene. All the boys and men who went to her had almost the same problems.

Many of the students had problems with their girlfriends. They complained that the girls preferred working men who were able to take them out and give them a good time. The boys had no money to do that. They came to her. Their teachers went to her too. Many were frustrated and felt an impotent rage towards the killer regime. They would come to her place and engage in anti-government talk and how they could assist in toppling the regime. Many academicians had either bad or failed marriages. And the men in such unions would go to Brown and her type. And she welcomed them all. She needed both their money and their company. Her type were lonely, lonely, lonely souls. Lonely and poor ....

When Genesis had drunk himself helpless, as if from a long distance, he heard her whisper.

"*Dadi*, the water, it is already."

He stared at her stupidly.

"*Dadi*, I said the water is already."

"What wa-tt-er"?

"For bathe. *Dadi*, we goes and bath."

"This woman is crazy!" he thought.

Then loudly, he asked, "Da-ddy? Your father ish is here?"

"No, me have no father. But from tonights, you my *Dadi*. You owner of this home, *zerefore* you *Dadi*. And you to call me *Mami*. Not Browni," she purred.

"Mummy? No. No. Not Mummy, my mm-other. No pleash Browni."

He had ever heard these men and women who addressed each other in the manner Brown was suggesting but he hated it and was damned if he was going to follow suit. It would be like committing some kind of verbal incest.

Somehow, 'Mummy' managed to take him for some kind of bath. He was too drunk to care whether she saw him naked. They went back inside the house and she gave him more of the cocktail until he lost his power of speech. And then she dragged him to bed, gently. She had first removed the spotless white sheets and replaced them with a not too clean, coloured pair.

She proceeded to undress him and when he was as he came from his mother's womb, a smile crossed her face. For a brief moment, a slight feeling of remorse pricked her conscience. Yet again, she was about to change the life of an innocent young man. But the brief moment of regret quickly vanished.

She too had once been a student. That was many, many, years back. She went up to only primary two and had to drop out of school because her father could not afford the fees. Later, she was brought by an Aunt to the city to become a housegirl so as to earn some money to help her parents and keep her brothers and sisters in school. He aunt's husband raped her and made her pregnant. Her Aunt made her abort and threw her out. There was no way she could go back to her home. She had no money. She had to find work and earn money. She ended up in Makivu with a woman who said she should serve crude

109

drinks to her customers. Most of the customers were men and as she served them, they would dip their fingers in her bosom or touch her womanhood. Wherever she protested, her boss would threaten her with eviction.

At the end of the month, she asked for her salary. Her boss looked at her in a strange manner: "Your salary is on your body, between your legs. If you don't want a salary from there, go and look for another job and good luck."

She had no money, nothing and slowly, she degenerated into a life of prostitution ...

As the cock crowed 3:00 am, Brown made the half conscious Genesis lose his virginity.

"Nkwanshi honee, you haa-ve agreed at lasht? Is it the wedding night? Honey, have your remembered to put the white sheet? Let themm not cut a big whole...and the clan, the fatted cow...Nkwash ... I laugh you..."

***

Meanwhile, Nkwanzi and *Mafuta* were at the Grand Imperial Hotel. He led her to a table in a dimly lit corner and beckoned the waiter.

"Make hole table black. Brings a crateful of beers," he ordered.

"But *Mafu* ... I mean Jack, why do you order for a whole crate when you are only one person? I do not drink so who is going to drink all that beer? Its a waste of money!"

"Don't worried about money. Money not my problem. How can I brings out a byutiful like you and I not make hole table black?"

Soon, the place was flooded with young men who wore huge-bell bottom trousers and high platform shoes. Their shirts were buttoned halfway leaving their chests bare. Their trouser pockets bulged with what were obviously pistols. All of them wore dark sunglasses, come day, come night, come sunshine, come rain. These were the intelligence boys and girls, that dreaded secret service that Duduma had put in place.

"Tell me how those so called intelligence people are supposed to get information when they make sure everybody knows that they are in state research. Who can talk in their presence?" Nkwanzi asked contemptuously.

"Shh my deer. For us, only eat, eat and drink our beer. No talk of such *tings*. Here, let *dem* brought you a bottle of Baby Campaign."

"No, thank you I will just take a soda."

"But anyways, infact, actually we go and danced" and he half dragged Nkwanzi to the floor. A waltz was playing, the music was good.

She was good at waltzing. They had learnt it in the entertaining society at school. *Mafuta* dragged her all over the floor, bruising her toes and humming the number out of tune all the time. He placed her near his fat belly trying to squeeze her but she felt repulsed and kept on pushing him away tactfully. How it would have been beautiful to dance to this tune with Genesis! Then they played a Zairois number and *Mafuta* got excited. He started jumping up and down, jerking as if he was being bitten by some invisible ants. The number plaing was beautiful. She liked it so much and got involved in the dancing. There is something invigorating about Zairois numbers, something that pulls one to one's feet to dance. With this music one's whole body dances, not just parts of the body.

"I glad you enjoyed darlings," shouted *Mafuta*.

Nkwanzi immediately recoiled and started dancing like a log of wood. It was as if he had caught her in a shameful act.

"My deer, I loves you. Will you give me? I am moody!"

My God! How terribly embrassing and nauseating. How she hated that question! "Will you give me?" as if she owed him anything. And by saying he was moody, he probably meant he was in the mood! How vulgar! She turned around embarrassed, to see whether anybody had heard. Mercifully, they were all engrossed in the dance.

"You not answer. I wants to marry you. You will be mother of my son. Maama Junior! He to be the one to tooks over when I dead. You marry me. What don't I have? Money, cars, women," he said as he burst out in coarse, uncouth laughter.

Then he lounged at her. She side-stepped his huge body and he went smash on the floor. He got up and rubbed himself foolishly. Nobody bothered about the great fall. Afterall, many were falling all over the floor in various stages of drunkness. Suddenly, she found herself laughing. The nursery rhyme of Humpty Dumpty, the egg, which fell and broke came to her mind and she recited it loudly:

Humpty dumpty sat on a wall
Humpty dumpty had a great fall
All the King's men and all the King's horses

Could not put Humpty Dumpty
Together again.

"What dat you saying about hempty, hempty?" he asked suspiciously.

"Nothing."

Suddenly disgusted with everything, she went back to the table and he staggered after her.

"Please take me back to the campus. I'm tired."

"I am not take you back to the camps. You going to asleep in my housh," he hiccuped.

"Sleep in your housh ... house? You must be out of your mind. I will walk back."

He laughed out loudly. He knew that she was merely threatening and that she could not dare. No civilian dared walk at that hour.

"More me dance," he broke into her thoughts. Before she could retort, commotion broke out at a table a few metres away. All of a sudden, the table was surrounded by about fifteen of the state research boys.

"I hear dis man clear. He guerrilla. He say Tanzania is more better country than Uganda," accused one sun-glassed fellow.

"That's not what I said," pleaded the accused. Naked fear stood out in his eyes.

"That what he say. I overhear him wid my eyes, dese one," sunglasses stressed.

"No, no. I was only saying that Tanzania is better off than our country Uganda because they have got a direct route to the sea. The problem is that you heard only half the sentence. You only heard 'Tanzania is better off than Uganda' and then you came."

"But why talk Tanzania? Tanzania is *aduyi*, enemy camp. You guerrilla."

And sunglasses aimed his pistol at the accused.

"But why to waste time? The man guerrilla. *Mucukuwe* outside ... *anataka Chakula* ... gave him pood."

The poor victim was checked and all his money taken.

"Bring density card."

Trembling, he gave it in. His tormentor held it upside down.

"Yiyi density card fake, wewe guerrilla kabisa. Twende."

A pregnant woman who was obviously his wife had listened, mouth agape with shock. She started screaming, "Where are you taking my husband, where are you taking my husband?"

Sunglasses gave her a big push which landed her on the floor with a big thud. Blood started oozing down her legs. The hotel staff stealthily carried her to hospital where she lost her child and eventually her mind...

Several months later, Nkwanzi was told that the poor woman used to move with all her children asking the soldiers, "Where is my husband? Where is my husband?"

The poor fellow was hauled to his feet and they started beating him as they laughed. They dragged him towards the door as he pleaded with them. The more he pleaded, the more they beat him.

"Crocodile to eat good pood tonight," sunglasses said.

They pulled him outside. A sharp scream rent the air and then there was a loud bang as the boot of a car was slammed shut. A volley of bullets rent the night air and the screech of tyres, as a car sped off, added to the music of death. There was a round of applause from most of the revellers as they took to the floor dancing more vigorously.

"We goes to dance," said *Mafuta*.

Nkwanzi shook her head and felt tears flood her eyes.

"My deer, don't cried here, we enter problems. Dries up your tear immediate. If you are seen cry, it mean crying for gorilla which they have taken it outside and we shall be kill instant."

For once, she agreed with what he was saying. The band struck what had come to be known as the regime's anthem – something whose meaning they had failed to decipher. It was in the language of the rulers but there was one word *nyama* which signified eating. As soon as this anthem was struck, everybody jumped to the dancing floor and formed a circle. They clapped and danced to the music. The men took out their pistols and held them up in their right hands. The dance of power was in progress.

"Quickly, lets goes and danced."

" I'm not coming."

"Girl! Don't be fool. If you don't danced this record, they kills you. It meant you gorilla," he hissed earnestly.

"I will run away from them."

"Girl, you mad up here, I tells you. Everybody starts to looked us like gorilla, we be killed like one who they tooks now to be ate by crocodile. Dancing that record only, we goes."

"I'm not going to dance that thing. I'll sneak out. Nobody will see me. Find me outside," and with that, she started crawling under the tables. *Mafuta* frightened out of his wits crawled after her. He tried to snatch the hem of her dress to pull her back but in vain.

"Nkwanzi, they sees us, killed us. Please ..." he panted.

Eventually, they, reached the door and tore towards the car. He quickly opened the car door and they entered and he sped off.

"You camps people mad, mad up here. Why you refuses to dance *Nyama yetu*? What it tooks from you if you dances it?"

"Please take me back."

"My deer that one we pinis. I tooks you home, my home, our home. You sleeps in my bed once, you not want leave again. I swears!" he cackled again.

Many thoughts run through her mind. Should she try and walk back? But she quickly dismissed the thought. She was sure to be gang raped and bayoneted by the soldiers. She had no choice but to go to his home. She opened her bag and felt the cold metal of the sharp *empindu* which she always carried. With this tiny weapon giving her comfort, she calmed down. They arrived at *Mafuta's* house. It was so big, at first she thought it was a hostel. He made it a point to take her on a tour of inspection.

"Here, your kitchen. This, the gas cook, this the electric cook. No *sigiri* here. You no dirty your bytiful hand. You no to cook anyway. I haves seven boi and housegirl. This room ..."

Nkwanzi was so bored. Where were his wives anyway? she asked him.

"Don't worry for them. They sleeps. Anyway from todays, they to be your housegirl."

By that time, Nkwanzi had given up on the fellow and could not even follow what he was saying. Eventually, the house tour took them to a massive bedroom. He immediately pulled her towards the bed and tried to undress her.

"Leave me alone," she told him murderously.

Like most men, he wrongly thought Nkwanzi was playing hard to get.

"I told you to leave me alone," Nkwanzi said and immediately got out the *empindu* which she held up murderously. He was taken aback by both the small instrument and the look on her face. Seeing that she was serious, he went native.

"You *malaya*. I spending my money on yours, buy *clozesi* and *shuuzi*. I boughts you drink and goods and danced you. I carries you in my Benzi and with my peterori and now you says no sleept wiz me? You must gave me the goods," he said knocking her down on the bed and almost suffocating her with his almost two hundred kilogrammes. Quickly, she stabbed his hand with the *empindu*. Holding his bleeding hand, he looked at her incredulously.

"Touch me again and I'll plunge it through your belly. Tomorrow, you can come and take whatever you brought for me. I have a fiance whom I love and it was a mistake to come out with you."

"But how you love *dat* boy which it have no shillings?"

"You will never understand. I will go and sleep in the sitting room."

"But tomorrows, I came for all *tings* I gaved you. All. You no drinks suga I bought to drink *wid dat* boy! No."

"Come for them all."

She left his bedroom and slept in the sofa. As soon as she heard the greeting of the morning birds, she walked out of the castle and back to campus. Atim was still in bed

"Atim, I have a long story to tell you. But the most important question is, do you think Genesis will believe that I did not sleep with the *mafuta*?" she asked her heart pounding.

Atim took time before answering.

"I don't think he will believe you," she said with finality.

"Atim!"

"He may in the long run, but right now..." and she shook her head.

Nkwanzi feared to go and see Genesis. She sought out Mzee after a week.

"Mzee, you think Genesis will believe me?"

He sighed.

"It will take a lot of time and convincing for him to believe that. Moreover, he has changed a lot since that incident. He's ..."

"He's what?"

"No. Forget it. But give him time to heal."

Nkwanzi could not get anything more from Mzee. She tried to catch Genesis several times. She would waylay him sometimes on his way to lectures. She would greet him warmly and he would reply with a cold, "How're you madam?"

Madam! That sent cold shivers down her spine.

After a month, Nkwanzi gathered courage and went to his room. She knocked timidly on the door. A female voice said, 'come in'. Nkwanzi's heart missed a beat as she entered the familiar room.

"You're welcome," said the voice.

115

Jesus, who was this welcoming Nkwanzi to her room, or was it her former room? Genesis was lying on the bed and he looked surprised to see Nkwanzi. The voice sat next to him and looked straight at her.

"Can I help you?" the girl asked Nkwanzi in a soft, musical voice, almost a husky whisper.

There are certain women one looks at and gets mesmerised. This was one of them. Tall with a velvet dark complexion, huge eyes accentuated by dark shades under them, the envy of most women. Hers were the eyes commonly referred to as those of a heifer, brimming over with love and kindness. Nkwanzi caught a glimpse of the inside of her mouth and thought of hers with a grimace. Her gum was pitch black making her teeth look whiter than the cattle egret. It was as if the teeth had never chewed any food, only constantly bathed with milk. Hers was the kind of beauty that halted traffic.

Nkwanzi looked at this masterpiece of God, of nature, and felt as if she had been created as an afterthought. She was plain and the only head she had made turn twice was Genesis' and now it was history. 'But I was created in God's image,' she thought proudly and this beefed up her self-esteem.

"Can I help you?" the beautiful voice, tingling like tiny bells broke into Nkwanzi thoughts. Nkwanzi must have been staring at this impeccable creation. She could not answer. She continued to stare at this Miss Uganda, who in turn stared at her as Genesis stared at both of them.

"Can I help you?" she asked the third time.

"Er...well... I ... well ... was sort of ... kind of looking for Mzee. We had a topic to discuss and er ... he said I should drop in after lunch," Nkwanzi murmured.

"Eh, that was funny of Mzee. To suggest that you come after lunch when he knows that's when he gives us time to be together!" she said as she ruffled Genesis hair fondly, her hand straying to stroke the hairs on his chest.

God! Nkwanzi was going to burst into tears. Her heart was pounding wildly. 'Father, help me please,' she prayed silently. Genesis looked uneasy. The tears were threatening to break out but Nkwanzi would not let this Miss Uganda see them. With an effort, she got up and murmured something about coming to see Mzee another time.

"Are you sure you're okay? You look poorly. Why don't you sit a bit while I get you some juice?" she said, genuine concern in her voice. She got up and put a kind hand on Nkwanzi's shoulder. Nkwanzi almost slapped her hand away but she restrained herself. Miss Uganda was kind hearted as well! That trebled Nkwanzi's jealousy. She would not have minded if Miss Uganda had been beautiful but bad mannered. In fact, Nkwanzi had hoped that Miss Uganda was that type. But to have a combination of beauty and good manners! That definetly unhinged Nkwanzi.

Nkwanzi knew she had lost Genesis. As she was going, she remembered Miss Uganda had asked her to stay on and rest a bit.

"No, no thank you. I'm all right. It's just a slight headache," she managed to say before she stumbled out of the room.

Blinded by tears, she crushed headlong into a figure as she rounded a corner in the corridor.

"Easy, easy. Why, Nkwanzi, what's the matter?"

It was Mzee. She couldn't let out a word. She just howled and howled. Mzee held her until the well of tears was dry.

"Let's go for a walk. Lets go to the swimming pool," he said.

He took her hand and slowly they walked to the swimming pool. They sat at the edge and looked at the still blue water. After what seemed like eternity, Mzee sighed.

"You know Nkwanzi, I'm deeply worried about this country, our future. Duduma's regime seems to have unleashed an invisible weevil in every corner, in every sector of our lives. Education has been rendered meaningless. Everywhere those *mafuta's* are boasting. Their gospel is; 'I never went to school or I had little education and yet look at me: I'm much better off than a university professor.' I don't blame them. They are right in a way."

"The young people have taken this gospel wholesale. Many are refusing to go to school saying they will do business and become *mafutas*. We are losing a whole generation. There are no health facilities to talk of. There are no drugs in hospitals, the only medicine there is, is only for the rulers. Roads are long gone. Most of the pot holes are as deep as graves. Morality is in prison. Sex orgies are the order of the day. They have sex with women, bayonet them and drink their blood. Firing squads are also another order of the day. A man of the ruling clan only has to covet your woman, land, house or car. He then labels you a guerrilla and you are put on a firing squad.

"There is no social life to talk of. People have long abandoned bars and nightclubs. In fear, people have retreated to drinking from small, hidden places. These places are run by women who hide drinks under their beds. And in the dim light, people go and drink from there and talk in whisphers. Women have taken to peddling assorted merchandise in offces in order to make ends meet. Maybe ironically in a way, this is the only good thing that has happened to our women folk. They never used to do business but now out of necessity, they have started and most probably, will never look back.

"People are dragged from their offices and shot on the streets like dogs. They are picked from funerals and told they were collecting money for guerrillas. They are eliminated. A soldier only has to lust for somebody's wife or girl friend and their man is killed. If anybody from the ruling class wants somebody's job, the person holding the job is killed immediately. Thousands of women are now widows, their husbands have been made to disappear. Duduma has brought a weevil that will take years and years to remove: the weevil of bribery and greed, of rape and inhumanity...Ah! Fear rules us, and Duduma's end does not seem to be in sight," Mzee concluded as he stared into the deep end of the pool.

Nkwanzi shivered as if a cold wind had blown over her.

They stared into the silent water.

"But Genesis, I'm sure he'll come back to you."

"When he has got that ravishing beauty?"

"She's a nice girl..."Nkwanzi's spirit hit sea level."But you never know what makes a man tick and apparently, something is failing to fit...something in their affair."

"Mzee, tell me more about her."

"Nkwanzi, I won't. You want me to comfort you and tell you negative things about her but I won't deceive you. She is one person who seems to have everything in place. But let us not talk about her. She will go in her own time."

In her own time! Nkwanzi knew then that Miss Uganda was still around. And all of a sudden, she wished she could go home. Whenever she got a problem, she always went home and within a short time, she would heal.

What was it about home that always acted like medicine upon her troubled mind? It was sitting with Maama in the kitchen as together, they prepared the evening meal. It was the song of the evening birds as they prepared themselves for the night's sleep. The low mooing of cattle as they were brought in for the evening milking, their adders full. The happy noise of the young girls as they skipped the rope and the cheer of the boys as they scored goals, passing their banana fibre ball from one to the other.

The quiet of the evenings, the gentle wind rustling through the banana leaves. The spirals of smoke from the kitchen fires and the music from the grinding stones. The sound of rain on the iron sheets which seemed to sing a lullaby sending everybody into deep sleep. Yes, the only way she could get over Genesis was by going home. She knew that once there, she would forget him and his Miss Uganda. The holidays came. Nkwanzi went home and at night, sat in the kitchen by the fireside.

Chapter Ten

Decline and resistance

Time had flown. They were now in second year at the university. The situation in the country had worsened. There was no love lost between the Makerere University community and the government. The government viewed the university community as enemies and the trigger happy soldiers were always itching for an opportunity to teach the we-know-it-all university lecturers and students a lesson that they would never forget.

Duduma who had now given himself so many titles and declared himself life president spat out his hatred for intellectuals while presiding over a graduation ceremony. In his usual jovial manner which disguised his deadly self, he conferred degrees upon the graduands:

"By de otority entrusted to me, I confer upon you the Degree of Bachelor of Ants".

"I confer upon you the degree of Master of sugarly".

When it was time for his speech, he spat out venom:

"Saasa Yinyi yote mwalimu of Makerere munafikiri who are you? When I was former current Chairman of AAU, you say I no fit to lead Africa nation in AAU. Lakini you piploz of Makerere Universe watch out! You will saw," he warned.

Makerere University kept dangerously quiet but at night, many groups met and discussed how to join in the struggle to oust the killer regime. Duduma became the most hated and feared person in the country. One day as he drove himself along the road to State House, an old woman stopped him.

"Can I helps you granny?" he asked kindly.

"Yes please. Just drop me at the next trading centre my son."

She did not recognise him. Duduma courteously opened the door for her and they chatted happily on the way.

"Tell me, what do piploz thinks of his excellenta President Duduma?" he asked.

"Oh, oh, oh! People are really living in fear and they hate the man. The man is a killer. The country is bleeding. Everything has come to a stand still. There is no sugar, salt, soap, paraffin, nothing. No medicine. Even transport is impossible. This is why I stopped you. It is difficult to get transport because petrol is sold on *magendo*. Eh, eh!

We have never suffered like this."

"*So what are piploz saying? Do dey want to removes Duduma?*"

She was lucky she was not looking at his eyes. They shone with a dangerous light and became mere slits. He gripped the steering wheel as if he would break it.

"Yes. They want to fight and remove him. We hear that there are many people training in the country of our neighbours Tanzania. They will come to remove this weevil Duduma." Then she dropped into a conspirator's whisper. "My son, this man they say he kills people and cuts off their heads. He keeps the heads in a fridge! He drinks their blood! My son, it is true he drinks human blood so that he can chase away spirits of those he kills. We heard that he went to a witchdoctor because he wants to rule forever. The witchdoctor told him that if he wants to rule forever, he had to kill his first son, drink his blood and eat his liver! This Duduma did it!"

"*Eh, dat is fanastic and great also! He eat his son blood and drunked his liver! What else he do?*"

"He has killed his wives as well, suspecting them of bringing bad luck. My son, join the rest of the people to pray so that this mad man can be removed. Oh if that murderer can be removed so that we sleep!"

Duduma listened attentively. When they reached the trading centre, she told him to leave her there but he insisted on dropping her at her house.

"*You are mother of mine. I took you to your house. Shall I overturn here to go your house?*"

She was touched by such kindness. He drove to her house and got out to open the door for her.

"My son, may God Bless you," she thanked him profusely.

Meanwhile her children had come out to see whom the car had brought. They were in time to see President Duduma climbing into his car.

Shocked, they run to her.

"Mother, do you know who has just dropped you?"

"Yes. It was a kind man."

"A kind man! Mother, that was Duduma!"

"What? My God! My children, then you better start packing and we shift to my father's village. Quick, pick what you can because anytime, we will be picked and murdered."

And as they packed a few belongings she told them her encounter with Duduma. They did not waste time. They picked the few belongings and fled for their lives. That very night after the family had left, Duduma's boys indeed struck the already abandoned homestead. Finding that the family had fled, they packed all the belongings which had been left behind and set the place ablaze.

It was around this time that President Duduma sent his son, who had gone only up to primary seven, to the university with a special chit. The chit read like this:

To the headmaster, vice chancellor
Makerere Universe.
I am sending my son to you. Give him to take the course to become Doctor or District Administrator also.He is read political science completely and also.
Thank you very many for what have you done.
For God and my country.
President Duduma, Field Marshall, Life President, DC, DSO, QC, Former current chairman of OAU.

The president's son came with a lorryful of furniture, music systems, TV sets, food, name it, and grabbed a room in the post-graduate hall of residence. There was a unanimous protest from both the dons and their students. A resolution was passed, there were to be no lectures until the president's son left the university. The air was tense. Government ordered the lecturers to go back to class. The dons refused. The students too defied an order to go back to the lecture rooms. Enough was enough. The university was not going to accept this profamity. As if that was not enough, Duduma's son added insult to injury by pitching camp in the **post-graduate** hall. What burst the lid was the murder of a student in cold blood, in broad daylight. The student who was coming from town reached the main gate and found two soldiers.

"Wewe! Simama. Tax ticket yikko wapi?"

"I am a student, I don't pay taxes," he replied producing his identity card.

"Don't spoke English. Sema kiswahili."

How the students and ordinary people had loved *kiswahili* in the past. But now it had become the language of violence.

"I 'm a student," he said again.

"Wewe student gani? Wewe grandfather! Towa vyato."

The poor fellow removed his shoes.

"Kaa chini. Towa socks."

He had put some money under his socks. He removed them. When they saw the money, their eyes lit up and they grabbed it.

"Ee,ee! wewe onakanyaga President? Wewe lazima gorilla."

"Please, it is not that I was stepping on the President. The head of the President on the money is only a picture."

"Shuts up! You peoples of universe yote gorilla. Shoots him!"

And the other one cocked, aimed at the student and as if he was about to eliminate a rabid dog, pulled the trigger. The bullet lifted the student, he spun briefly around, threw up his arms in an involuntary gesture of surrender, came to rest down in a featal position and with a surprised look on his innocent face, he breathed his last. The soldiers dipped their fingers in the warm blood that was spurting out of the student's side and licked it. They walked away leisurely, counting their loot. The shot had been heard all over the campus. Word quickly got round and everybody trooped to the scene of the tragedy. A cry went up from the assembled community, a cry of anguish. The bats at Bat Valley were thrown out of their cosy nests in their thousands and flew over the city making what sounded like a cry of protest and war. The students decided to demonstrate against the killer regime, come what may.

"Down with the killer regime!"

They were joined by street urchins and many other people and the crowd swelled. They marched all around the city. The trigger happy soldiers itched to mow them down but, on hearing about the protest march, Duduma had sent word that there was to be no shooting. Apparently, this uprising scared him.

However, the army descended on them that very night. It was about 3:00 am and Nkwanzi was deep asleep. Suddenly, she was woken up by heavy pounding on the door.

"Fungua mulango!" ordered many voices. Atim had also woken up. They looked at each other frightened out of their wits. More kicks and the door caved in. Soldiers entered, armed to the teeth. They hauled them to their feet.

"Mutoke! You wants to overthrew government eh? Tonights, we shown you."

They pushed them out of the room. Thank God they were in their long, cotton night-dresses. There was commotion every where. All the students were facing the same fate. Many other soldiers stayed behind in the rooms ripping mattresses and pillow cases on the pretext of looking for grenades and bombs. They loaded their trucks with students' belongings. They vandalised books, they defecated in the rooms and corridors and smeared faeces on walls. The students were ordered to walk to the Freedom Square. The unlucky ones were made to "walk" on their knees on the tarmac! By the time they reached there, their knees were masses of bleeding flesh. All the students had been rounded up and were at the square.

"The whole Uganda army must be here," whispered Atim.

"We are doomed," Nkwanzi whispered back.

The commander then shot a volley of bullets in the air and the Square fell silent. He started speaking.

"*So. You are the we knows much. The actually. And munataka to overthrew us. Using what? Hands? ha, ha, ha! Tonights, we shown you power. Book no power, pen hakuna power. Power yiko happa.*" Another volley of bullets went off and other soldiers madly followed suit. The students all fell down.

"*So you fears guns. Then why wants to play wiz fire? It burn you.*"

"*Now, have sex each wiz ze azer. Boy wid boy, girl wid girl,*" he commanded.

Shocked, the students looked at each other incredulously.

"I said each get wife quickly!" he said murderously.

"You are sick!" shouted Mzee.

There was dead silence.

"*Who say we sick?*" asked the commander in a deadly voice. "*We gonorrhoea eh? Get wife same, same. Men do men and women do women. And boy, who say we sick, I kills you now,*" he said as he cocked his gun.

"*Afande, big Daddy say no kills. If kill, muzungu will coup us. Muzungu will come with much guns and go to bus-park of aeroplane then coup us,*" said one frightened soldier.

"*Hockay, give dat boy who say we sick, give it tea.*"

Mzee was given a tin of beans.

"*Opens it,*" he was ordered.

"But I have no opener!"

"*Use teeths.*"

As Mzee started on the impossible task the commander shouted, "*Sings and dance. Sung, sung a song immediate!*" he bellowed.

Atim started an old spiritual and the rest joined in, relieved that the commander had dropped the sex order, firmly holding up their hands in a sign of triumph:

Oo freedom, Oo freedom
Oo freedom, over me
And before I be a slave
And be buried in my grave
And go home to my Lord
And be free.

"Changed song! Not good data one," shouted the commander sensing something sinister, some hidden message in the song.

Atim's strong voice immediately rang out and the rest joined in singing:

We shall overcome, we shall overcome
We shall overcome, some day
Oo deep in my heart, I do believe
We shall overcome some day.

They sang with vigour, with hope. They got emotionally involved, the song fortfied them. Many of the soldiers who had been gulping down all types of alcohol, and smoking marijuana now started fondling the girls. The male students began to be restless, unable to stay put as the worst crime against humanity seemed about to take place but in the same moment, the commander shot in the air.

"Quick. Everybody gets on truck and we went. Big man says operation over."

Confusion broke out. They shouted, rushing to board their trucks. As Nkwanzi made to run back to the hall, she felt somebody hold her back. She looked up and stared into Genesis' eyes.

"Genesis." Relief flooded over her.

"There's no time to waste. Let's go," he got her arm and they started running. Soon, Mzee and Atim caught up with them.

"Where're we going?" Nkwanzi panted.

"We're going to meet some of the people who are struggling to topple this insane regime."

They run up to Katanga, one of the slums in the city. They went through winding, narrow paths and reached a tiny mud and wattle house, roofed with papyrus mats. Genesis knocked three times on the rickety door.

"*Ni nani?*" asked a voice from inside.

"Baba Candle," answered Genesis.

Nkwanzi swallowed. Did this mean then that Genesis had fathered a child? But she quickly dismissed the thought. Things were too serious for that kind of flippancy. A woman opened the door and they entered.

"You can put your guns down. Genesis and Mzee have brought new members," said the woman.

About six men put down their guns and then they sat in a relaxed manner.

"Mama, we have brought the new members" said Genesis.

"We welcome them. Oh, they are in their night dresses. Here, tie these *lesu* around yourselves," said Mama.

They did so. Nkwanzi peered at Mama closely. She was of medium height. Her natural hair was cut short, almost giving her a boyish look. Her face was oval and there were numerous thought lines on her brow. She had a strong, square chin and her eyes were sharp, missing nothing, always focused, alert. Later, they learnt that she was a teacher in one of the primary schools in the city but in the evenings disguised herself and sold crude spirits. Most of her customers were soldiers who usually shot their mouths off after drowning glass after glass of the firely liquid. She would then get information from them and this would assist in strategising for the underground movement to topple the regime. Mama's voice brought Nkwanzi back to the new situation.

"The operation on campus, were any students killed?" she asked.

"No, Mama. Apparently there were orders from above that there should be no killing. But many were brutally beaten and need immediate medical attention," replied Mzee.

"Songa, alert our medical team. Let them go to the university immediately and attend to the wounded. Any rape?" she asked, a dangerous glitter in her eyes.

"No Mama. It was just about to take place when the commander ordered his soldiers to scram and we were saved," answered Atim.

Mama's tensed up body relaxed and she wiped the sweat that was running down her face. Mzee excused himself and went through a back door.

"Let me introduce you to the other members. For the sake of all of us, we're baptized with new names as soon as we join the struggle. This is for the safety of everybody because if you are caught and tortured, you may reveal the real names of your comrades. This *Ndugu* here is known as Songa. He is a medical doctor."

126

"Eh, how's this one a doctor? He is covered with charcoal! I don't believe it," Atim whispered to Nkwanzi.

"You may not believe that he is, seeing him in this state," Mama said, seeming to have sensed the contents of Atim's whisper.

"I'm a medical doctor. During the day, I do my duty at the hospital. Then in the late afternoon, I take on my other duties of a charcoal seller," and he chuckled.

"Yes. You will see him on top of a charcoal lorry, looking blacker than the charcoal itself, dressed in rags and chewing away happily at sugar cane. He commands a group that gathers information and takes drugs to our fighters who are deep in the forests. And this *Ndugu* here, is Mbele. He is actually a Lt Colonel in the army and a communications expert. He is the one who informs government about the movement and whereabouts of the enemy, giving government wrong information. For him, he does not need to disguise himself. Everywhere he goes, he says he is on duty, sniffing out the enemy."

The Lt Colonel nodded gravely. In a situation where all the soldiers were feared rather than respected, Mbele commanded the latter.

Somebody came in through the back door and sat in a corner.

"And this *Ndugu* here, is Simba." The Ndugu growled.

"But he is a madman!" exclaimed Atim

"I have seen this madman somewhere," Nkwanzi said.

Mama laughed. "He is a university student, together with you at campus. During the day, he's very busy with his books. In the evenings, he comes here, removes his clothes, puts on those rags and his madman's wig. Raving mad, he goes to pick rubbish at the most strategic places. Simba, from which rubbish pits do you go to pick your food?"

"Near the barracks, state research offices and such other places where they eat good food," snarled the madman as he moved threateningly towards Atim and Nkwanzi as they stifled frightened cries.

Mama laughed. "Simba, remove your disguise." Simba did so and they were shocked to see who he was.

"Mzee!" they both exclaimed.

"Shh, not so loud although nobody will hear us. Yes, Mzee is the maddest madman in the country now. You did not think much about the fact that when you people came in, he sneaked out. He went to change his clothes and sneaked in with his costume."

"Mzee! It's incredible!" said Atim shaking her head in disbelief.

"But of course, you must have realised that these days, there are so many mad people roaming everywhere. Do you think they are all mad? Many of them are our operatives," said Mama.

It was indeed true and they had all realised it. But they thought because of the killings and torture going on, more and more people were going berserk. Many women whose husbands were picked and disappear without a trace, ran mad. Many people who were picked and tortured also ran mad: But now Mama was telling us another category of mad people.

"And by the way, last but not least, Baba Candle here," and she passed a fond secret smile to Genesis, "is a *cura* in state research headquarters. Do you know what a *cura* does?"

Atim and Nkwanzi shook their heads in ignorance.

"Those days before the flushing toilet came, people in the city used to empty their bowels in buckets. A *cura* would very early in the morning, go for the bucket and carry it on his head. If you met him, you wouldn't look at him direct in the eyes. If you did, he would pour the contents of the bucket on you. The water system is in shambles now. There is practically no running water anywhere. Baaba Candle has to do a lot of toilet cleaning in the early morning. And nobody can look him in the face. That way, he gathers a lot of information and has saved many lives."

Nkwanzi felt proud of Genesis.

"And now I have to initiate you into the struggle."

She went into an inner room and returned with a big, white chicken. After murmuring a few words, she quickly severed off its head with a sharp knife. Atim and Nkwanzi were made to sit in the middle of the room. Mama passed the chicken over them as she chanted some words, the blood dripping on their heads. Atim and Nkwanzi were frightened by the ritual and the fright showed.

"Comrades," soothed Mama, "we're not wizards. But we believe in doing things of our fore-fathers. Those things which weren't bad. Whenever there was war, and the clan warriors were called upon to set off, blood would flow. The blood of a live thing : be it bird or animal. Blood must flow and melt in the earth from which we come, from which we eat and return when the breath ceases in our body. It is this earth which will give us the strength to struggle. Earth is nature : God is nature. And we must look to Him for guidance. We feed on ourselves, food grows on our own bodies and this soil is our father and mother and our God and so our struggle must be tied with the earth our parent, our God. Do you understand?"

"We understand, Mama."

"From now, your name will be Nguvu," she told Atim who nodded agreement.

"Yours'll be Udongo." Nkwanzi too nodded agreement.

She then went to an inner room and came back with a thin, long stick. She broke off two pieces and gave one to Atim and the other to Nkwanzi.

"You'll always carry this small stick. Every member of the group has it. It's only for identification purposes. If you're in a difficult situation, say at a roadblock, you just pull it out of your bag and brush your teeth with it. If any member of our group is around, he or she will also pull out theirs and will try to help you out of whatever difficult situation you're in." She handed them the sticks. "Make sure you don't lose it. It's a unique piece of stick. So keep it well."

Then she went to the inner room again and came out with a small envelope.

"There's a powder here. It's lethal. It's the crushed liver of a hyena which if you take, causes instant death. I'm giving you a quarter of a teaspoonful of this powder. Always travel with it. And listen carefully: if you're ever caught by government soldiers and they torture you, you'll release all the information about the organisation."

"No, no. We wouldn't, could never release it however much we were tortured," Atim protested for both of them.

"Comrades, that's what you say. But the flesh is weak, the flesh can be hurt until one screams for mercy. Jesus Himself, the very Son of God when the hour for His crucification drew nearer, said He wished God could take away the cup of suffering and death. How can we human beings then not succumb to pain? Moreover, they can torture you until you lose your mind and give out information involuntarily, or they will give you drugs which will make you unconscious and you disclose everything. Therefore, that is why I am giving you this lethal powder, not only to save other members of the underground movement but also to save you from very painful death. Therefore, should you ever be caught and stare death in the eye, pop this small piece of paper into your mouth, bite it and you will immediately join your maker, painlessly. Do you understand?" she asked as she looked straight into our eyes.

"We understand, Mama," they replied as they took the powder of death and yet life from her.

"Lastly, from now, you will wear your hair short and **natural**. Never hot-comb it. The women of the struggle believe they should be natural and not waste money making artificial images of themselves. Our barber will do the needful now."

This was done immediately.

"Welcome to the struggle," she said as she embraced them.

The others all came and hugged them in turn as they murmured, "Welcome to the struggle sister."

Genesis took the opportunity to press Nkwanzi hard to his body, in an octopus embrace which made her feel an electric current of pleasure run through her.

"Your work will be to help in pamphleteering. I'll tell you how to do it. We in the women's wing also have to get food for those in the bush. I'll tell you all that's needed to be done," Mama said.

After the ritual was over, Nkwanzi asked what pamphleteering meant. It involved writing anti-government literature and throwing it in parts of the city and posting it to all government departments in order to cause panic in government.

They stayed in the tiny room, each one of them receiving their assignments for the following day. At 3:00 pm, they started moving out. Genesis changed his clothes and put on a dirty overall to go and clean toilets at the state research bureau. Atim and Nkwanzi went back to campus to start writing anti-government literature. By six thirty, in the morning, Genesis was back from his task. He bathed thoroughly, put on fresh clothes and came to Nkwanzi's room.

The custodian at the hall office teased him, "You have come to listen to BBC focus on Africa?"

"Yeah man. The early bird catches the morning worm."

Atim opened the door for him.

"How's the weather?" they greeted him. This had become their new greeting.

"It's a sunny day," he replied.

They knew all was well.

"Nkwanzi, let's go and have coffee in my room and read Milton's poem; **Paradise Regained**."

Nkwanzi hit heaven. She knew their relationship was back on course. On the way, she asked him a question that had been nagging her.

"Incidentally Genesis, what happened to Miss Universe ... eh, that

130

Miss Uganda ... the ravishing beauty I found in your room?"

The whole world stood still as she waited for his reply.

"Oh, that one. Forget about her. She never made me tick," he said matter of factly.

Nkwanzi's breath whistled out in relief.

As soon as they reached his room, they found Mzee who hastily left. Genesis looked into Nkwanzi's eyes and asked: "The conditions have changed, have they not? We can now go for the apple?"

"No Genesis, the apple still remains for our wedding night."

"Whew! That's a long term investment. But I'll wait."

They intensified the struggle against Duduma.

And the country bled. Parents and widows waited in vain for their children and husbands. After sometime, they would give up and bury banana stems to symbolise the bodies. And after this 'burial', an empty blank look would appear in their eyes, never to be erased.

***

The four friends graduated from Makerere University. Atim went to teach in one of the secondary schools in the city, Genesis took up the post of District Commissioner also in the city. Nkwanzi went to the Law Development Centre for a diploma. Mzee stayed at the university to pursue a Masters degree and hence start on an academic career.

"Mzee, why have you opted for an academic career? You can see how since Duduma took over the reigns of power, university dons earn pea-nuts while school drop outs with connections in government have been given factories and big posts and are now millionaires. You better reconsider your decision," advised Genesis.

"I've thought long over it. This business of our earning pea-nuts is because we are being ruled by people who do not value education. After this regime is toppled, an enlightened group will come and pay us well. You imagine, the whole Vice President of Uganda went armed to the teeth to the Central Bank and bellowed, 'Where Mr Foreign exchange? I wants to see this man. Everybody is looked for him, he is mostly important man in country after President. What he looks like I wants to know.' If you are ruled by such illiterates who think foreigh exchange is a person, how do you expect them to value education and educators?"

The group kept on with the underground struggle, sometimes

131

having very close brushes with death. One night while at *Mama`s* she told them that she was worried.

"What is disturbing me is that there're so many groups fighting Duduma and we are not uniting under a common umbrella. As long as we remain fragmented, the struggle will take longer".

Her fear was put to rest soon after. The government spokesman came on air one morning. By then, his command of English had greatly improved and so had that of Duduma.

"Fellow citizen, this is a speso announcement. Life President and former current Chaiman of AAU wises to inform everybody that Tanzania country is gorilla. In fact, Dr Duduma no problem with Tanzania. Infact also, Dr Duduma he say if President of Tanzania was to be woman, he Duduma would to marry him except President of Tanzania, he have grey hairs. But he tooks our land. And Uganda can't just be to looks when they stole our land. Uganda is, therefore, going to fought Tanzania to bring our lands back. The fight it start now, now. End of speso announce ment."

Then they knew that Duduma's end was near. It was madness of him to declare war on Tanzania. All the fighting groups resolved to put up a united front. The city rumbled with the noise of heavy military vehicles on the way to attack Tanzania. The soldiers were shouting and shooting sporadically in the air.

First went lorry-fulls of infantry followed by the commanders. The commanders were all in open-roofed Mercedes Benzes. All the commanders reclined in the back seats, drinking and romancing with elegantly dressed girlfriends. The girlfriends wore knee length, evening dresses, their ears, noses and arms sagging under the heavy weight of imitation gold.

A story doing the rounds had it that one such a girlfriend had sulked and declined to escort her commander boyfriend to the front-line on account of the fact that she did not have gold.

"I don't have a gold watch, ear rings and chains. And yet all the other women of the commanders have gold. I can't come with you to the front line unless you get me gold also," she pouted.

"Oh, you wants gold. Hockay. Let us went. You gets all the gold you wants."

The girlfriend's face creased with smiles. He drove off. The commander cruised at two hundred kilometers per hour in his limousine. They flew past the city shops and headed east.

"But why are you driving away from the city? That's where we should buy the gold and now you are driving towards the countryside!"

she cried.

"You says you wants gold. I tooks you for it," the commander rejoined, smiling secretly.

He sped on the highway until they reached an extensive, thick forest called Namanve. Then he branched off and took a ragged murrum path.

"But is this not the terrible Namanve forest?" she asked terribly frightened now.

He kept quiet.

Goose pimples appeared everywhere on her body. She had heard about Namanve forest and so had everybody else. It was a common secret that it was the killing field of the regime. People were taken there, left to starve or shot dead. Others were shot in the legs and left to die a slow, painful death. Hundreds of corpses were dumped there.

If the trees of Namanve forest could talk, they would tell the worst horror story under the earth. And this was where the commander was taking her! She knew she was finished. She thought of opening the door of the speeding car but knew that he would crash her with it.He drove deeper into the forest and the stench of decomposing bodies assailed her nostrils. He stopped at the edge of the clearing.

"Get outs," he ordered.

He opened the door and dragged her out. Numbed by fear, she stumbled along. Then a long scream escaped from deep down her lungs as she tripped over a decomposing body. As she got up, she stepped on another and the rank flesh stuck on her shoe. She screamed louder.

"You wants gold. Pick, pick gold. There from dose peoples. Pick gold watch, pick hundred. Pick shoes, pick handbag. Pick..." he said as he laughed horribly and sent a volley of bullets in the air.

The vultures cackled and scattered, their screech mingling with the girl's scream. The rest of the bullets made a thud as they hit the live target and he never looked back as he drove off in his limousine...to pick another girlfriend to escort him to the front-line. Yes, these were the valiant soldiers setting off for the front-line.

They went for the big war in Tanzania. They came back with lorry-fuls of chicken, goats, iron sheets and women. They drove through the city and sang songs of victory. The people watched silently and prayed harder. Stories were told of how many of the captive women committed suicide rather than become concubines to their captors. Fear and hope hung in the air. Mama called a meeting.

133

"I've called you here for good news which calls upon us to be very vigilant at the same time. The last days of the bloody regime are at the corner. Tanzania has moved. She's been attacked and cannot keep quiet. Her army is on the move and so are all the groups of our people who've been in exile, fighting to get rid of Duduma's regime. They've all combined with Tanzania's army. Victory is sure but be alert lest you fall at the eleventh hour, our hour of victory."

And the war raged on. With Mama leading, their group took *panya* routes and supplied drugs and information to the liberators. Duduma tried to put up a brave show. He brought in mercenaries who, it was rumoured, were prisoners rather than soldiers. They were wiped out within no time even as Duduma kept on announcing through the goverment spokesman that the government was doing very well.

"Our gallant soldiers are doing very well and defeating the enemy. We appeal to all civilan to remain calmly. Your big Daddy itself is at front line. President Duduma wisez to informed everybody that he is still your Daddy, big Daddy of fewer words, Professional solder. Stay calmness . Your big Daddy protect you, your life president, former current chairman of OAU still protect you... Field Marshall, Conquerer of the British empire, Victory Cross, DSO, MC..."

People said yeah, he is actually an MC – mental case.

Nobody listened anymore.

And finally, the liberators took the city of Kampala. The guns had pounded away the whole night. The morning was clothed in a slight drizzle as the guns of war slowly fell silent...a new government was in place.

"Let us go for the swearing in ceremony," said Mama.

They trooped to Parliament for the swearing in ceremony of the new President. Thousands and thousands of people were trooping to the same place. They waved branches, they sung praises for the liberators. The weather was funny. One minute, the sun was relentlessly sending her naked rays down and baking them the next minute, a heavy downpour with ferocious thunder followed.

"Is this crowd bigger than the one that came to see Duduma sworn in nine years ago?" asked old man Yakobo.

"It's definitely much bigger and more mixed in terms of tribes," replied his friend Dombo.

"This thing of crowds. I hope they will not change soon. For remember how we saw crowds milling to go and witness Duduma's numerous firing squads?"

"But I think Yakobo, you misunderstood many of those people. Quite a big chunk were forced to go there out of fear. Woe to whoever refused. Most of our people are not that callous. Its just that they were ruled by fear."

The new president was an eldery, calm, soft spoken, gentle, civilized man. He now took the microphone.

"I Professor Polle swear that ..." he swore to thunderous applause.

"From an illiterate buffoon to a Professor! This is no longer a country that God forgot. He has remembered us, heard our prayers, forgiven us our trespasses and we live again," many said.

That night, the group trooped to celebrate at Mama's. Like everybody else, she was in ecstasy. She had changed from her usual skirt, blouse and sweater and wore a bright coloured *Kitenge*, complete with a huge head-gear. The dingy place had been cleared and electricity installed. No longer was there need to hide in the shadows cast by a kerosene *tadoba*. There was nothing to hide anymore. The neighbours joined in and soon they were on the floor in a traditional dance. Mama was paying special attention to a middle aged man with whom she danced with abandon.

"Mama, is that him who has been in exile?" Nkwanzi asked in a whisper.

"He is," she said casting a love look at him and they were happy for her.

They celebrated until the wee hours of the morning.

"Come with me Nkwanzi," urged Genesis. They went straight to his bed. As they fused into each other in a searching kiss, their hearts pounding as one, Nkwanzi knew they would have to be wife and husband very soon.

"Nkwanzi, is it not yet Uhuru?" he asked his voice slurred with emotion.

"No, Genesis. Not yet. But we can start making wedding plans."

"All right, Mrs Rwenzigye-to-be. When should be the big day?"

"Soon, Genesis. Soon."

"But there is something I want to warn you about, Nkwanzi. That is about this thing of your virginity. You want to carry the custom to the end. But let me warn you, there is also a custom that should a woman die when still a virgin, they push a banana stick into her private parts and bury her with it embedded there. The banana signifies a man's tool."

Nkwanzi did not react although what Genesis had said was terrible. But she wanted to remain in her happy world and as she gradually fell asleep in his arms, she wondered what else she needed to ask from God. With Duduma gone, Genesis in her arms, what else did she need?

Chapter Eleven

A new start

Slowly, the country settled after Duduma's exit. There was a fresh scent in the air, a clean scent. No longer could one smell the stench of death. The groans of death that had permeated the night air were replaced by the hilarious sounds from nightclubs and drums of the ordinary people. The hitherto constant howl of the dogs, the peculiar cry of the cats as they imitated human beings, that cry of theirs which portends danger, the hoot of the owl that had sent chills down the spines of the listeners, all fell silent.

The vulture made its exit from the city, its gruesome sumptuous meal of human fresh now conspicuously missing. The animals which had fled the chaos returned from exile and settled once more in the national parks. The beautiful birds, which had also migrated returned in their millions, their song mingling with the blare of juke boxes and drums.

Genesis and Nkwanzi walked down to one of the big markets in the city. The market was a hub of excitement and activity. With the advent of the new government, the market people had slashed the food prices. The goodwill was a miracle.

"Genesis, all this is incredible. Do you think this slashing of food prices is happening only here in the central region because that is where the new President comes from?"Nkwanzi asked.

"It seems to be happening everywhere. And remember, moreover that these market people are not only from the central region. The're from all over the country."

At that moment, a soldier accidentally upset a basket of tomatoes belonging to one of the market women and they got crushed in the process. The woman almost took off thinking the soldier would shoot her to smithereens. Instead the soldier apologised profusely.

"Madam, I'm very sorry. Forgive me for my carelessness. Here, let me pay for the tomatoes. How much is the whole basket?" asked the uniformed man taking out money.

"No, you don't have to pay. It was an accident. After all, you have already paid by having fought to liberate us," said the woman amazed that a soldier could be so civil.

"Madam, you have *watoto* to take care of. You had come to sell your tomatoes. I'll pay," and he did.

137

All those who watched shed tears of joy. Indeed God had remembered their sad country.

Another soldier had stopped when his car hit a ditch and splashed dirty water on a wheel-barrow pusher.

"*Ndugu*, I'm very sorry. Let's go and I buy you another pair of trousers," the soldier who was obviously of the Tanzania stock said.

"I hope things'll remain like this," said Genesis.

The soldiers became everybody's darling. Many of them fathered thousands of children as happens wherever soldiers camp. Many of them did not even know about their children and did not care to know either.

But the honeymoon did not last long. After a few months, many of the soldiers became hungry for money and comfort. They started robbing people in broad daylight.

One man told of an incident which left everyone agape. He had been on his way to a watering joint, as they called their drinking places, when he abruptly came upon a roadblock. The 'liberators' who had erected the roadblock came out of the bush.

"*Reeta hera*," they barked.

His pockets were emptied and he was told to drive off 'fastest'. He tore off to his joint and narrated the ordeal to his colleagues of the bottle, who all offered him one-one in sympathy. As the handful discussed the sad trend the country was taking, a handful of 'liberators' entered. They were in a jovial mood looking like the cat which has caught a juicy rat.

"Give everybody a drink," they offered.

Naturally everybody was happy with the generous offer but not so the man who had been fleeced at the roadblock. He gave an involuntary scream of rage and all turned to look at him.

"What's the matter ?"

"Those so-called liberators who have given us a round! They're the very ones who took my money. And now they're offering me a drink using my own money! What liberators are these? These are thieves !" and he walked away in disgust.

Mama sounded the group for an urgent meeting soon after that.

"We have serious problems. I'm sure you've all heard about it. There're still a lot of killings going on in the country," she started.

"Yes, Mama, we have all heard," rejoined Mzee

"In fact in my own village, two families have been wiped out. They were of the same religion as deposed President Duduma! People are being buried alive, hacked to death, and women gang-raped," said Mzee.

"People are taking the opportunity to settle old scores, land disputes, petty jealousies. One of the biggest problems is between the *returnees* and the *stayees*. The returnees think all the *stayees* are guilty, some kind of accomplices to the atrocities that took place. They believe the *stayees* were conniving with Duduma. The *stayees* think the returnees have come with a 'holier than though' attitude. That they want to grab jobs and throw out the *stayees*. There is mutual suspicion and bad blood between the two," said Mama.

Chaos reigned in the country and the fight for power raged on. All the fighting groups were suspicious of one another and each of them wanted to rule and before long, President Polle was overthrown and a commission put in charge of running the country. After Polle's removal, rumours were rife that deposed Opolo was planning a come-back and this came true sooner than later. A few months after, there was an announcement that there were to be general elections.

A few days after this announcement, Genesis woke Nkwanzi up one early morning. It was 5:00 am when she heard a knock on the her door. She knew that somebody at home must have died, for surely it was only a carrier of such bad news that would go to anybody's house at such an ungodly hour. Bracing herself for the worst, she went and opened the door.

"Genesis! What's wrong?"

"Does anything have to be wrong? Is it a crime for me to come and visit my future wife?" he asked playfully.

"Do you by any chance know what time of the night it is?"

"You mean what time of the morning? You are talking like a village person. According to the rural folk, as long as it is still dark, then it is night."

"They are not wrong. Darkness is synonymous with night. Anyway, what brings you so early?"

He moved towards her, targeting her lips for a kiss but she averted her face.

"Genesis, how many times shall I tell you that people should only kiss after both have brushed their teeth? But you men don't seem to care. There're many husbands who turn to their wives early in the morning demanding for a kiss before both have brushed their dental formulas. Let me tell you, it's unhygienic and nauseating."

"Yes, Mrs Rwenzigye. I understand and while we're on the topic of dos and don'ts, when you become my wife, what else should I not do?" he asked teasingly.

"It's not a joking matter. As my husband, these will be your don'ts. Number one: don't urinate on the toilet seat. Men urinate while standing and splash the whole toilet seat with their lousy urine. They don't even bother to clean it. How are women supposed to use the toilet then? Squat on your stinking urine?"

"Point number one taken, Mrs Rwenzigye. Number two?"

"Number two: when you come back home after duty and take off your shoes and socks, don't throw them anywhere and then ask me later about their whereabouts. I will not have married you to pick up your socks, shoes and slippers. Number three: when both of us come from work tired, in the evening, don't put up your feet and ask me to make you a cup of tea."

"Yes, madam. Anything more?"

"Definitely, there is a lot more. So here comes number four: when you fail to get sleep in the middle of the night, don't wake me up for sex. Most husbands use their wives as a sleeping tablet – valium."

"But, madam, how do you know all these things when you have not had the experience?" he asked in mock suspicion.

"I keep my ear to the ground. And number five: never leave your underwear for me to wash. If I left mine in the basin, would you wash it? If you aren't going to wash mine, don't expect me to wash yours. Many men say it's degrading for them to wash a woman's underwear. How come you don't find it degrading to lodge in the part which that very underwear covers?"

"I understand, Mrs Rwenzigye," he said and burst out laughing.

"What's so funny?"

"I'm just imagining how your Ssenga will tear your dos and don'ts to pieces. She'll give you a talk before our wedding and you'll come and tell me. But Nkwanzi, on a more serious note, there's something 'political' I've come to discuss with you," he said frowning.

"You mean we are going underground again?"

"No," he paused. "There was announcement over the radio. You must have heard it. There are going to be general elections."

"Yes?" she prompted.

"Nkwanzi, I'm going to contest for a parliamentary seat. I want to represent my people."

"What?" she said, unconsciously dropping the cup which she was holding. It fell on the cement floor and shattered into a thousand pieces.

" I hope that's not an ill omen," laughed Genesis trying to sound light hearted.

"Genesis, you are going to what?"

"You heard me correctly. I'm going to run for parliament."

She sighed heavily. Then she went towards him and sat on the arm chair. She took his head in her hands and looked earnestly into his eyes.

"Please, Genesis, don't enter politics."

He laughed, a harsh, rasping sound.

"What the hell do you mean that I should not enter politics? You know very well that you and I're already there. We actively participated in the struggle against Duduma. So the question of joining doesn't arise."

"But why, why should you go into active politics? You have a good job. A moderately well paying job. We are happy. We are going to get married. Please, Genesis, let's live a humble life."

"What humble life when our people back home are suffering?"

"So, if you join politics what will you do for them?"

"A lot. I'll improve their lives."

"How will you do that without money? No. Genesis wait." She held up her hand as he made to interrupt her. "Changing their lives is a dream. And, Genesis, you know our politics is terrible, there's something almost satanic about it. It's surrounded by evil and corruption, it's dangerous, dirty ..."

"Precisely, that's why some of us want to go there and change the system, clean it up. And as for its being dangerous, I don't know what's not dangerous in life. We are told that the very food we eat is dangerous. They tell us sugar is dangerous to our health, salt is the same, red meat. Cooking oil is bad news, sponge mattresses cause back ache. Travelling in a car needs one to say prayers first and flying needs one to sing *Nearer my God to Thee*. What is not dangerous?"

"Please let me finish. Let me tell you what will happen to you the day you win. Success will go to your head and, like most politicians, you'll not know how to handle it. The weevil of corruption will invade you. You'll have lots of money and your social status will have changed and you'll get many concubines. The more money you get, the more corrupt you will become and the more women you will acquire. That is how politicians use and exploit women because the women are poor. Then, you'll be involved in taking bribes."

141

"Nkwanzi, you have little faith in me. I am going there to change things, not to be part of the dirty players!"

"Genesis, leave it to the crooks."

"Oh, so we should be led by crooks?" he asked, a note of annoyance creeping into his voice.

"So you insist on going on?"

"I am determined to go on and change things for the better."

"Then my dear, you will go on without me. Since you insist, carry on minus me. I can't marry a politician who will abandon me sooner than later or worse still, heap other women on me and treat me as a doormat. You are only going there for money and the glare of public life."

Genesis was visibly annoyed. He stood up abruptly.

"You can leave me. I'm fed up. After all, what am I getting from you? Behaving like you are an identical twin sister to the Virgin Mary."

"Genesis!" she exclaimed, shocked.

"Yes. I come here with a noble idea, you throw it to the winds. You can get yourself another fiancee."

"Genesis!"

"Yes. I'm fed up with your holy attitude. Simply because some old fashioned aunt of yours told you about some damned sheet, you then torment me."

"Genesis! It's not just the sheet. I believe we should keep our bodies intact until marriage. Virginity should be treasured, not despised."

"Oh, the gospel according to St. Nkwanzi! Spare me. Virginity indeed! I'm not even sure whether you are one! I'm not allowed to prove it. Virgin? Hmm!" he snorted.

"Genesis, I never knew you were like that."

"Now you know."

"Is that why you went to Katanga or is it Makivu to pick prostitutes?"

"Oh! People who live in glass houses should not throw stones! You spent a night in the same bed with that *mafuta* of yours. So what were you doing? Reading the Bible or playing Snakes and Ladders the whole night?" and he laughed harshly.

"Genesis! Please get out of my house and my life. You already sound like a corrupt politician. I told you that at *Mafuta's* house I spent the night in a chair!"

"Spent the night in a chair indeed! Some chair," he snorted, his voice heavy with sarcasm.

"Yes, I'm going. And I'm going to run for parliament," he announced and he got up angrily, opened the door, went out and banged it with so much force that the house shook with vibrations. Nkwanzi's body trembled with fury and she threw herself into scrubbing the house.

"Let him go and good luck. I'd rather remain single than marry a politician ... But I love him ..."

Genesis did not go to see her and she could not go to his place either. Mama, being in the know of what had happened, called them for peace talks. Nkwanzi refused, at first saying the peace talks would turn into peace jokes. Mama convinced her that it would not be the case.

"Nkwanzi, since you people are going to be husband and wife, you might as well throw your weight behind Genesis. I support his bid to go into politics, we've had crooks there for too long. Moreover, since we've founded a new party which isn't based on religion, we need many candidates to contest on its ticket. The new party will change the face of politics in this country. Let Genesis represent us."

After a long discussion, Nkwanzi agreed to stay with Genesis and back him in his bid for the parliamentary seat. They discussed the logistics of going down to campaign. Mama would come with them for although she was not from that part of the country, there was a way in which she transcended tribal barriers and reached the people. Atim too was coming as a morale booster.

"Now, the big question is, who'll be the campaign manager?" Genesis asked.

"He'll have to be from our party and home. He has to be able to reach the grassroots and convince the rural folk," said Mzee.

"I've seriously been thinking of Rex," said Genesis.

"Rex!" they all exclaimed.

"I'm serious. Rex has broken from the old party. He is with us in the new one. He has a language, the kind of language the person in the village understands. He is a smooth operator."

"Too smooth I'm afraid! I don't like Rex, I've never liked him," Nkwanzi said.

"Nkwanzi, you've never forgiven him for having taken Genesis to Makivu to drink away his frustrations. You remember that time you went out with *mafuta* and Genesis and Rex went to Makivu? That time...," Mzee was saying.

143

"Please let us leave the past alone. The subject under discussion is the choice of Rex as my campaign manager. Nkwanzi, why don't you like him?"

"There's something about him that reminds me of a creepy reptile. He is not straight, he is always looking down. He can't look you in the face," she said uneasily.

"Well, the question of how he looks at people is another matter. As for me, I see him as the best option," said Genesis.

"All the same," said Atim, "there is something, something that is not right about him. I cannot put my finger on it. The fellow is a crook I'm sure. Even though we're told those are some of the best politicians."

"Please don't say that. That's what we are trying to change. Now, since we do not have much choice anyway, I am going to inform Rex and then I will let you know his reaction."

Genesis came back after a few days.

"Well, how did Cigarette receive the news?" Nkwanzi asked.

"Cigarette?" asked Genesis perplexed.

"Oh, I mean Rex," she said laughing.

"Well, he was happy, excited about it all. In fact we better move to the village.

Genesis, Nkwanzi, Mzee, Atim, Mama and Rex went to the taxi park and boarded a taxi which would take them right to Genesis' village.

At the back of the taxi, the words CONCORD ON THE ROAD smiled at them. All the taxis had words all proudly proclaiming that they were the fastest on the road. One had: NO-ONE CAN OVERTAKE ME another HAVOC SPEEDOMETER, and yet another screamed: YOUR PARTNERS IN SPEED. Two young men sat in the front seats. The first had cut his hair leaving only a circular patch in the middle of the head, which gave him the look of an eagle. The second wore huge trousers with the waist line pulled up to his chest while a tight belt made sure the trouser would not fall from the chest cavity position. His jaws moved in wide gnashing movements as he heavily ground a chewing gum making noise in the process. The movement of his jaw reminded one of a giant shark ready to turn its victim into minced meat. His sleeveless T-shirt which generously exposed his bulging muscles had the words: LOST GENERATION. The second one was more or less dressed in similar attire with: IDENTITY CRISIS printed on his T-shirt.

As the driver manoeuvered the taxi out of the park, the young men could not hide their impatience and restlessness. Eagle Patch told the driver in a drawling voice, "Hey man. Step on the gas. We're late ya know".

"How can I step on the gas when we're in the city traffic?" asked the driver as he weaved in and out of the traffic.

"The way you do it is your business. We, we pay the dough. You, you step on the gas, right? Right."

"Hey pilot, give us some music men. We no going for a funeral fella. Give us some hot number."

The 'pilot' obliged. By then, the car was on the smooth main tarmac road. It was a beautiful morning. The 'pilot' must have felt the beauty for he inserted good music in the player. Jim Reeves' soothing *Precious memories* came on the air. Most of the people lay back, closed their eyes and savoured the sweet music, many of them singing along with Jim Reeves.

A smile of bliss engulfed their faces. The record ended too soon. *Across the Bridge* followed. Again serenity was the atmosphere in this CONCORD. Jim Reeves words rang out clear:

Across the bridge
There is no more sorrow
Across the bridge
There is no more pain...

All of a sudden, the music rudely stopped. Identity Crisis removed the tape from the player and furiously hurled it at the driver.

"Pilot, what sort of people do you take us for? You think we are centurians? Why do you play for us archaic music as if we are ancients?"

And he begun to mimic Jim Reeves.

"Across the bridge, there ish no more shorrow, the shun will shine, acrosh the ri-iver -. You think we are crossing the bridge into the next world eh? Let me tell you, it is you oldies that are about to cross the bridge not us youngies. Isn't that so, buddy?" he asked his friend.

"Obvious case," replied Lost Generation.

"They play that outdated music to remind themselves of their days of sin. Precious memories. What memories? We are living in today not in memories. Give us some hot number men."

The driver complied. He put one which was the darling of the youth then. Both Identity Crisis and Lost Generation begun to wriggle in their seats, obviously enjoying themselves. Rex joined in ignoring Genesis' protests.

"Louder men, louder," shouted Identity Crisis as he turned up the volume button.

The more mature passengers put fingers in their ears. The taxi became a moving discotheque. The young men urged the driver to step harder on the accelerator and the driver, taken up by the mood did not need a second bidding. After all, he too wanted to make money for himself, and what better way than doing two journeys?

Yes, Concord was on the road. Twice, they were stopped by Traffic Police for overspeeding. The conductor would get money and form a fist with it. As he reached the Policemen, he would extend his hand in greeting to one of them and drop the money in his hand.

"Have a `safe journey'," the policeman would say, his face creased in smiles.

When they reached the flat terrain of Lweera, the young men urged the driver to move faster.

"Pilot, let the speedometer hit the peak. Why do you think that maximum speed was put in the car? Was it just to decorate it? Me, I have to reach home, go back to the city and come back again," said Identity Crisis.

The driver complied.

Mama got mad. In an authoritative hard hitting voice, she spoke out.

"You so-called Pilot, reduce speed immediately or the rest of us will quit your car and board another."

There was a murmur of agreement from the other passengers but the two young men and Rex were obviously displeased.

"What do you think you are driving? Animals? Even cows going for slaughter deserve to be driven carefully. Is it because of these names they give you that you drive recklessly? When you're called Pilot, you want to fly the car? And you young men who say you have to go to your destination, come back and go back again. If you were in such a hurry, why did you not start on your journey yesterday? And we passengers are the worst culprits. We fold our hands and keep quiet or urge the driver to speed on recklessly. This man, if he wrecks the car he can buy spare parts for it. But does life have spare parts?"

The driver and the two young men felt chastised. The Concord fell quiet and moved soberly along.

The group arrived at Genesis' home in the evening.

Chapter Twelve

Change of guards

The next weeks were hectic as they held consultations with the authorities and the local people. But one thing was beginning to bother them: Rex's constant disappearances. They would make an appointment to go and meet people and then wait for Rex in vain. Then Rex would show up two hours later, sweating and apologise profusely. They would dash to the venue and more often than not, find that the people had left after waiting in vain. Some people who had been disappointed in this manner begun to say that Genesis lacked seriousness.

"Rex, we can't go on like this. Nomination is close at hand and we've not interacted with all the people," Mama protested.

"Men, don't worry. You know sometimes at night I organise meetings which I address. You don't have to be everywhere. Some of these meetings I can address on your behalf."

Nomination day was around the corner. A meeting was held to decide what was to be done on that important day.

"We've got many people to sing your praises, your escorts on that day. The more we have the better. The other candidates on seeing our big convoy will feel as if they've already lost and maybe jump out of the race," said Mzee.

"No, men. I don't agree. We're people with a difference and we want to show that difference. We belong to the new progressive party. We don't want to behave like those people in the old parties, showing off with a big convoy of cars and mammoth crowd. Let's cut all that out," said Rex.

Everybody was surprised by his attitude because they all knew that he loved pomp. What had made him change drastically?

"Rex, I disagree," said Mzee. "Those crowds are necessary. As our candidate is going for nomination, he has to be escorted by cheering supporters. This is morale boosting. And after nomination, we have to come back home to a big do."

"What big do?" inquired Genesis.

"Well a bull has to be slaughtered and local beer brought for the people. It will be a feast. Nomination is a very important occasion."

"Why men," Rex countered, "why do you want to waste our money on bulls and booze? Man, we can instead put that money to better use.

We should just go for nomination, just the few of us, come back home and lay strategies for the campaign. Feasting should be out completely," stressed Rex.

"You know every day I develop more and more respect for my campaign manager," put in Genesis. "Why should we waste the scarce resources we have on useless things like throwing a feast after nomination?"

"Genesis, I rule that we shall have the crowd and I'm offering the bull for slaughter," Genesis' uncle offered.

The rest clapped and shouted with joy apart from Rex and Genesis. Rex looked as if he had received bad news. An expression of suppressed fury clouded his face and he looked dangerous.

"I'm the campaign manager and I'm the one to decide what should be done. We've come to change the face of politics. And the beginning should be to cut out such useless showing off and feasting. That's for primitive, illiterate people."

"Please don't insult our people. It seems this young man has another thing in mind, not because he wants to change things," said the uncle.

"What other thing do I have in mind?" Rex asked suspiciously, looking a bit frightened.

"You know better."

"Anyway I agree with Rex. We shall have a few people going with me for the nomination and we shall come back here, the few of us to an ordinary meal," ruled Genesis.

This made Rex put on a banana grin.

"I have won," he said.

"Won what?" queried Mzee. "Rex, your attitude is puzzling. We're together. So what is this about winning? Let me warn you; your opponents will make big dos on that day, and people will be impressed."

"The matter is over," said Rex getting up.

Came the D-day, they got ready to escort Genesis to the nomination centre.

Apparently, Genesis' woes had just began. Just as they were about to set off for the DC's office, Genesis' father came breathing brimstone and brandishing a *panga*.

"Rwenzigye, what shame is this that you want to bring upon my household? I'll chop you to pieces, I swear by my grandfather's name. What's this I hear?" he thundered, his eyes dancing dangerously, his

148

fury finding an outlet in thick saliva that foamed at either side of his mouth.

The group was taken aback by this outburst. What could the old man have heard to enrage him to this extent? They looked at him, uncomprehendingly.

Genesis' mother whom everybody called Kaaka braved the situation and asked, "Mwami, what is it with you?"

"What is it with me? Ask what is it with your worthless son. I'm telling you he'll not stay in my compound," said the old man, his gnashing teeth sounding like a buffalo trying to chew a piece of rock. He chopped something imaginary with the sharp *panga*.

"Put away that *panga*. It'll bring bad luck," Kaaka told him firmly.

He refused. Then with a deadly calmness, he turned to Genesis:

"My son, is it true what I've heard? Is it true that you've abandoned the party of this home, the party of your father and mother and taken on this new one we hear about?"

"But, old man, I've been telling you about it for the last two weeks," Mama said.

"Shut up you! I am talking to my son. You have been talking but I did not think my son had taken on this madness until today. Now you so-called son of mine, is it true that you are going to be nominated under your new thing?"

"Yes, father, it is true. As Mama says, we have been telling you about it. We told you that the new party will bring people of different tribes and religions together."

The old man looked like a dark thunder cloud about to explode. For several minutes, he heaved with suppressed fury, tried to speak and failed, only emitting unintelligible sounds. Then finally, the storm broke.

"Rwenzigye, Rwenzigye, if you carry on with that madness, you're no longer my son. How, how do you, my own seed bring this terrible thing upon my household? How can you, whom I fathered, be the one to come and divide our people with your nonsense?"

 Father, listen. This is not nonsense. It's..."

The old man put up his hand to halt Genesis' speech.

"All I want to know is whether you're going on with this madness or dropping it. And if you're truly my son, this very minute, you'll deny this party of yours."

"Father, I can't. This party is the only hope for our country."

"Shut up before I shut you up for ever! We've had our two main

149

parties for a long time. We know that the Democrats Party has been for Catholics. Us the Protestants, ours has been the Congress Party and many of the Moslems have been together with us there. Now, you come with yours which has no religion! A thing like that without religion belongs to the devil. It is for the *abakominista*. For which religion is it?"

"Father, that is precisely why we started it. It is wrong for parties to be based on religion."

"I don't have time to waste. We have our party and we shall stay in it as a family and village. Rwenzigye, do you leave this *communista* party of yours now?"

"Father, I can't. I won't," Genesis answered calmly.

"Then you will leave my house and compound. You are no longer my son," the old man pronounced with a deadly calmness.

"Mwami, you are wrong to act that way," said Kaaka. "If Rwenzigye has chosen to go for this new thing, let him. In fact, I am also following him there. The way I have been seeing these things, our parties are not good. Just think, we never talk to our neighbours who are in different parties, different religions. They never talk to us either. What sort of life is that? Me, I am following my son to this new thing."

"Woman," he fumed, "you dare to talk like that? Just leave my house in the same way you came. Our parties are not good indeed! There is nothing wrong with our parties. If anything is bad, it is ourselves. You brought nothing to this home, you will leave with nothing. I want you out of my house now!"

"Old man, you're carrying this thing too far. Let's...," begun Mzee.

"Shut up! Shut up everybody! I am a man with two testicles and my word is law. Rwenzigye and his mother must leave my house now if you people don't want to see blood."

Everybody knew that when the old man mentioned his two testicles, then the matter was indeed serious.

"A woman to question my authority! I will not hear of it. A woman listens to her husband and goes wherever he goes. But this one wants to take a different direction from me. Just remember, when you change from the food you eat in old age, you lose your teeth. Get out."

"Let's go for nomination and then we can come and explain quietly to the old man," said Mzee.

"A wise decision," agreed Genesis.

"But then where is Rex?"

150

"He'll find us there," Genesis said.

They set off as the old man hurled insults at them. He got out a broom and started sweeping the compound furiously.

'Let them go and go forever. And that mother of his. They warned me long ago that she comes from a clan of mad people but I never listened. How can a woman whom I paid for with my own cows disobey me? Let her go back to her clan of mad people and they give me back my cows. And this boy Rwenzigye, I don't even know whether he is my seed. Maybe his mother whored him."

The group had just moved a few metres when Genesis' uncle came panting,

"Genesis, your campaign manager has betrayed you!"

"What?" they asked in unison.

"I was at the District Headquarters where the nomination is taking place. We kept on waiting to see you and wondering why you were not coming. Then we saw a very huge crowd of people dancing and singing. The slow procession stopped and the decorated car was opened for the candidate to step out. Then out stepped Rex and he went straight to the office and was nominated. He came out and people cheered him and chanted his name and that of his party. Then they started insulting you."

Everybody was shocked.

"Unbelievable. But anyway, let's proceed and go for nomination. We shall go to see Rex immediately after ..." said Genesis.

Genesis had already put his papers in order so all they had to do was move to the District Commissioner's office. Mzee was so enraged about Rex's betrayal.

"That Rex will pay for his Judas act. It may not be today or tomorrow but one day, he'll have to pay," he swore.

"Mzee, get such thoughts out of your mind, I don't expect you of all people to talk that language of 'paying'. These things happen, you know. Even brothers, from the same womb can and do stand against each other in an election. In any case, this is politics, hatred does not need to come in."

"You sound like a preacher but please keep the sermon to yourself. As for me, I'll never forgive Rex. Anyway, let's go for nomination," the enraged Mzee said.

After Genesis had been duly nominated he said, "Let's proceed to Rex's home. I want to tell him right from the beginning that since he has decided to contest against me, we should be civilised about it. We should show people that two friends can contest with each other and retain their friendship."

"You see Genesis, you're an idealist," Mzee rejoined. "There is no way you will retain that so-called friendship. Whatever little friendship you had with that lizard is gone forever,"

Mama stepped in: "Genesis is right. We are going to Rex's home. Our politics are not of confrontation. Since he has jumped in, we shall go and tell him that together with him, we should be an example to the rest of society."

The noise of the revellers at Rex's nomination party caught their ears a few kilometres away from the home.

"Let's go back. We're just making fools of ourselves," said Mzee.

"We are going there," Mama replied with determination.

When they reached the well-lit place, people were in various stages of drunkenness. They were drumming and singing on top of their voices.

Genesis Rwenzigye,
Go back to Kampala and sweep your office.
You have no vote here.
Rwenzigye without a car,
Rwenzigye on foot,
Rwenzigye no money, no wife,
Rwenzigye *chini*,
Rex *juu*!

"Let's go back. Genesis this is a mistake!" Nkwanzi pleaded. Mama took her arm and resolutely moved her forward.

Rex had already seen and approached them with an oily smile.

"Well, well. If it isn't the candidate. You're welcome ..."

"Shall we beat them up chief?" asked the crowd.

"No. You don't beat up visitors. Give them food. I'll talk to them. Well Genesis ...," he begun expansively.

There was absolutely no hint of shame in him.

Rex had meanwhile turned to Genesis : "Well, well, Genesis, the groom. What a pleasant surprise! Even though I'm more than happy to receive you, I'm at the same time wondering how a groom can move from his own celebrations on such an important occasion. Whom have you left your people with or is there no such a crowd in your own home?" he asked with heavy sarcasm, his hand describing a curve as he swept it over his people.

"Rex," begun Mzee speaking between his teeth.

"Oh, and Nkwanzi is here? My dear I had not seen you. Come, a word in your ear," he said pulling her a distance away. "Nkwanzi, why do you stick to a loser?" he asked with a contemptuous gesture towards Genesis.

"He has never been a loser and he will never be. He will even defeat you in these elections," she said with feeling.

Rex burst into his characteristic laughter.

"Defeat me? Beautiful, you're a dreamer like him. If he's lucky he'll get two votes. His and his mother's whom I hear has decided to join him in the new party. No more."

"You'll be surprised. People know what's correct. He'll trounce you."

"I've already trounced him in the first round. I outwitted him didn't I ?"

"Through crookedness," she shot back.

"It doesn't matter what methods I used."

"The end justifies the means, eh?"

"Precisely. But Nkwanzi, that isn't why I called you aside. You know I have lusted after you since time immemorial. You've become like a project to me. I must get you," he said, his voice thickening. The he-goat smell on him grew stronger and she was reminded of Matayo, the herdsman who had defiled her years ago.

"Matayo, you're sick," she spat at him.

"Matayo? Who is Matayo?" he asked suspiciously.

"Oh never mind. You are Matayo and Matayo is Rex. You're all the same. What does it matter? Let's go back to the others. It was even a mistake for me to come here."

"Nkwanzi, wait. Nkwanzi! I'll get you one day. It doesn't matter how long it takes."

"Oh, so that you can complete your project? You interfered with Genesis' political bid and now you want to interfere with his fiancee? Well Rex, you'll have to wait forever."

"That's what you think," he said as he made to get hold of her hand. She threw his hands away, and went to stand by Genesis' side.

"Genesis, old chap, I was merely telling your fiancee to persuade you to stand down."

"Rubbish. He'll do nothing of the sort. We shall defeat you. The people'll not allow you to hoodwink them," Mzee replied.

"Which people? These people?" he asked as he threw a contemptuous gesture towards them.

"How can you want to represent a people whom you clearly despise?" asked Mama with annoyance.

"It's not that I despise them but I can do whatever I want with them. Listen Genesis, step down. You can't defeat government, you can't defeat the state. My party is sponsored by the state and the people will vote for the state."

"And you think these people love you? They don't. They just fear you," Mzee butted in.

"What does it matter? Better to fear me. But they love me. Let me tell you people, you'll never get any votes. We have ninety nine tricks from which to pick in order to win. In fact, let me ask these people to sing an important song for you."

Rex called upon what he called his choir to come and entertain the visitors. A choir of sorts assembled all dressed in rags. Opening their mouths wide, they broke out into the following song:

Play, play
Ee
Play with the ballot
Ee.
We shall play with the ballot.

Rex, taken up with the song stood up and started conducting the choir. The whole crowd burst out singing "Play play".

"This is disgusting. These people are actually saying they are going to rig the elections. It's the leaders who have taught them the song!" remarked Mzee.

When they were spent, Rex came sweating and slumped in his chair.

"Rex, what sort of leader are you? You're openly telling people that you'll rig the elections. Let me tell you, our party has resolved that if you rig the election, we shall go to the bush," Mama said heatedly.

"And we shall follow you there," Rex shot back.

"But, Rex, we started the new party together. Why then have you abandoned it?" Genesis asked.

"Simple. I can't go on the losing side. Why should I? Most of our people still believe in their parties, so why not stick with them?"

"Were they singing about God or about Rex?" wondered Mzee.

Elections were held a month after. Genesis got a few votes, Rex 'won' although it was widely known that his party stole the votes of the Democrats Party. Opolo's congress party won the controversial elections and he would be sworn in as the new President.

On the day of swearing in, thousands of people trooped to the parliamentary buildings. They sat on top of lorries and buses. They climbed buildings and trees. It was the month of July, the hottest month of the year, and the sun relentlessly sent down her scotching rays. Opolo came amidst ear-shuttering ululations. He stepped calmly out of the car and waved to the people in the same manner. If he was very excited, he managed to conceal it.

He was now middle aged. His rather bushy hair was asymetrically parted with precision in his characteristic style. He carried himself gracefully. He walked slowly, majestically, with the support of an ebony walking stick. For the second time, he was sworn in as President of Uganda.

"Speak to us, *nyamurunga*. Our miracle, speak!" an excited crowd prompted him.

With a fixed smile, he surveyed the mammoth crowd and put up his open palm symbolising his party. He spoke slowly, cautiously, as if he had been meticulously trained in the art of speech. He was definitely a first class orator and the first language interference in his speech made it sound rather exotic than ridiculous.

"Today, I'm *hepe* to *stend* before you, *efter* being sworn in *es* your President for the second time."

The applause and ululation threatened to uproot the trees and bring down all the buildings in the surroundings.

"*Thenk* you, *thenk* you. Before I proceed to *eddress* you, I *ferst* wish to *cerry* out a roll call to see whether all the districts of Uganda *ere* represented. I'll go in *elphebetical* order."

And he went through a detailed roll call of all the districts in the country.

"Aa, aa," he chanted and they replied with equal fervour.

"Ee, ee," he chanted and they replied after which they broke into thunderous applause.

"Well, my friend. Is this crowd bigger than Duduma's or Polle's?" asked old man Yakobo of his friend.

"I don't know what to think. I'm now confused," Dombo replied.

155

Opolo's second coming became the subject of debate for many months. Some people said it was a blessing for the country since his first regime had been largely peaceful and developmental. Others said his second coming was likely to create chaos. He had ruled once, why try again? They further reasoned that the second half of his rule had been bad anyway.

The President subsequently formed his cabinet and Rex was made minister for Turbulence Affairs.

Members of the new party held an emergency meeting.

"We warned these people that if they rigged the elections, we would go to the bush. They have done so thereby tampering with the lives of the people. We are going," said their pencil-thin leader.

Members of Democrats Party refused to go underground. They were branded cowards, hypocrites, being without fibre. Many of them joined Opolo's cabinet.

"We don't want bloodshed. We can solve our problems through peaceful means," they said.

Soon after this, Genesis came to Nkwanzi's house very early one morning.

"I've come to tell you that I'm going away," he began.

"Where are you going?"

"To the bush."

"I'm coming with you."

"No, Nkwanzi you are not. You are staying."

"Genesis, what the hell are you saying? I'm definitely coming with you."

"You're definitely not coming," he replied authoritatively.

"Oh! And what gives you the authority to stop me? I'm not yet your wife you know and even if I were, you know very well that I wouldn't allow you to order me around as if I were a minor. In fact, I'm surprised at you. I didn't think you're the type of man to behave in this manner. Anyway, I'm coming with you to the bush."

"No. You aren't Nkwanzi. You must stay behind and keep the fort. Both of us cannot go. Suppose we get killed? I'll go alone."

"Genesis! Now I'm confirming what I had always suspected. You don't love me."

"Honey, its because I love you that I am asking you to stay behind. Staying here does not mean that you will not be involved in the struggle. The struggle we are undertaking is not the same as the previous one. Then we remained and attacked the enemy from within.

156

This time it is different. We may stay there for one year, we may stay there for ten years! Many of us may never come back. Stay here and wait for me."

"You talk as if we will not be in contact!" she protested.

"Of course we will not be in contact. And please don't try to find out anything about me. You know these fellows. If they suspect you have something to do with rebels, I hate to imagine what they would do to you. If anybody ever asks you about me, tell them I went to Finland for further studies."

Genesis told her that they were leaving at midnight that night. They stayed glued together on the sofa and tears coursed down her cheeks and Genesis kept leaking them off with his tongue. When it clocked 9:00 pm, she struggled out of his arms.

"Let me prepare something for you to eat."

"No, love, thank you. It sounds like the last supper," he laughed.

She did not join in the laughter. She kept on looking at the clock, her heart pounding wildly. At midnight, there was a knock on the door. Genesis held her more tightly and the only sound around was their heartbeats.

"Nkwanzi, I'll be back," he whispered.

"And I'll be waiting."

"Deal?"

"Deal."

"Thank you for being strong."

Genesis opened the door.

"We've come," said Mzee.

"I'm ready," replied Genesis.

"Nkwanzi is coming with us a bit of the way. She'll come back with the car."

They were in a small Renault and Mama was at the wheel.

"Now, there is one roadblock on our way, it is a *kaali* roadblock.," Mama warned. "Just relax and do not show any tension. I will speak to the soldiers. Genesis, you have lost your father and that is where we are going. Understand?"

"Understood," they chorused.

"Nkwanzi, you're Genesis's wife. Happy?"

"More than happy," she replied.

"Here goes," she said as she turned the key in the ignition and the Renault set off.

Mama sang snatches of militant church hymns, mixing her own

words with those of the original:

Stand up stand up for freedom
Ye soldiers of the bush
Lift high the flag of freedom
It must not suffer loss
From victory unto victory
Our army shall us lead
Till every foe is vanquished
And the people are free indeed

Stand up, stand up for Freedom
The strife will not be long
This day the noise of battle
The next our victory song...

Then suddenly, she said, "Shh. There is the dreaded roadblock."
Nkwanzi's heart started beating loudly. Genesis squeezed her hand gently and the wild beating slowed down. They stopped a few metres from the roadblock.

"*Zimmya taa,*" shouted a voice. Mama complied. Then the surrounding bushes started moving. Out came about fifty soldiers all armed to the teeth. They flashed torches at the group. Looking at the red glow of their eyes, the group did not need any light.

"*Ttoka inje,*" they shouted as they flung the car doors open.

"Make line *Mmoja*. And where are you going at this time of the night? To the bush eh?"

Mama laughed light-heartedly.

"Afande, how did you guess so correctly? Actually we're on our way to the bush," and she and Mzee laughed again. Nkwanzi held her breath. The soldiers joined in the hearty laughter.

"*Aya, leta kitu kidogo.*"

"*Yikko hapa Afande,*" said Mama handing over a bundle of mainly small denomination shilling notes. The soldiers converged upon the bundle like children fighting over grasshoppers.

"*Aya Mwende,*" they said waving them off.

Mama tore off amidst a silence that lasted for over ten good minutes. The silence was broken by Genesis.

"Eh, where did this pool of water down here come from? I have nowhere to place my feet!"

"You aren't the only one. Me too here, there's water on the floor of the car. Where did it come from?" Mzee wondered as well.

"I urinated. Both before the road-block, and immediately after," Nkwanzi said.

They burst into laugher.

"You've started Lake Nkwanzi," said Mzee.

They drove in silence a few kilometres.

"You will leave us here," said Mama.

The terrible hour of parting. Nkwanzi did not want to shed tears.

"Nkwanzi, I will be back. See you later."

Nkwanzi bit her trembling lower lip.

"Goodbye, Genesis."

"Nkwanzi, never say that again. Never say goodbye. Just say see you later at any parting."

"Okay, Genesis. See you later," she whispered.

He squeezed her hand and followed the others into the bush. The darkness and tall grass swallowed them as Nkwanzi proceeded to the next trading centre where she would spend a night and drive back to town the following day.

Chapter Thirteen

Change of players

The next two months were hell for Nkwanzi. She became restless, she could not sleep properly. She would lie tossing on the bed, listening to every sound outside. The fall of a leaf on the roof, the scratch of a grasshopper on the window pane, the dogs that howled for hours on end. It was only as dawn approached that she would fall into an exhausted sleep.

Meanwhile, the situation in the country was getting worse. State-inspired terrorism was on the increase. And the target was the civilians who were labelled collaborators. Many of the security operatives used the opportunity to extort money from innocent people, well to do ones. The security people would earmark one such a person, proceed to his home, armed to the teeth and tell him he was a guerrilla. They would demand for a lot of money saying if he did not produce the money, they would get rid of him.

The guerrillas launched a relentless attack against the government. The more aggressive they became, the more the government forces vented violence against civilians that they suspected to be in collaboration with the rebels. There was one particular area where the ordinary people were massacred like animals. This was the area where the guerrillas had set up their base. Wherever the guerrillas struck at government forces, government would send there a battalion of soldiers. It was alleged that these soldiers would spend the night before the operation smoking marijuana and drinking local potent gin mixed with red pepper.

By the time they reached the operation zone, they would no longer be human beings. They would cut to pieces any living thing, rape women, the old and babies. They would split open the bellies of pregnant women as they claimed they were looking for grenades hidden in the stomachs of the women. They cut off men's penises and ordered the men to eat them. They made people eat their own shit, made them dig their own graves and buried them alive. In short, the atrocities that took place especially in that area called the Triangle were no different from those that were meted out to the populace during Duduma's days. Many daring people told off several government officials about the blood bath.

"What do you expect when you start a war in your mother's

house?" the soldiers would reason. "The whole family will suffer. Once war breaks out in a certain area, for sure innocent people will die. What happened in Vietnam? Weren't the so called civilized Americans carrying out atrocities against innocent civilians?"

"Because the American soldiers did it in Vietnam does not mean that it is correct! It is horrendous! Why doesn't government fight the guerrillas? Why pick on innocent, unarmed civilians? Even in the past, women and children used to be spared in war. But now, they are victims."

"Guerrillas cannot operate from a certain area unless the people there support them. If the people reject them, refuse to give them food and so on how can the guerrillas operate?"

"The guerrillas do not have to ask the permission of the people before they can operate there! If the locals deny them food, they will just go to the gardens and get it."

"Not unless they do not want their good will and support and if they do not want to take over government. But if their aim is to take over power, they will treat the civilians well and show them that they are better than those in power."

But the powers that be never listened. They kept on hammering in their point of view.

"Look, in areas where there is no insurgency, the people are peaceful. There are no roadblocks. But once there are guerrilla activities in an area, people have to suffer. What do you expect government to do? Fold their hands and not fight back? It's like when there is a snake in a beautiful pot. You cannot kill the snake without breaking the pot. Moreover, the people who are being killed there, how can you tell whose bullet has killed them? The bandits are also killing."

The situation worsened. Soldiers who wanted to rob would place say a tin of margarine in the middle of the road. Woe to anybody who walked or drove past this tin. He would be tortured or worse still killed for having by-passed the 'roadblock'. He would be labelled an outright guerrilla. Prisons were filled beyond capacity. Most of the inmates were accused of being guerrillas. They were given no food, no water. They drank their urine, ate their shit and eventually when there was no shit because there was no food, they turned to eating the flesh of their dead colleagues until they themselves died ...

***

The fighters in the bush fought relentlessly. Mama, who was put in charge of the women's wing welcomed all. She would talk with small groups of women in the fields as they cultivated together with her, as they weeded gardens or harvested.

"My fellow women, apart from being providers of food for the struggle, you will also act as informers. And now listen very carefully: If you ever sight government troops, get out your mortars, quickly put in ground nuts or millet and start pounding away. Pound and pound away. The sound will be picked by our fighters and they will know the whereabouts of the enemy. Is that clear?"

The women nodded in agreement and the struggle continued.

***

It was more than a year since Genesis had gone to the bush and Nkwanzi had not heard anything of him. Then one evening, as she sat watching TV, she heard a knock on the door.

"May I sit?" asked the Honourable Minister for Turbulence Affairs, after entering.

She was taken aback.

"Honourable Minister, what brings you to my humble quarters?"

"Come, come my dear. You haven't even offered me a seat even though I put in my request," he laughed as he sat down.

"Thought you needed company. You seem to be so lonely. Nkwanzi, why don't you ever give me a ring?"

"What can a poor, humble civil servant like me have to do with a demi-god like you, a minister?"

"Oh come off it. And you do not have to be a perpetual civil servant. I can give you a job you know" and he winked.

"Mr Minister, sir, I like my job. And now may I ask you once more what brings you here? I've a lot of work to do."

He laughed out loudly.

"Still the same, still the same."

He looked at her penetratingly, naked lust in his eyes. She felt disgusted and showed it. His expression changed instantly and he looked murderous and she felt a shiver of apprehension ran through her.

"Incidentally, where is your famous fiancee?"

Her heart skipped a beat but she played calm.

"He went to Finland for a masters degree. I thought you would

162

know since you keep your ear close to the ground," she said and went for a glass of water.

"Wrong, madam. He's in a room at the Nile mansions which is preserved for interrogation of guerrillas."

She dropped the glass and it shattered into pieces.

Rex laughed loudly.

"If you care to have him alive, you should come to room 109 at the Nile Mansions tonight at nine. Madam, the ball is in your court. And if you can please release your octopus grip on me so that I can go."

She had not realised that she had clutched his legs in earnest. She removed her hands and he laughed loudly and stepped out.

"God help me!"

Genesis at Nile Mansions! The stories from there would make the bravest person faint with fear. The torture room at the mansions – and that's where Genesis was being held! The electric machines, snakes which were brought to torture people... The room at the mansions was reserved for rebels of 'high rank'.

Nkwanzi sighed heavily. She had no choice but to meet Rex that night. She knew that somehow, she had to pay for Genesis' release and the payment Rex expected could only be material .... Oh, if only Mama was around to advise! The whole day, she thought and thought. Then as the sun was setting, she got ready. She put on her best dress. She knew Rex liked smart women. At 8:00 pm, she sent for a taxi and stepped out of her house.

She reached Nile Mansions and proceeded to the reception, armed people surrounded her immediately.

"Where're you going?"

"Whom have you come to see?"

"Who're you?"

"Produce your identity."

They searched her from head to toe. They violated her privacy, going as far as asking her to spread her legs so that they could check for any bombs or grenades that she might have hidden down there. 'At least if they could get women security personnel to check their fellow women,' she thought. She was escorted by three heavily armed men to room 109.

She took a deep breath as they entered the room. The luxurious room was well lit. On one long sofa sat two girls who were hardly out of their teens. They were in school uniform and looked as frightened as rabbits. When the security left them alone, Nkwanzi asked these girls in a whisper what they were doing in a hotel at that late hour.

"We were at school when we got a message that we were to come and meet a minister. So, we were brought here," the girls kept quiet and looked down.

"Then what happened?"

"The minister took us to his bed inside there and has been doing shameful things to both of us." Both broke into silent tears.

Oh my God! Rex had degenerated to this? One had heard of ministers picking school girls to use but hearing and seeing it were two different things.

"So where is the minister now?"

"Inside there."

Whatever it took, she would tell Rex off. A soldier came and told the girls,"*Twende*" and the poor girls followed him fearfully. The door to the inner room opened and Rex emerged naked except for a small towel tied round half his torso. He was shocked to see Nkwanzi and yes, embarrassed. Quickly, he darted into the bathroom and dressed.

"Nkwanzi! Well, well, my dear. This is the happiest day of my life," he began gleefully rubbing his hands.

"I'm sure it is Honourable, sir," she rubbed.

"Nkwanzi, now to business," he said briskly. "I will have Genesis released on one condition," he said as he looked deep into her eyes.

"Yes?" she prompted her heart thudding.

"That you spend tonight with me. The choice is yours."

"Sir, Honourable." She kept on stressing the sir and honourable because she knew they liked to be called such. "Have you not had enough for the night from these poor young girls?"

"Madam, these young girls had come to meet an Ambassador," he answered coldly.

Their eyes locked until his fell.

"My question still stands," he resumed. "Are you spending the night here for the release of Genesis?"

The sound of the tick-tock, tick-tock became more pronounced. A cricket shrilled outside and shut up. From somewhere, a muffled scream filtered through the night.

She looked at Rex.

"Yes, honourable. It'll be my **pressure** to spend the night with you."

"Did you say pleasure or pressure?" he asked with suspicion.

"What does it matter sir, I have agreed."

He laughed.

"Let's go."

He led and she followed. In tow were about seven heavily armed guards. They walked along a thickly carpeted corridor and then down steps into a dark alley. Thud, thud, thud went their steps. They went down still another staircase and down into a dungeon. From within, muted groans of creatures in intense agony could be heard. Involuntarily, she clutched Rex's hand. He laughed.

"You think fighting a government is like having a cocktail party, eh?"

Fear clutched at her heart. She began to discern the sound of whips as they made contact with bodies. One of the guards pushed open a door and they entered. The stench from the room made her almost retch. Urine, human waste, decomposing flesh ... She turned to go back but Rex propelled her forward. And then she saw the poor prisoners at different stages of starvation. They were mere ribs, many stretched out their hands, their deep sunken eyes begging for food, for life.

"Rex!" she whispered in shock.

"Yes, lovely. This is the price of rebellion."

"Treat them humanely, Rex. Give them a fair trial."

He laughed harshly.

"There is nothing fair about war. These people have waged war against government. Government has to protect the state."

The walls were spluttered with blood and brains.

"Call out rebel number 73," Rex told one of the guards.

"Rebel No 73. Come here."

An emaciated figure dressed in only underwear emerged from somewhere in the shadows. Slowly, weakly, the figure led by the guard picked its way, carefully stepping over the forms which lay groaning on the floor. The guard would step on them mercilessly putting in the boot.

"Genesis!" she said as she moved forward.

Rex pulled her back. Genesis looked shocked to see her with Rex.

"Let me at least greet him," she pleaded with Rex.

He laughed.

"You might as well do so. Your greeting will be your farewell. Remember the deal?" he winked knowingly.

She approached Genesis and stretched out her hand in greeting.

"Genesis," she tried to say but no words came.

"Nkwanzi," his dry lips said.

As she grasped his hand, she pushed the tiny piece of paper into his palm and their eyes interlocked. Hope sprung into his eyes. But for the sake of Rex, he wore a hurt, jealous expression. Rex gave him a wide smile and then abruptly, his face became a cruel mask.

"Has this rebel confessed?" he barked at one of the soldiers.

"Yes, *Afande*. But he refused to name the collaborators."

"Oh, he has refused, has he? Give him the test of manhood. Bring all those that are refusing to name their collaborators."

Rex prodded Nkwanzi to move on and they entered another room. A well lit room. There was a long chopping board across the room and a cruel looking *panga*. As Nkwanzi stood wondering about what Rex was up to, a man opened the inner door. In filed seven prisoners, in dirty underpants, all weak and starved. Genesis was among them and again Nkwanzi started walking towards him but Rex held her back with an iron grip.

"Name your collaborators." the man ordered. His question was met with silence and unfocused stares.

"Name your collaborators!" he bellowed again.

Blank stares.

"All right, since you are all refusing, you will have to pay heavily for shielding the enemies of state. Place your penises on this board."

"I say, place them on the board this very minute," he screamed with fury.

They took out their shrivelled things and gingerly placed them on the board. The man picked up the *panga* and sharpened it against the wall, as if he was getting it ready to slaughter a bull. Urine ran freely down the prisoners' legs.

"Now, name your collaborators," said the man dangling the *panga* menacingly. As he made to bring it down, the prisoners begun to scream out names:

"Ssebaddu, Okello, Atuheire..." the list tumbled out.

Nkwanzi heard Genesis mention names but they sounded ficticious.

Rex ordered the 'executioner' to take down the names mentioned and release the rebels immediately. Nkwanzi concealed the relief she felt.

"Let's go," Rex said abruptly.

He laughed and led the way out.

"This way my dear. I've booked the Presidential suite. My dear, you have the makings of a first lady."

Soon they were in the said Presidential suite. When she looked at the table, she opened her eyes with astonishment. Every drink was there.

"Astonished at the drinks? Beautiful, you're worth more than a million guests. Drink to your fill," he said as he popped open a champagne bottle.

He poured the sparkling liquid into two glasses, handed one to her and holding up his, said with grandeur, "Cheers, beautiful. And from tonight, we shall be lovers. None will put us asunder."

"Cheers," she said with forced cheerfulness.

He mixed all manner of drinks and gulped them down and soon, he was drunk. He then called out to her with slurred speech and beckoned her to the Presidential bed. He rolled off his trousers and threw them at the foot of the bed, the rest of his clothes following suit.

"Come my dear. I want to feel your body next to mine, *bosh* in their original forms," he hiccuped.

"Don't worry honey. I'll remove the clothes later. I want to work you up first."

She forced herself to kiss away his protests. She caressed his hairy chest and he moaned with pleasure. He purred like a cat and brought her face down to his.

"I can't wait for you to take off your *closhes*."

The cow smell on Matayo of so many years ago hit her nostrils and she felt an onrush of nausea. Somehow, he had managed to take off her pants and he stood poised above her, his manhood glistening, trembling with a silent tremour. 'The poised serpent,' she thought once again.

"Let me come on top of you," he whispered with heavy lust as she quickly changed position.

She moved her hand down to his crotch and felt him stiffen and suck in his breath.

"Forgive me Genesis. I have to do this for your sake otherwise you are dead meat."

Like a cat making a leap for the milk, he got ready for the thrust and as he heaved towards her very being, she raised her knee and jammed it between his legs. She squeezed, squeezed against the organ of his seed. Shocked surprise mingled with pain sprung into his eyes. And then in an agonised, strangled voice, he cried out "Maama" and clutched at his now shrunk manhood before he doubled over and spewed all the contents of his stomach on the presidential bed. Quickly she jumped from the bed and put on her shoes. She cast a last look at the form groaning with pain, unable to utter a word. The form, coiled like a feotus, would probably not be able to walk or do anything for the next two days.

"Enjoy yourself, honourable," she flung at him as she hurriedly opened the door and took off, the soldiers saluting her. Yes, she was the big man's madame, *'chakula ya wakubwa'*, and had to be given respect otherwise she could report them and then they would be in hot soup.

She half walked, half run through the thick darkness until she reached Mama's place. She knocked three times and Genesis opened the door. She fell into his emaciated arms and their lips met in a long kiss.

"Quick Nkwanzi. We don't have much time. Put on this habit of a nun and let's get out of here quickly. As soon as I got out of that hell and read your note, I organised everything."

"But Genesis, you're weak. Will you manage to walk back to the bush?"

"It's only that I was almost starving but my strength will come back. I have to go anyway. I have no choice. Nkwanzi, you know what'll happen tomorrow morning. The Honourable Minister for Turbulence will mount a thorough search for both of us, there is nowhere we can hide and not be found. For sure tomorrow a *panda gari* operation will be mounted. You must have heard what happens in such operations. Homes are turned inside out as the soldiers look for arms, rebels and their collaborators. The looting, raping and killing that takes place in these operations makes everybody's blood chill. Nkwanzi, I still don't want you to come with me to the bush. You have seen how dangerous it is. You will go to Kenya for a few months. I will give you our contact there. We are about to liberate the country, there isn't long to wait."

She consented.

"See you later, my dear," he whispered.

"See you later, Genesis," she whispered back.

The following day, all radio stations blared out Nkwanzi and Genesis' descriptions. They were branded enemies of the state, dangerous rebels. Their portraits were plastered on every electric pole, on all the buildings in the city. The words screamed at all:

WANTED!

Genesis Rwanzigye and Nkwanzi.

Dangerous bandits. If seen, contact the nearest police station or

army detach. A big reward awaits.

Against all odds, the two escaped though.

Meanwhile, the government began a man hunt for Kazi, the rebel leader. On many ocassions, people who resembled him were arrested and tortured. The security situation deteriorated further and further. The centre of government began to crack. Soldiers started refusing to go and fight. President Opolo was urged to talk peace, but he declined, seeing it as a weakness if he negotiated with the rebels. The army eventually split into tribal groupings and the centre cracked.

A palace coup followed soon after. Opolo was overthrown by his own army. The new government led by a good natured but illiterate general tried to talk peace to the rebels who initially agreed. But after some time, the rebels refused and said the new government was the same as the old one. The rebels overthrew it, took over power and President Kazi was sworn in as President.

Chapter Fourteen

Change of actors

Clad in tatters but with the strength that accompanies victory, the soldiers who had for many years been referred to as rebels, marched into the city of Kampala to a tumultuous welcome. The people had heard of the exemplary discipline of these soldiers and welcomed them whole-heartedly. For the first time in the history of the country's coups, there was no looting. All shops were guarded and there was a special announcement that anybody caught looting would be dealt with harshly. The leader of the new government, Brigadier Kazi was to be sworn-in outside parliament that afternoon. Nkwanzi had already met Genesis who had told her Mama was in charge of the Presidential Protection Unit. Mzee had come back in one piece too.

Long before the swearing in hour, the crowds started trooping towards parliament chanting praises for the new government and its leader. There were no roadblocks and people breathed a sigh of relief that at long last, these permanent fixtures had been removed. Nkwanzi joined Atim and they went to parliament.

A soft drizzle mildly showered the excited crowd. There was not a single tree which was not laden with people. They were on top of all the buildings adjacent to parliament and sat on top of all the cars available. The people looked with awe at the women soldiers, smartly clad in their uniforms with AK 47 strung on their shoulders. The women combatants were something like a tourist attraction; the eigth wonder of the world, for never in the history of the country had women been combatants. After a few minutes, they heard the noise of many jeeps and in the lead was Mama driving one. She parked it and jumped out quickly, briskly. The other open jeeps arrived and Mama was already at the side of one saluting Kazi who was clad in military fatigue.

People ululated and chanted, "Kazi our Messiah!"

They wept with joy, some fainted from excitement.

Kazi was a trim, tall, bald-headed man in his late forties, with small alert eyes that seemed to be everywhere at all times. They darted in all directions, taking everything in, missing nothing. He had a high forehead and even though his lips opened in an occasional smile, one could tell from them that here was a good man who, however would not tolerate anything that stood in the way of his mission. He walked briskly, with a spring and there was a kind of restlessness about him. It was apparent that he suffered from first language interference when he spoke English. He added a vowel at the end of most words, pronounced /l/ as /r/ in most words and spoke with a pronounced stammer which worsened when he got annoyed. As he shook people's hands, he called out some names.

"Ee, Yakobo, it is good to see you. My friend, Do... Ddombo, you are still alive! *Congraturations* for *havingi* survived. And you, my old woman Mariza, thank you for *havingi* sent me the boys."

Somebody heard this and muttered that Opolo had afterall not arrested some people for nothing. They had been guilty of collaborating with the rebels. Nobody heard the grumble though.

Finally, he was sworn-in as president.

"I Kazi, swear that..."

Ululation, thunderous applause and the sound of drums threatened to bring down the skies.

"Speak to us Messiah, talk chosen one, saviour!" the crowd begged, many on their knees.

A cloud of something akin to annoyance crossed Kazi's face.

Abruptly, he took the microphone and his stammer worsened.

"*Wanainchi* of our country, for us in t-the M-Movement, we don't want t-to be ca-called such names *sijuyi* Messiah, *sijuyi* S-saviour. S-so for me *p-pprease* don't call me such names. I am not Jesus, don't put me on the level of a semi-god. Even I shall not put my head on the currency notes. Why should I?"

The crowd was silent.

"*Wanainchi*, I first want to *conguraturate* y-you for *havingi* survived Opolo and got rid of him." Thunderous applause.

"Eh, this one does not know that some of us still support Opolo. Now he's here thanking us for having got rid of him! Me I can't stay to listen to such profanity. Opolo brought us independence, he built roads, hospitals and schools and now this one is insulting him," said one man walking away immediately.

"Comrades, me I have no time for *roll-callingi* like this Opolo has been d-doing. This business of *callingi* out different districts in order to see whether people from there are present, *sijuyi* Arua, Arua! Bundibugyo, Bundibugyo! Me, I don't have time for that. Th-that is for the classroom not for the head of state while *add-addressingi* the nation."

People burst into derisive laughter. Kazi put up his hand and they fell silent.

"Comrades, we have come with a mission; we have a vision for our country. Our mi-mission is to bring sanity back to our country, to put it back on the world map. Our country is known as a slaughter house world-wide and we are putting an end to that. We have brought a f-fundamental change. We have planted a m-mustard seed which will positively change our country for ever. O-ur ppeople have been subjected to state inspired *vv-viorence* for too long. *Rapingi* our women, our mothers and sisters. There is a *sayingi* in my language that, if you look in your mother's private parts, you have nothing to say. These murderers had no respect for our taboos and brought disaster. They not only indulged in criminal acts but also indulged in obscurantism. You know this obs- obscurantism – not tackling the substance."

He paused for a few seconds.

"Don't witch-hunt anybody *sayingi* that, 'Oh! this one supported Opolo's government.' If anybody's guilty of any crime, take them to court. Don't take the law into your hands. For us, our *poricy* is *reconciriation*. If you have a T-shirt with the picture of Opolo, don't fear to wear it. It is your right to dress as you please. If any soldier attacks you, report him *immediatery*.

"Indisciprined armies have been our greatest probrem not *onry* here in Uganda but the whole of Africa. There has been a situation where sordiers were told the gun is your father and mother, use it to get money! Madness, madness *onry*. Lastly, for us, we have analysed our history, the history of our people, the history of the African people, and we know that *imperiarism* is the cause of most of our *probrems*. These *imperiarists*, they came and divided us. They drew the boundaries badly and divided people who had things in common. They set us against each other. They came and said they h-had discovered our lakes, rivers and mountains. How can you s-say you have discovered a river which had always been there, seen by the people of the a-area? This is *ins-insultingi* our people! Therefore, guard against the cancer of *imperiarism*, their propa-propaganda."

He went on to tell the nation that political parties which were one of the major causes the country's many years of upheaval were henceforth suspended. They had divided people along ethnic, religious and regional foundations, he said. Morever, the democracy that the Western world talked about was only condusive to their situation and not for African countries because the contexts pertaining in these

172

continents are different, they are at different stages of development.

"Well, we hope he'll not take on the economic policies of the developed nations since he has discarded 'their' democracy," an elitist voice commented.

"The President is right. Why should the West always impose upon us their mode of democracy? That is like re-colonising us," others said.

The ones who were not happy with the suspension of political parties kept quiet because they had heard of the exemplary discpline of the new army, and right then what was number one on the agenda was peace.

The trees swayed, the buildings thundered with the echo of the applause and the soft drizzle steadily showered the crowd as Kazi drove off.

"So now, which crowd of those who have come to witness the swearing in of our presidents is bigger?" Yakobo, the old man, asked.

"I think Opolo's second coming was the biggest," said Dombo.

"No. No. Duduma's still beats all of them," asserted Bwana.

"I beg your pardon, this is the biggest crowd ever in the history of Uganda," Yakobo said after a pause.

"But this President, how does he start insulting our friends from abroad and calling them bloody imperialists? These people have always helped us," Dombo grumbled.

"It is because he is a communist. They all talk like that, those communists," replied Bwana.

"*Communista?* What is that? Is it these people who suck other people's blood?" Yakobo asked, alarmed.

"Communists are those who don`t believe in God," Bwana said with disgust.

"You mean we are going to be ruled by a Godless person? Then why is our motto: **For God and my country**?" Yakobo cried.

And the debate on the new regime raged on.

"But the man speaks vernacular English!"

"So what? Opolo was a fantastic orator and yet see where he landed us."

"It is not Opolo who landed us there. If this Kazi had not waged his guerrilla war, Opolo would have ruled us well. Once there is war, nothing moves, the situation gets bad. Moreover it is common knowledge that Opolo was not a bad man. It is the people around him that were."

I don't buy that rubbish. Could he not discipline those bad people who used to surround him? In any case, you can see that Kazi has a disciplined army."

"Don't tell me about a discplined army. Disciplined, ha! All soldiers are the same. Have you forgotten how many of the soldiers who removed Duduma were disciplined at the beginning? What happened soon after? They started behaving like the ones they had got rid of."

That night, people celebrated the new lease of life. For two days, they ate, drunk and made love with abandon. Nkwanzi, Genesis, Mzee and Atim converged at Mama's place. Mama's man friend was also around and there was a glow of love in her eyes.

"Mama is in love like a teenager," Atim said in an audible whisper and all broke into hearty laughter.

"Know what, I thought she had given up those things long ago," said Mzee.

"What do you mean, 'given up'? She is a human being. Or did you think she is too old? Even old cows eat grass, you know," Genesis said.

At the height of the merry making, one of the young men came and told Mama that there was a freedom fighter who had arrived and wished to greet them.

"Bring him in quickly. That's a comrade in arms."

Immediately after, a flamboyant, smart soldier entered.

"*Karibu* Comrade," Mama welcomed him expansively.

Had Nkwanzi not seen that comrade somewhere? There was something very familiar about him but she could not tell properly because half his face was concealed by his military cap. He removed the cap.

"Rex!" she shouted in disbelief.

"Rex?" echoed Genesis and Mzee.

"Hello, comrades! I missed you in the bush because I was in another platoon. But I am glad we are here together comrades, celebrating the fall of the dictatorial regime," said the soldier in a booming voice.

"Well, well. I don't ... can't ..., " started Mzee throwing up his hands in a gesture of incomprehension.

"Don't look perplexed, buddy. Thought I would abandon you to struggle alone? I would not be worth my name then, would I? I could not stay in Opolo's dictatorial regime any longer and I came to join you. Our country badly needed liberation. I saw the light and hearkened to the clarion call of my people," he said in a hasty voice, his eyes avoiding contact with any of theirs.

"He saw the money not the light. Thinks there is going to be a lot of eating in this government," muttered Mzee.

"Well, comrades ain't you gonna welcome your fellow freedom fighter?" persisted Rex.

"But of course you are welcome, brother. It's just that you took all of us by surprise. When did you join the struggle?" asked Mama.

"As soon as I realised that our government was no good. And, men, was I mad at them! But I don't want to dig up history. Let us move with the times. Hey, you know some of us are stupid. Wanting to stick to the past. But me I tell them, look, the one married to your mother is your father. The Movement has married our mother, he is now our father."

There was a long pause which Mama broke.

"Oh well, Rex is right in one aspect: Let us not concentrate on the past but look at the future of rebuilding the country even though we cannot stamp out history. Well, Rex, you are welcome."

The rest of them had a lot of misgivings about Rex, and knew him as opportunistic. However, he kept on forcing himself into their company wherever they were.

Later, Nkwanzi and Genesis discussed their future plans.

"Nkwanzi, before the end of this week, I want you to go and inform your parents. I'm also going home to inform mine. Within a month, you'll be Mrs Rwenzigye. We shall have a quiet wedding attended by a few people," he whispered close to her lips.

She pushed him away gently.

"Honey, what's the matter?"

"Genesis, I don't know what you mean by quiet wedding."

"My idea is that we should have a small, quiet wedding and an equally small reception consisting of you and I, your matron, my bestman, my parents and yours. Finish."

"You know what, Genesis, you're crazy. That is not the wedding of an African. The ceremony is not just for family and close friends. It's a clan affair. I'm not a daughter of just my father and mother but of the clan. Call me backward if you wish, but I want a big wedding."

"Honey, you amaze me! Sometimes you talk as a woman who is not educated! Apart from anything else, we can't afford a big wedding! Do you want us to use the limited resources we have and then starve? Morever, my dear, the Movement has brought sanity back to the country. We, the new breed of leaders, should show the way and we

175

should not indulge in lavish feasts like used to happen in the past. Such lavishness is an exhibition of corruption. Where do you get all this money to throw extravagant parties?"

"But you know a wedding is not made by two people only. Friends and relatives contribute to it."

"Oh, you want us to go begging like some of these couples who fundraise for underwears, ties, handkerchiefs and even rings! I can`t stoop that low."

"We can provide for our attire but the feast will be taken care of by the clan."

"You know what, next you'll be saying that I should pay dowry for you!"

"But of course you have to."

"What? You want me to buy you? Honey, that's like buying a sex worker!"

"Genesis! How dare you! To me it isn't buying. It's only now that the whole thing has been turned into a business. But if you give my parents, say, one heifer, I have no objection. The only thing I'm against is when the groom-to-be is asked to pay a lot of cows and money and also when husband and wife divorce and the man asks the woman's family to refund his cows."

"Nkwanzi, you shock me. It's not that I cannot afford to pay dowry for you. I can. But I am against it because it transforms women into slaves. You know very well that some men batter their wives on a daily basis simply because they paid bride-price for them."

"But of course you would not treat me like that simply because you will have paid dowry. And these men who batter their wives do so not mainly because they paid dowry. They're just beastly. Anyway, Genesis, let us end the argument. You will pay dowry but it will be a token. I'm going to request my parents that I be there when the negotiations are going on. That's what every bride should do and in that case, you will not be overtaxed."

He shook his head.

"As you wish, my dear."

"Genesis, it's not just as I wish. Now that we are going to be one, my wish should be your wish. And look, actually in our culture, part of the cows you pay are sold and the money used to buy gifts for our home. The bride's people too buy a lot of things for the young couple. So it's not as if it's a one-way traffic."

He paid dowry. One heifer, two sheep, two goats and a few other

176

items. After that, Nkwanzi went home to prepare for the marriage and Ssenga was called in to talk to her on how to be a good wife.

"Child, never turn your back on your man. Whenever he turns to you, consent. No matter what time of the night it is."

"But really ..." Nkwanzi started to say but Ssenga held up her hand.

"I am talking, you listen. Never go to bed when you are dressed. If you do, it means you are telling your husband not to touch you. Always go to bed in the same way you came from your mother's womb."

"But really, Ssenga, you mean I should throw away my night dresses?"

"What is that night dress for? It's for girls who are not married. Those dresses for the night, keep only for the hospital."

"Ssenga, please..."

"Don't argue. Leave your arguing. That's when you'll make a good wife. I'll tell you a short story. A woman was having problems with her husband and they were always quarreling. Things became so bad that the woman visited a witchdoctor. She told him the problem. 'Your problem is very easy to solve. Everytime you are with your husband, put water in your mouth and close it tightly,' the witchdoctor advised. Child, do the same and you'll never get any problems if you have water in your mouth. You will not talk back." She paused.

"Here are herbs which you will be boiling in a small pot. Every evening, you should squat over them so that their steam can perfume your womanhood. Your husband will like you better that way."

"Are there herbs for him to perfume his manhood too so that I can like him better?"

"That's a foolish question. It is you trying to please him. Otherwise he will go to other women who will do anything in this world to make him happy."

"Really, Ssenga, how can you talk like that? He should strive to make me happy too! Happiness is not a one-way traffic."

"You shut up with your nonsense. I am here to talk sense into you and your job is to listen. Now listen carefully. Do not allow these young girls whom you call house-girls to cook for your husband and serve him. It must be you to do it. And more importantly, do not allow those house-girls of yours to make your bed. Remember that the person who makes the bed sleeps in it. If you make her do it, she will become your co-wife.

177

"Always give visitors something to eat or drink, however small it may be. Our people say that when you have nothing to give a visitor, you say 'have this little salt and leak it.'

"Respect your father-in-law and never mention his name or any object which has a similar name to his. If his name is Rain, never mention the word 'rain'. Or if his name is Spear never mention that thing. Call it the hunting knife or something else."

"But really, Ssenga! Suppose his name is Rain. Then when I want to say that it is raining, how do I say it?"

"Simply say that the heavens are urinating. Lastly, never, ever trust a man. They are all the same, they all go to the same school when it comes to how they treat women. Don't trust him and tell him all your secrets. Do not make him your pillow and blanket."

"But, Ssenga, how can I marry a man whom I don't trust? I trust Genesis completely."

"You'll live to regret it. It's better not to trust him so that in future when he goes with another woman, you'll not be suprised." She paused. "My gift to you is a sheep. Go and keep quiet in your home like a sheep. Be humble like it. Lastly, I want you to be as proud as a leopard. You know, the leopard is so proud of its beauty it cannot allow anybody to spoil it. So, when it is wounded, rather than bleeding outside and spoiling its beauty, it bleeds from inside. Child, like a good woman, you should bleed from inside when problems come."

"But Ssenga, that is internal bleeding and it is dangerous. It kills!"

"You shut up with your nonsense. If you follow what I have told you, your marriage will never break."

Ssenga talked to her everyday. Meanwhile, she was being overfed and pampered. The month flew by and soon, the big day was at the corner. The night before the great day, there was no sleep for Nkwanzi. Mama came home and they spent the night talking away. Her cousins too kept on urging her to cry because she was going to leave home and brides were supposed to cry. She just laughed at them although they tried very hard to sing extremely sad songs.

And, finally, the great day, the wedding day dawned. Ssenga bathed her amidst protests that she could do it herself. She left Nkwanzi to oil herself and murmered something about going to pick a good luck leaf from behind the kitchen.

While alone, as Nkwanzi gently massaged baby oil on her body, she began thinking of the pleasure that awaited Genesis and her that night as they consummated their marriage. She was happy that she had kept herself for him. That white sheet would be found with blood ... Genesis, how she loved him! He had exhibited the patience of Job and she knew there were few like him left in the world.

She imagined him stroking her that night and her body tinged with ecstasy. It had been worth the waiting. Tonight he would appreciate how great it is for a woman to maintain her virginity. He would respect her forever. She looked at the watch. 10:15am. Engrossed in her thoughts of ecstacy, she never heard the knock on the door and somebody's subsequent entry... He stood transfixed on seeing her naked. His breath whistled out through an open mouth. He had only come to bid her farewell and cynically wish her well in her marriage. But to find her like that!

'My God!' he whispered to himself as he gulped down the saliva that filled his mouth. 'She looks like a Greek goddess!' And this was the body she had denied him, the body which he was now looking at in its original form. 'No. No,' he thought blindly, his heart pounding, overpowered by lust.

He made one quick spring and before Nkwanzi realised what was happening, he had covered her mouth with his hand and thrown her on the bed. Within a split second, he had opened his fly, and his huge manhood sprung out like a venomous reptile. Her eyes opened in horror before she felt a searing, tearing pain, a pounding into her very soul. Before she could sink her teeth into his hand, he suddenly groaned as if in great agony, cried out for his mother, jerked a few times and then his whole weight sagged on top of her. He was like a python which had just swallowed an animal and could not move.

Filled with the deepest loathing and hatred she had ever felt for any living being, she pushed him away violently and he fell on the floor with a thud. 'Scream, scream!' an inner voice urged her. But something held her back. How could she announce to the whole world, a few hours to her wedding, that she had been raped? Would Genesis wed her? No.

"Get out, get out you pig before I kill you," she said between her teeth, her eyes frantically searching for a knife, any object that she could plunge into his stomach. The fact that she could not see any weapon made her more frustrated.

"Nkwanzi, you were actually a virgin!" he whispered, surprise in his eyes. "What was Genesis doing all the time? And imagine, I always thought he was chewing with you!"

Anger, loathing, frustration and impotence all conspired to deprive her of speech momentarily. Then she burst out,

"Get out you, lousy pig. And let me tell you, one day, you will pay for this." She aimed a vicious kick at his stomach and as he bent double with pain, he farted. A loud, foul fart.

"Get out, you farting pig! You're full of shit," she yelled and she gave him another kick as he limped out.

As if waking from a nightmare, she looked at the watch: 10:20 am. The pig had not taken more than two minutes to shatter her life. God! She had to think fast. Ssenga was about to come back. She should not find her like this. Moreover, there wasn't much time left to go to church. Nkwanzi's body trembled with gasping sobs and rage as blood flowed down her legs. Quickly, she got a *lesu* and wrapped it around herself, filled the basin with water and emptied a whole bottle of dettol into it. Would she ever feel clean again? Would she ever disinfect herself enough?

As she was about to go to the bathroom, Ssenga entered and exclaimed, "Well, this bride! You are going to bathe again! Child, you are going to turn into a frog. It is the one which does not want to leave water."

The sight of her made Nkwanzi burst into fresh sobs, big gasping sobs. Ssenga came over quickly and embraced her.

"Child, hush. I know leaving home is not simple. Its like cutting the umbilical cord. At first you tried to be strong but when I left you alone, you thought about leaving home forever and felt sad. But hush, child. That is not how to cry. A bride cries as if she is singing. She does not cry alone but with other girls. You are crying wrongly, as if somebody has died. You should not cry as if your heart has been pierced by a cruel hand. Child, you will be all right. Your husband will love and respect you. You have kept yourself for him all these years ... intact," she whispered.

Nkwanzi broke into fresh sobs.

"Hush, hush. Don`t mourn. You are mourning! Shh, shh. We are getting late."

"Ssenga, please bathe me. Bathe me with those herbs."

Ssenga laughed. Nkwanzi had refused her to bathe her and now here she was begging her to. Before the two could proceed to the bathroom, Mama entered and exclaimed.

"Well this bride! I had come to dress her and yet here she is going to bathe again. Since you obviously think one basin of water is not enough for you, maybe we better go and dip you in Lake Victoria!"

180

And she laughed.

Throwing herself on Mama, Nkwanzi broke into fresh sobs. Mama was shocked. As Nkwanzi sobbed, Mama cast a question to Ssenga, using her eyes. The latter shook her head in perplexity. Mama sat Nkwanzi on the bed.

"Nkwanzi my dear, what is it?"

"Nothing, nothing, Mama," Nkwanzi said and broke into fresh sobs.

Mama held her to her bosom.

"Sweet Jesus, Nkwanzi, something *is* the matter. It is big, it is heavy. Please, tell us what it is. A problem discussed is half solved."

The clock ticked on in the uneasy, troubled silence.

"Nkwanzi, we are even getting late. Since you don't want to talk about it, let me dress you and we proceed to church. At least you should feel proud that you are the first bride in so many years to wear a white bridal attire, symbolising sexual purity."

Nkwanzi flinched with pain and bit her lip to stop herself from screaming out. She insisted on bathing again.

"There is no time for that now. The bath you had is enough," Mama said firmly.

"I must bathe again. I must," the bride insisted.

Mama and Ssenga got more perplexed.

"All right child, let's go."

They went to the bathroom and Nkwanzi removed the *lesu*. Then Ssenga screamed. Mama dashed there immediately and surprise sprung on Nkwanzi's face.

"What is the matter again?" Mama asked.

"The blood, the blood!" Ssenga gasped.

"What blood?" Nkwanzi and Mama asked simultaneously.

"Why, there, running down the bride's legs!"

Ssenga sighed wearily, and in a tone of resignation, said, "This is bad. To see the moon on your marriage day is bad. Tomorrow morning, your husband will have no sheet to show the clan. The people will think he is not a man. They will whisper with evil tongues and say your man threw away the knife long ago; that his manhood is not there."

Nkwanzi quickly put in that it was not the moon. Then as quickly realised her mistake and tried to retract the statement but it was too late. She looked down. A long pause followed.

"Nkwanzi, we don't have much time. Please tell us what has

181

happened to you." Mama pleaded in a quiet but firm voice. There was a long pause and then Nkwanzi lifted up her eyes to the two women who meant so much to her.

"I have just been raped," she stated in a voice devoid of any emotion.

"What?" the two exclaimed incredulously, both holding Nkwanzi from either side.

"Yes, I have been raped."

"It can't be ..."

"But who ..."

"Rex."

"Rex?"

"Yes," answered the embattled bride.

"Oh, oh! We are cursed! How can this be? What crime have we committed? Oh my poor child! Oh, oh, oh!" wailed Ssenga.

Mama tied her *lesu* more firmly around herself and said with grim determination, "Nkwanzi, we must act quickly. The wedding has to be postponed and, more importantly, we must report the matter immediately to the police."

"What?" exclaimed Ssenga springing into action.

"I can't ..." begun Nkwanzi.

"What police are you talking about? Look, you so-called Mama, this matter will not leave this room and I want you to listen very carefully. This terrible matter is buried in our stomachs, the three of us. No one must ever hear of it. We must all swear never, ever to breathe it to anybody. This is a shame that should never, never be known by anybody else. This unspeakable act of rape is a weevil and the only way we can keep this weevil buried is by keeping quiet. If we talk, we shall make the weevil come to the surface." Ssenga said, her pleading eyes focused on Nkwanzi.

"I agree with you Ssenga. This thing should never be disclosed to anybody else," the bride said.

"Nkwanzi, no, you can't talk like that. Rape is the worst crime against humanity. The rapist must be netted and the only way of doing it is by you going to report the matter to the police. Nkwanzi, if you a lawyer keeps quiet, then how will we fight this evil which is on the increase? How will you tell women to report rapists when down inside, you know that you kept quiet thereby shielding a criminal? Lets go to the police station," said Mama as she made a resolute move towards the door.

182

"No, Mama, we won't. The minute we report the matter, the whole country will come to know of it. You know with the freedom of speech there is nowadays, every newspaper will carry a screaming headline about me. I will go through a second psychological rape. People will sneer and laugh at me saying, 'There goes the woman who was raped on her wedding day.' And then how do you think Genesis will take it? He will drop me," she said with finality.

"We will explain to him. He will know that it was not your fault! He will understand. Let's go."

"My child will not go anywhere near the madness you are talking about," Ssenga said with a lot of heat. "You, Mama, you're a bad woman. I don't even know who gave you that good name. It is this *Puresidenta* Kazi who brought us problems. He made a mistake when he made women hold the gun and fight. When a woman behaves like a man as you did, then madness has entered the country. That is why your type who fought in the war cannot get married. Which man can marry you? Haven't many of your type remained cooking in your fathers' houses? No man can take you for a wife. Which person, whose head is straight can say that a terrible thing like this one which has happened should be told to people? It is only a mad woman like you who can talk like that. You want to ruin my child's life. Child, come. Let me bathe you, then you dress and go to church. Come, child. "

"The decision is yours, Nkwanzi. But remember, you and I should show the way. We must be role models for the youth, we must fight the traditions which doom women to passivity. We must fight against outmoded ideas and prejudices and then the young will follow suit." Mama paused. "So, do we go the police or do we go to church?"

Time was static as Nkwanzi stood in the middle of the two important women in her life, both waiting for her word. For the nth time, Nkwanzi sighed and the two held their breaths.

"I will go to the police."

Ssenga collapsed in a heap on the floor, mumbling incomprehensible words, her eyes rolling in a trance-like manner.

"Let's go,"Mama said as she took Nkwanzi's arm. "We shall send somebody to look after Ssenga."

"At least let me wash her first," Ssenga said in a tearful voice, recovering momentarily.

"No, Ssenga. I can't bathe. That will be destroying the evidence. I must go as I am," Nkwanzi told her gently.

Ssenga broke into uncontrollable weeping, talking unintelligibly.

They went to the police station. The statement was taken down and a few minutes later, the specimen for the medical examination taken from Nkwanzi. Rex was arrested and put behind bars to wait for his trial.

"We still have a few hours. Let me go and call Genesis, we sit in a neutral place and you tell him. Everything now depends upon him," said Mama.

Genesis came and found her at the agreed place.

"Well what is this? We are supposed to meet at the church and not here. And in any case, we are getting late. Nkwanzi, what is this SOS?" inquired the groom.

Nkwanzi broke into a fit of trembling and Genesis registered shock.

"Let's leave them alone. There is something they have to discuss," Mama told a perplexed Mzee.

Left alone, Genesis asked Nkwanzi what the matter was. Unable to talk, she could only murmur incomprehensibly.

"Nkwanzi, don't tell me that it is the thought of tonight that has caused this hysteria. I'm not going to eat you ... I am not an ogre!"

After another fit of uncontrolled trembling, she composed herself and told him without emotion.

"Genesis, Rex has just raped me."

"What?" Genesis exclaimed in shock as he gripped her by the shoulders, his nails digging into her flesh. But she never felt the pain. And she told him the whole tragedy, omitting nothing. At the end of the tale, the silence hung thick and heavy. After what seemed like eternity, Genesis spoke.

"We shall go on with the wedding. What has happened is not your fault. I'm glad you reported the matter to the police. Rex must pay," he said, his eyes narrowing dangerously. "If it was not that we have brought the rule of law, I would have shot Rex immediately," he said between clenched teeth. Then he gnashed his teeth as tears of rage and hatred coursed down his face and Nkwanzi flinched at his naked pain. After what seemed like eternity, he said, "Let's go my dear. Go and dress up. We are already late as it is."

Nkwanzi's tears had already dried up. She looked at Genesis with wonder and quietly walked out.

The people at her home were very worried not knowing what was happening. Mama had a hard time convincing Ssenga to bathe the bride again, but eventually, she agreed.

"Scrub me harder, harder, aunt, with the sponge," Nkwanzi begged.

But the grime, the vermin, the weevil was really in the inside where the sponge could not reach.

Then a wave of fear swept over her. Suppose the pig had made her pregnant? No, it could not have happened. God could not be cruel to her, she consoled herself.

Mama dressed Nkwanzi who had long decided that she would not use any make-up. She was to remain herself.

"My, Nkwanzi, you look a dream."

Nkwanzi stepped out and the mild morning sun greeted her. Her father was waiting outside to take her hand and escort her up to the car. Her cousins were ready with their drums and started singing a sad song to make her weep.

"You stop those songs. Can't you see that she has wept enough and her eyes are swollen? Sing a cheerful one," Mama commanded.

They took in the message. They changed to a cheerful one, teasing her and she smiled and the tension on Mama's face melted.

Slowly, they drove to the church and later Tingo led Nkwanzi down the aisle to where Genesis stood. Outside, the weather had changed and a heavy downpour pounded on the church roof. When Nkwanzi looked at Genesis, her heart did a somersault. He wore a white *kanzu* with a navy blue coat on top. Mzee, the best man wore a cream *kanzu* and black coat. Nkwanzi had told Genesis she hated the tradition of the groom and best man wearing identical clothes. There should be a difference in their dress. He stood confident and firm and looking so handsome. He forced a smile when he saw her and she too forced one.

The moment for her second baptism arrived, and later she signed the register as Mrs Sayuuni Rwenzigye. The service ended and slowly, they walked out of the church as the congregation clapped and sang.

The rain had stopped and the sun smiled down at them.

"Kiss the bride, kiss the bride!" some of the young people in the crowd chanted.

Genesis and Nkwanzi had decided not to do this. It was not good for people to kiss publicly, in full view of elders.

"Now, we're going home. Our home," her husband whispered, trying to sound cheerful.

And the small volkswagen slowly drove them towards her new

home. The air was fresh, as it always is after a shower, and the land was green. The hills stood proud and rounded, like the breasts of a young girl. Genesis kept pressing her hand gently, understandingly and she would press his in the same manner. Apart from momentary flashes of the pig, she felt her heart almost burst with happiness and love for Genesis.

They arrived at his home where a big crowd awaited them. After the day's festivities, they were led to the small neat, beautiful hut Genesis had built. Mama and Mzee quietly bade them goodnight. Genesis led her to the very neatly laid bed and they lay close to each other. She waited for his touch but he lay with his hands folded under his head, looking at the ceiling. For a long time they could not sleep, and they both kept to their thoughts.

Eventually Genesis said with a long sigh, "I'm sorry, Nkwanzi. Let's give ourselves time and things will straighten out in the end."

'The white sheet, the blood...What a big laugh! Some people are accident prone, others are scandal prone. Is it that I'm rape prone?' the bride thought wryly as sleep finally stole over her. She was woken up later by Genesis' gentle kiss on her eyelashes.

"Mrs Rwenzigye, you have to get up you know and go to grind millet," he laughed. "On a more serious note, there are rituals you have to go through. Mercifully, that white sheet thing is now a buried custom," he said with pain causing her to cringe.

She could see that he was struggling hard to be natural. She got up quickly and took a bath. Later, she was led to the main house where she was introduced to the whole clan. And then, Genesis' paternal aunt took over.

"Now come and sit down here and we shall give you what will be your marriage name. These days, you find that when a girl gets married, she is called Aunt by everybody. Or others call her *mugore* from her day of marriage until she ages and dies. But for us here, we shall follow our ways. From now, your marriage name shall be *Bacureera*. The name means a calm, quiet, humble, woman. You will bring peace and tranquillity to your home. The home will be respected because of you, because it is a woman who carries the dignity of the home."

All this time, Mama, had been looking very unamused. She whispered furiously in Nkwanzi's ear,

"You're not going to accept that name, are you?"

"Why not?"

"It will make you a slave. It is supposed to make you shut up and accept all wrong done to you, no protest, nothing. Don't accept it. With that name, you will not be assertive."

"Mama, how can I refuse? And do you really think a mere name can make me accept injustice?"

"Nkwanzi, a bad name damns its owner. Those marriage names chain women. They are supposed to beat you into behaving 'properly', beating you into line. Names like Babukaara meaning, the calm one, Bafungura, the one who always provides a refreshment, Bayoroba, the soft one, Batatsya, the one who welcomes all. They are all terrible names for women. They doom women to passivity. Don't accept."

"Mama, I cannot be a rebellious bride over a simple name."

Mama shrugged her shoulders in resignation. Nkwanzi took on the name and there was jubilation. Immediately after the ceremony, Mama went back to the city.

The couple stayed home for a month while Nkwanzi got to know her in-laws. Her mother in-law, whom everybody fondly called Kaaka, immediately took to her and Nkwanzi saw in her a truly loving mother. After a month, Genesis and Nkwanzi went back to the city too and to their jobs.

Genesis was put in charge of the country's secret service and Mama remained in the army. Mzee still opted for an academic career and went back to Makerere University and Nkwanzi continued with her law practice.

It took a few weeks for Nkwanzi and Genesis to consumate their marriage because Genesis still had a problem. Every time he approached her, he would in the same instant groan, turn over on his back and stare at the ceiling. Nkwanzi, though worried, still understood. Slowly, he healed and it was not long before Nkwanzi conceived.

Chapter Fifteen

Signs and symptoms

The government had meanwhile embarked on bringing sanity to the country. Stringent measures were put in place for government officials. No minister was supposed to own a luxurious car like the Mercedes Benz as had been the case in the past governments. All ministers were supposed to use small cars. Ministers were supposed to buy local furniture. No liquor was to be served at government receptions. This was the correct line. President Kazi himself set the example. He identified with the simple ordinary people and discarded pomp.

Many people jubilated at these measures, others sneered and said this was mere eupohoria and that when realities welled up, they were bound to change. As time moved on, Kazi tightened his grip on ministers and army officers who misbehaved towards *wananchi*. It did not take long before some of them did. One minister was overtaken by a taxi and it annoyed him so much that a 'mere' taxi driver should overtake him.

"Who does this man think he is? I am a whole minister and he dares overtake me? Overtake the idiot immediately and stop him."

The driver did as he was ordered. The taxi stopped. The minister himself hauled the driver out and started beating him.

"Stupid idiot! You people now think you are so free you can show disrespect to ministers! We brought you freedom and now you think you should insult us. Take that, and that," fumed the minister as he kicked the poor fellow.

The minister's bodyguard joined his master in battering the driver. People witnessed the incident with disgust. They reported it to the press and it hit the headlines. President Kazi took action. Investigations were carried out and the minister found at fault. He tendered in his resignation...

***

Nkwanzi's time came and Genesis took her to hospital. Ssenga had already come to be with her and counselled her on how to handle labour pains.

"Child, giving birth is the greatest test for a woman. It is the most painful thing in the world but it is also sweet. You have to bear that pain like a brave woman. When the pain grips you, never scream. That would show that you are a coward and your husband's people will despise you. So child, if the pain is very bad, just hold the bed very tightly but don't say a word that will tell people what you are going through."

"Ssenga, I think there is nothing cowardly about screaming when one is in pain. You may keep quiet and die!"

"Child, I'm telling you what to do. Do you want to ashame our tribe like those women of some tribes who while delivering start shouting and saying they will never have sex with their husbands again and scream the whole hospital down?"

At that very minute, the first labour pain hit Nkwanzi and she let out an involuntary scream. Ssenga quickly put a hand across her mouth which without thinking, Nkwanzi bit. Ssenga flinched with pain and withdrew the hand immediately.

"Child, child!" she groaned.

Mama too came and told her, "Nkwanzi, this is another frontline, but be strong. If the pain becomes too much and you feel like screaming, just holler your lungs out. At least the era when women used to be beaten with thorny twigs and have grinding stones placed on their chests if they cried during labour, is over."

Ssenga heard and got livid with anger accusing Mama of trying to ashame Nkwanzi. Mama laughed much to Ssenga's annoyance.

Nkwanzi grew weary and the pains went on a brief holiday. Then sleep overtook her...

"Congratulations! You got a lovely baby girl. Lovely. She is a beautiful half-caste."

Shocked, Nkwanzi heard the midwife announce what to her was a death knell. So Rex the rapist had afterall been successful in leaving a permanent scar on her. Oh, God, if indeed you do exist, please take me now, she prayed. The midwife was stitching her and the pain she felt in her heart blotted away the pain of stitching.

"Here, let me place the angelic infant in your arms. You must be longing to hold her," said a figure in a white uniform.

"I don't want it, I don't want to hold that thing in my arms! Please take it away. I hate it, I loathe it," Nkwanzi screamed. God, how she hated the wriggling thing!

They were all shocked at her outburst and stopped whatever they were doing.

189

"I know why she is reacting like that. Her blood pressure must have shot up and disturbed her brain. We must give her a jab to bring it down immediately."

Meanwhile Genesis had come in with Mzee. Genesis came and planted a kiss on her sweating brow.

"My dear, I understand you were brave. Now, where is my famous daughter? Oh, there in the crib," and with a radiant smile, he went to the crib and lifted the infant. He peered at it closely, a perplexed look on his face.

"Nkwanzi! But this can't be our baby! This one is a half-caste. There must have been a mistake. They must have exchanged our baby!"

Fear made her freeze.

"It seems there is a problem here. Apparently this is the husband and this is one of those cases where he planted tomato and is now reaping onion," the figure said in a loud whisper.

Cruel, mocking giggles followed. Genesis heard the words and his breath got imprisoned somewhere in his chest. For a few minutes, he stood speechless, unseeing. Then he broke out in maniacal laughter. Then in one spring, he flung the door open, rushed out and banged it. The noise reverberated through the entire hospital.

"Genesis, Genesis for God's sake! Genesis come back," she pleaded as she tried to get up but the figures in white pushed her back with cruelty.

Mzee had stood by, shocked, immobile. Nkwanzi's words sprung him into action and he dashed after Genesis. Genesis ran on, his maniacal laughter rising to a crescendo. An old woman selling assorted goods took his arm and halted him.

"Son, tell me. What is the matter?"

Genesis paused, sense momentarily returning to his demented mind. He looked into her concerned eyes and a tremor shook his body.

"Old woman, the matter is, I sowed tomato and reaped onion," and he sprung into the air and resumed his maniacal laughter.

"Yees, I sowed tomato and reaped onion. Ha ha ha haa! I sowed tomato and ..."

The sound reached Nkwanzi's ears and went to her brain. She pushed a finger in each ear to block it out.

Meanwhile, Mzee was close on his heels.

"Genesis, Genesis for God's sake! Genesis come back. Genesis don't cross the road. There is a car coming! Genesis, Genesisss...!"

There was a screech of tyres and a thud as metal met flesh. Then silence ...

***

Nkwanzi woke up from the brief slumber screaming.

"Where is he? Where is my husband?"

"I'm here my dear. Calm down," he said as he looked down at her with concern.

"Genesis, you mean you have not been crushed by a car?"

"Which car? Oh I see. No, I am all right. Calm down my dear. You fell asleep and had a horrible dream."

Relief flooded her whole being. Then fear clutched her heart again.

"What about the onion and tomato?"

"Onion and tomato? Honey, calm down."

Before she could ask anymore questions, the pain gripped her again. The uniformed figures told Genesis to go out. He protested and said he wanted to be by his wife's side as their child came into the world but they refused and said that was out. Within a few minutes, the baby was wailing.

"She is ebony black. Beautiful," said one of them.

Nkwanzi's breath whistled out in relief.

Genesis came in shortly afterwards. He held the tiny baby in his arms briefly and declared:

"The little angel is so beautiful and peaceful. She has your eyes and my nose. Her name is Ihoreere, meaning peace."

"Nkwanzi, I told you God is not our enemy," whispered Mama in her ear.

***

Genesis was a fantastic father and over the years, his life revolved around mother and child. Every evening, he would come home and play with Ihoreere, talk to her like an adult. He refused her to go for pre-nursery school, saying that was tantamount to child abuse. In the evenings, he would come straight home to talk to her.

"Nkwanzi, Ihoreere is just incredibly clever. I'm sure she will become an astronaut," he would state proudly.

He supervised her while she did her homework unlike many

191

fathers who left their wives to do all the homework with the children.

The country moved on and indeed many agreed that there was a definite change in the way things were being handled. This situation, however, was slowly being disturbed by a mysterious malady that nobody had yet comprehended. Nkwanzi had heard in a way of passing that there was a mysterious disease which had come from nowhere and had no cure. But she had not yet seen any of its victims. Then one day while walking along the streets of Kampala, she met Mbele with whom they had struggled in their modest group to remove Duduma. Nkwanzi had been meeting him on and off. And now when she met him, she got a shock. His face was gaunt, his arms were drumsticks. His lips had gone red and pulled away from his teeth in what looked like a sneer of cruelty. His hair was scanty and thin, his eyes deep sunken and his cheekbones stood out. His clothes hung on him, the coat hugging his thin frame. God, how wasted he was!

" Mbele! What's eating you up?"

His lips murmured something inaudible. God! He could hardly stand! "Mbele, come take my hand," Nkwanzi said gently as she led him to the nearest cafe. His chest heaved with exhaustion and beads of perspiration appeared on his upper lip. Quickly, she ordered a glass of juice for him. His hand shook so badly she had to hold the glass up to his lips. He took a sip and immediately went into a spasm of coughing. A rasping, dry cough that left him gasping for breath.

"Mbele, what's the matter?"

"Typhoid, typhoid fever, my dear."

"But typhoid responds to treatment. You mean the one you have is resistant?"

"It would seem. I have swallowed antibiotics until their very sight makes me more sick than the disease itself. And instead of getting better, I get worse."

"Mbele, go home and rest. Come, I will hire a taxi for you."

She went and told Genesis about it and they went to see Mbele. Mbele indeed looked worse. Even his skull had shrunk. His relatives believed that he had been bewitched. They took him to a witchdoctor who said it was witchraft. He made very many small cuts on Mbele's body and rubbed in medicine. He said all the other members of Mbele's family had to be cut in the same way too. Using the same razor blade he had used on Mbele, he made many small cuttings on their bodies and rubbed in medicine. Mbele kept wasting away, fading until he breathed his last. People wondered what type of disease had

192

eaten him up. His body, lying in bed looked like that of a tiny, long baby. After his death, his wife was allocated to one of his brothers... Many other young people suffered and died from the same ailment as Mbele. They would complain of malaria which was on and off, develop a rush all over the body, cough, vomit and get chronic diarrhoea. Within no time, they would waste away and die. Many of Mbele's family members died.

"This new disease slims people," somebody said.

And they started calling the disease 'slim'. What plague was this that had no cure? And where did it come from? People however, had hope. Soon the white man would discover the medicine for it and there was no need to panic.

Meanwhile, another kind of panic had gripped the country. A serious insurgency broke out in the northern part and spread to the east. Stories of government troops killing innocent people indiscriminately began to filter in.

One particular incident left the country condemning the army vehemently. The army had rounded up about a hundred suspected rebel collaborators. These were peasants who were found busy in their fields.

"Tell us where the rebels are. You know where they are."

The peasants said they did not know.

"Oh, so you don't want to talk? We shall make you talk."

They were herded into a stationary train wagon. Its capacity was about twenty people but all the one hundred or so were crammed in. They could hardly breathe.

"Do you want to talk? If you don't talk now, we shall close the door and warm the cold wagon for your comfort."

The wagon was far from cold. The district has one of the hottest climates in Uganda, at times registering desert temperatures. The inmates of the wagon kept mum.

"All right, get out first for some fresh air," the soldiers ordered.

Relieved, the peasants hurriedly jumped out of the wagon.

"Each of you go and collect fifty big pieces of firewood. Remember, you try to escape, the bullet will eat you."

None dared escape anyway. Too happy to go and do an errand for their captors in the hope they would be released, the peasants ran to the open grassland and started gathering firewood. Soon each got the required number. They competed each to be the first to bring the firewood, so that they could please their captors, like children trying to please their teachers.

"Good. Place them under the wagon."

Puzzled, they did so and waited for the commanders to set them free.

"Now, does any of you have any confession to make as to the whereabouts of the rebels or whether you are a rebel collaborator?" The question was met with blank stares.

"Nothing to say? All right, you will tell it to your maker. Get inside. Quickly."

And the soldiers fell upon them and herded them into the wagon hitting them with gun butts. When the last of the peasants had squeezed himself in, the soldiers banged the door shut and bolted it from outside.

"All right now, it is party time. Light the bonfire. We shall heat them up a bit and after a short time when we open the door, they will be willing to sing."

The soldiers took up the order. They lit the dry embers which quickly leapt into flames fanned by the hot wind that whistled through the dry savanna grass. The thirsty fire leaked the sides of the wagon.

The inmates groaned. They hit the sides of the wagon, their voices unable to reach the outside world. They gassed, they excreted, urinated, vomited and the water drained out of them in torrents. Children clutched their mothers' scorched bodies, men and women packed like sardines could only groan. It was one cry, " Mama!" The cry of agony torn from the very soul. The hands hitting at the wagon dwindled and soon a silence fell within. The hitting ceased. The only sound was of the flames leaking the wagon.

"Good. They have had enough *chai*. Now they will talk. Open the door," the commander ordered.

They opened the door and bodies tumbled out as if in protest and fell at the feet of the soldiers. Dead bodies, their eyes wearing a look of shocked suprise stared horribly at the soldiers.

"My God! They are dead! President Kazi will roast us. We have brought a bad name to the army. Quickly, let us bury them in a mass grave."

They pulled out all the bodies from the wagon and then quickly went to dig the shallow grave. A few of the 'corpses' were not dead though. When a slight breeze blew over them, they managed to revive and they crawled away to tell the story later.

The country cried out for justice. Some of the culprits were put on trial and unfortunately others escaped to a neighbouring country. The war raged on until government realised it was easier to talk peace than to keep on fighting.

***

The weevil that had struck at the centre of life began to take its toll. Soon, it was announced that it was contracted mainly through sex, and then callous people became cruel to the victims. The urban lumpens were particularly the most cruel. They would stand with their backs against a wall chain-smoking. And then they would sight their victim: an emaciated one.

"Hey you! Slim, slim case, sorry. There, take *mabugo* to help in your funeral expenses!"

And they would throw dirty, five shilling notes at the victim and then burst into derisive laughter.

"Use some of the money to buy goat's meat so that you can eat and fatten!"

The victim would cringe and flinch from the inhumanity, trying to disappear into herself/himself.

The lumpen would lounge off, laughing hilariously at their comic act and with their wide trousers swinging in the wind, they would stroll along the city streets in search of more victims whom they could use to while away their time. The government opened up and launched an awareness campaign. Quack doctors sprung up everywhere claiming they had a cure for the terrible disease. People claimed to have received visions. One said she had got a vision in which God told her that the soil in her banana *shamba* was a cure for the terrible plague. Soon, thousands of people were trooping to this woman's home, desperate people with hope that the miraculous soil would cure them. They went, they were given the soil. The place became a health hazard and government stepped in. By the time it convinced the people that this was mere rubbish, the patients had eaten more than a hundred tons of soil. The pit which started with a scoop of a tea-spoon was as big as a huge crater lake.

It was during those troubled days that Nkwanzi was made Deputy Minister of Foreign Affairs. The government had put in place a policy of affirmative action which resulted into women being appointed to high offices among other measures. This policy made women visible. One of its major drawbacks, however, was that for many of such women, they were mainly given positions of deputies, an exercise that made the whole thing look like mere tokenism. This set a negative trend in that for most jobs, a man would take the chair and then the appointing officials would get a woman as his deputy.

Deputy or no deputy, Nkwanzi's appointment was received with jubilation by all her friends and relatives. Genesis was the happiest of them all.

"My dear, you have brought me pride. You have been picked on pure merit," he said as they melted into their characteristic kiss.

Nkwanzi's busy schedule began. Most of the time, she was on the move.

"Genesis, I feel bad not being in the house all the time. I'm beginning to feel guilty as if I'm abandoning you and Ihoreere," she told him once.

"You shouldn't worry. You're doing your job. Suppose it was me in that job, I would trot all over the place without feeling guilty."

Six months went by and Nkwanzi's heavy schedule grew even heavier. She started flying out of the country and she was so busy that even on a normal working day, she would reach home long after Genesis and Ihoreere had retired to bed. Things went on smoothly until Genesis' uncle poured a drop of blood in a pot of milk as the saying goes, and then the blood and milk could not be separated.

The uncle had come to pay them a visit. He stayed for two weeks and on the morning of his departure, he demanded an audience with Genesis.

"Son, what I have to tell you is grave. I'm concerned about you for you have no wife."

"What? Uncle, I advise you not to talk disparagingly of my wife," Genesis threatened, his eyes narrowing dangerously.

"I will speak, it is up to you to take it or leave it. I have been here for two weeks and I have not seen your minister wife all this time. Everyday, she is away, on the road or in the air. She is not here to cook for you, to look after the child and the home. You're married to air, embracing your pillow at night. When she goes to all these places, doesn't she go with men?"

"Shut up, uncle! What you are saying is bad. Supposing I was in her position, would I not be going on *safari* with some women colleagues? Here is your transport money. Go back home."

Genesis was livid with anger but the seed of discontent, jealous and suspicion had been sown in his mind. It grew by the day, a tiny fraction at a time until eventually, it took root in his heart. He begun to complain about Nkwanzi's perpetual absence from the house and complained that Ihoreere was not getting enough motherly care. He complained that he was tired of food prepared by a housegirl. And he complained of a sexless marriage.

Nkwanzi was shocked and tried to explain. Whenever she got a free moment, she would go home and try to make it up to him. But clearly, the issue had become a case of spilt milk. Whenever it was announced over the radio that the honourable Minister of Foreign Affairs was to go on a trip accompanied by his deputy, Genesis would become moody and irritable.

"Where will you spend the night?" he would inquire from Nkwanzi.

"In a bed, of course," she would answer irritably.

Such answers irritated him the more.

"And where will your boss stay?" he would continue the interrogation.

Nkwanzi began to become apprehensive of these interviews. But she refused to feel guilty about her numerous *safaris* because they were part of her job description. She told Mama and Mzee about it, they talked to Genesis but he remained in a perpetual sulk.

Then, he began to behave funny and Nkwanzi knew that he must have got himself a mistress to 'hit back at her'. And how she wept! A job which should have been a source of happiness had instead done the reverse! She got to know the mistress when she went to pick Genesis from the airport. He had gone to attend a Conference in London. She went to the airport and straight to the VIP lounge.

"I missed you so much honey it hurt," he whispered huskily as soon as he saw her. She was surprised at his sudden return to expressions of love.

They sat in the VIP lounge as they waited for his luggage. There was a mix up in the luggage and a porter said could she go down with him and identify it. In the Movement government, most ministers behaved in a simple way, they were part of the ordinary people. And so Nkwanzi went with him and when they reached the customs check point, they found a woman quarrelling furiously with the staff.

"You people are nothing but thieves! You have ripped my bag open and I am going to report you to my husband. Thieving useless fellows, wait until Rwenzigye hears about this. Heads will roll in this place."

Nkwanzi stopped short. Had she heard correctly? She had to find out. Her heart pounding, she approached the woman.

"Hello, Madam, how are you? I heard you complaining about these people. At one time, they did the same thing to me."

The woman was happy to get a sympathiser.

"How are you madam? Yes, these people are terrible!" she replied. It was obvious that the woman did not know Nkwanzi. President Kazi kept on appointing ministers and dropping them at such a fast rate that it was difficult for people to remember all of them.

"What did they do to your luggage?" Nkwanzi probed.

"You know, madam, I had gone with my boyfriend to London," she said in a conspiratory whisper.

"Oh, aren't you lucky! There are few men these days who can afford to take their girlfriends for a trip abroad!"

"I know I'm just lucky. Mine is a director of the secret service organisation. The man is simply great. My, what he did to me in London! Now he is up there in the VIP lounge with his wife who came to wait for him. The wives come to wait in the VIP lounge not knowing that the girlfriends who accompanied the husbands are here below," and she chuckled maliciously as Nkwanzi seethed inwardly.

"And does his wife not know about you?"

"Nah. She is the type that doesn't socialise. It is office and home for her. And she bored her husband stiff. Know what, madam, such women are phonies. Cold as a fridge," she whispered and laughed contemptuously.

Nkwanzi forced a laugh. All the time, she was scared that people would hear her loud beating heart. Pump, Pump... She was scared that it would burst. But she tried to keep cool. She had been looking at this woman who had stolen Genesis' heart. She was not a stunning beauty but there was an animal sexuality about her. Her lips were big and sensuous and when she passed her tongue over them, Nkwanzi was reminded of a bitch on heat.

She had big bums and when she moved, she exaggerated them and they moved rhythmically, obscenely. She wore what was obviously a wig and she had bleached her skin, it was an unhealthy yellow.

"Incidentally, what do you do?" Nkwanzi asked.

"I'm self employed. Rwenzigye has given me money to do business with," she whispered with happiness.

Genesis to have succumbed to this! To a woman who had bleached herself so! She felt like smashing the trash, wanted to beat her into pulp. Gouge out her lust-filled eyes but she knew as a big person, fighting was out. Moreover, it must have been Genesis who seduced her so in a way, if any beating was to be done, it should be Genesis to get it. The man was the hunter and guilty party. She composed herself and went back to the VIP lounge.

" Honey, you got the luggage?"

She nodded agreement, not trusting herself to speak.

"Anything particular you saw down there that depressed you?" he asked with concern and something akin to fear in his voice.

She put on the coolest smile. She had decided not to let him know that she knew.

"No. Just a funny woman who looked like a putrefying mass of humanity quarrelling with everybody."

He relaxed visibly and they set off for home. As soon as they reached home, he picked his briefcase and murmured something about going to office. At something past midnight! And then she felt deep revulsion and loathing for him. To make matters worse, she knew she still loved him. They had not had sex most probably ever since he got his trash of a woman. Now that she knew for sure what had been going on, she swore that he would never have her in the flesh. So when he approached her one night, she faced him and told him bluntly that he would have to use a condom.

"I can't use a condom with my wife! You either accept me as your husband or we separate. It is as if you suspect me of being sick!"

"No condom, no sex and that's that."

"My friend, have you forgotten what you vowed in church? That you married me for better or for worse? If this is for the worse part, you have to bear it. You vowed to love me in sickness and in health. So even if I was sick, you'd still have to love me."

She held her ground. Their friends were all shocked at this sudden turn of events and tried to intervene.

"I don't understand this species called men," Mama wondered. "Ever since we came from the bush victorious, several of them have turned out their wives and taken on new women. The children are the worst hit. Unable to take the crises in their families, they have left school and are decaying in slums, hooked to prostitution, drugs and crude spirits. What pleasure is there in seeing the mother of your children suffering?"

Ssenga heard and came to give Nkwanzi tips on how to claim Genesis back.

"Daughter, I don't want to say that I told you so. I have come to tell you how to get your husband back."

"Aunt, I need a miracle to get him back."

"You just have to do something simple. And this is it. You have seen crested cranes. Have you ever seen a crested crane walking alone? Never. They are always in twos: a man and his wife," she paused.

Nkwanzi began to wonder what Ssenga was driving at.

"So now, I want you and Rwenzigye to start being together, never to be apart. This is how it can be done. You will get the eggs of a crane and fry them. Then you will eat them together. From then on, you will always be together like the crested cranes. Simple."

Nkwanzi laughed and Ssenga frowned with annoyance.

"Why do you laugh at me?"

"I'm not laughing at you. It's just that what you are saying is ridiculous. It has no scientific backing. Aunt, we educated people don't believe in such things which have no scientific backing."

"Daughter, I believe in God but can your *sayansa* show us that He is there? No. You can't see God, you can't touch him but we know He's there. It's the same with these things I'm telling you about. They're there, their power and spirit are there, you can't see them or touch them. So you look for those eggs and with your husband eat them. They are not harmful, nor poisonous. I can't tell you to give bad medicine to your man or to both of you. I have spoken and I am going back home."

"Aunt, what pains me most is that he has lost interest in Ihoreere as well!"

"Love for a child comes from its mother's private parts. Since he is not sleeping with you, he can't have love for the child."

Genesis continued with his behaviour and as time went by, he started battering her. In his drunken stupors, he would come home and demand for sex. She would feel repulsed but because she wanted to maintain the family for Ihoreere's sake, she would try to put a condom on him. Then he would rage and hit her.

"You think because you are a minister you are everything? I'm the head of this house," he would fume and then commence to hit, scratch and bite her.

She decided that enough was enough and prepared to leave him. But just as she was planning to do so, he went down with malaria and she could not abandon him. He was listless, he was unhappy. He stayed in and out of bed for many months and meanwhile, his weight was going fast.

During this time too, the virus became vicious. It struck right, it struck left. It felled down both the mighty and the wretched and in many areas, it devastated entire families. Every night, the fires of vigil could be seen scattered in the front compounds of various homesteads. The forests were dwindling, AIDS was finishing the trees, taking them to light the fires of vigils. In the deep of the nights, groans of the dying could be heard as parents beat their breasts in agony, crying out to God.

Their children continued to fade and wither away like flowers in the noon-tide heat. The young widows would move and go into other towns and get new husbands. The young widowers would also shift and move to other towns and get new wives. It was a vicious cycle, and the virus hit. How the accursed invisible weevil devoured the children of Adam and Eve as if to mock the new-found peace in the country!

***

Genesis' health deteriorated over time. He started coughing and the doctor gave him all sorts of drugs which he failed to react to.

"I have to do a TB test," the doctor said finally.

"What! TB? Doctor, it is not necessary. Where could my husband have picked TB from?" Nkwanzi protested.

"Well, these days you never know. TB is all around us."

He took the test. Nkwanzi did not give it much thought as she knew it would be negative. It was positive. Genesis and Nkwanzi were both shocked. She felt fingers of fear clutch her heart momentarily and disappear as quickly.

"Genesis, let's not worry. TB is curable these days you know," she said forcing a cheerfulness she was far from feeling.

"You think so, honey?" he asked with doubt.

"I know so."

Genesis started on the TB drugs and begun to improve but after a few weeks, he went totally down. There was no doubt in anybody's mind: he had the accursed weevil.

"Nkwanzi, honey. I'm sorry, Nkwanzi...," he could hardly speak.

"Shh, please. We shall fight on. Genesis, many people are living with it positively. You too will do it."

Whenever he felt a bit better, he would force himself to go to office. However weak he looked, he would still go. Nkwanzi tried to dissuade him but he would not hear of it.

"Genesis, you are going because you want to show people that you are okay. Please, don't try to prove anything. Just stay home and rest."

He would refuse and go. Then one day, Nkwanzi received a call that he had collapsed at the office and they had taken him to the hospital. The doctor advised Nkwanzi to take him to the village.

"He doesn't have long to go," said the stethoscoped figure.

They took him back to their official residence where he spent what Nkwanzi knew would be his last night there. Grief made her speechless and she was glad Ihoreere was at school. The doctor advised her to take him home by air. The following day, Genesis was taken home, his last journey home.

Epilogue

It was going to be the sixth night of Genesis stay at home since they brought him. Dusk was beginning to fall. The low mooing of cattle as they were being brought in for the evening's milking, their udders full, cut across the homesteads. The twittering birds slowly fell silent and the only noise that remained was the shrill voices of boys happily passing the banana fibre ball from one to the other. The spirals of smoke rose from the kitchen fires and curled up, up, to mix with the gases of the atmosphere.

The women of the neighbourhood began to come, their mats folded under their armpits, ready to spend the night by Genesis' side.

"How passed the day?" they greeted.

"The sun has gone down, and the patient is breathing," the old man replied.

Genesis' dry cough made everybody dash inside.Nkwanzi held his chest until it subsided.

"Nkwanzi, give me some water," he whispered.

She got it quickly and he gulped it down.

"Ihoreere?" he whispered.

"She is here. She came from school today."

Ihoreere put her hand in his.A happiness, mixed with some kind of remorse and sadness suffused his face as he looked at his daughter. Ihoreere looked at him, not understanding why her daddy, who always protected her could himself be so weak now. Nkwanzi noticed that his heart beat very fast and she said so aloud. Kaaka tried to give him a little of the honey syrup but he failed to take it. Mama got a towel and started wiping his sweating brow. Nkwanzi held his other hand. The old man, Runamba, was seated quietly in the corner, his chin in his palm.

"Let us pray and then I can go," said the parish pastor who had come to see Genesis. Everybody bowed their heads.

"Father, you can see that your servant, Rwenzigye, is at the mouth of the grave..."

"Curse you pastor," Nkwanzi said inside herself seething with anger. "What sort of pastor was this? Talking so, in Genesis' hearing."

Mama squeezed her hand in a manner that said, "Ignore him."

"Father, there is nothing we can do to change your will. We are like the frog that was trapped under the huge hoof of a cow. It looked up at the cow, looked at its long horns and big body and knew that it was at the mercy of this gigantic animal and said: 'as you will long horns'. Father, as you will. Amen."

Before they all said, "Amen," Genesis whispered, "Nkwanzi, when Ihoreere has become an old woman, see you later."

In the same breath they said Amen, Kaaka all of a sudden clutched her lower abdomen as if in great pain. Nkwanzi felt Genesis' hold on her hand loosen but she did not pay attention to it. She was worried about the look of intense pain on Kaaka's face.

"Kaaka, what's the matter?"

"I fe-fel-felt something like labour pains. I felt as if I was about to push out a child," she said, now bent double with the 'labour pains' as sweat run down her face.

"Let me take you out for fresh air. At least Genesis is asleep," Nkwanzi said casting a look at him.

Mama got hold of the top sheet and calmly covered Genesis up to the head.

"Why have you covered him up to the head? He will suffocate!"

Mama looked at Nkwanzi strangely. Then in a quiet voice, she said, "Its over. Genesis sleeps forever," she whispered.

Nkwanzi was confused. Then she heard Ssenga wail and the other women started wailing too.

"You mean he's gone? Is that why he said, 'Nkwanzi, see you later when Ihoreere has aged?'" Nkwanzi asked fearfully, incredulously.

"Yes Nkwanzi. Take care of Ihoreere. Be strong for her sake. She needs you," Mama said as she held her tightly.

"Jesus, please take control," Nkwanzi cried out silently.

* * *

One evening, a week after the funeral, Nkwanzi sat with Kaaka, Mzee Runamba, Mama, Ssenga and Ihoreere in the middle of the compound where the fire of the vigil had been lit. What remained was the stump of the tree trunk that had been lit and the ashes. They sat quietly, not talking. Runamba smoked his long pipe, the spirals of smoke winding high up. Nkwanzi sat staring into space, aware that Ihoreere was looking at her, trying to get the meaning of what had happened. Nkwanzi felt inadequate for she did not have any right answer either.

Dusk began to fall. The children of the village could be heard screaming with pleasure as they passed the fibre ball to each other. The music of grinding stones resounded from the homesteads. The low mooing of cattle as they came in from the fields, their udders full, broke the stillness of the evening. The cooing of the lone dove magnified the loneliness.

The next day was the day for the ceremony of removing the ashes left after the fire of vigil. It was also the day when the widow's hair was to be shaved, signifying the end of official mourning. After this ceremony, close members of the family could go to their gardens and dig.

Nkwanzi got up as dawn approached and woke up Ihoreere as well. They sat on the verandah and soon, Kaaka, Runamba and Mama joined them.

As the ceremony was being performed, Nkwanzi watched the red glow of the rising sun as it came out of its slumber to smile upon the earth. From a radio nearby, she heard the happy voices of school children singing:

> For a number decades now
> More dead than alive were we
> Africa's Pearl a laughing stock
> Ugandans in exile ashamed
> To acknowledge their native roots –
> But now in openness we live
> The gun dymestified
> And AIDS no longer a mystery,
> It too shall be conquered.

— presentation

As she listened to the happy voices, she smiled. Then she picked her bag and held Ihoreere's hand ready to go back to her duties. But a question nagged at her: "Yes, a mustard seed had been planted in the land, but would it survive the invisible weevils?"

She hoped so; so far so good.

But it was too early to predict what would happen after.

The sun bathed the land with its increasing warmth as the Deputy Minister of Foreign Affairs entered her car, with Mama on the other side and Ihoreere cushioned comfortably between the two.

Glossary

Abajungu	white people
Abakominista	communists
Bogoya	sweet bananas
Chakula ya wakubwa	food for big men
Chiini	down
Diisi	District Commissioner
Juu	up
Kanzu	long flowing robe won by men
Mabaati	iron sheets
Magendo	black marketeering
Matooke	green banana
Mugore	bride
Murrum	beans and peas
Naikondo	bore hole
Omujungu	white person
Panga	machete
Sigiri	charcoal stove
Tadoba	small kerosene lamp
Tonto	local beer from bananas
Tukutenderezza	Glory Halleluyah

CPSIA information can be obtained
at www.ICGtesting.com
Printed in the USA
LVOW01s0122111216
516760LV00010B/57/P